THE PROFESSOR
OF DESIRE

THE PROFESSOR
OF DESIRE

PHILIP ROTH

FARRAR, STRAUS AND GIROUX

NEW YORK

Sections of this book appeared,
in somewhat different form, in *American
Poetry Review, Harper's, Penthouse,* and
The New York Times Book Review

For Claire Bloom

THE PROFESSOR
OF DESIRE

Temptation comes to me first in the conspicuous personage of Herbie Bratasky, social director, bandleader, crooner, comic, and m.c. of my family's mountainside resort hotel. When he is not trussed up in the elasticized muscleman's swim trunks which he dons to conduct rumba lessons by the side of the pool, he is dressed to kill, generally in his two-tone crimson and cream-colored "loafer" jacket and the wide canary-yellow trousers that taper down to enchain him just above his white, perforated, sharpie's shoes. A fresh slice of Black Jack gum is at the ready in his pocket while another is being savored, with slow-motion sassiness, in what my mother derisively describes as Herbie's "yap." Below the stylishly narrow alligator belt and the gold droop of key chain, one knee works away inside his trousers, Herbie keeping time to hides he alone hears being beaten in that Congo called his brain. Our brochure (from fourth grade on composed by me, in collaboration with the owner) headlines Herbie as "our Jewish Cugat, our Jewish Krupa—all rolled into one!"; further on he is described as "a second Danny Kaye," and, in conclusion, just so that everyone understands that this 140-pound twenty-year-old is not nobody and Kepesh's Hungarian Royale is not *exactly* nowhere, as "another Tony Martin."

Our guests appear to be nearly as mesmerized by Herbie's shameless exhibitionism as I am. A newcomer will have barely settled into a varnished wicker rocker on the veranda before one of the old-timers arrived from the hot city the previous week starts giving him the lowdown on this wonder of our tribe. "And wait till you see the tan on this kid. He's just got that kind of skin—never burns, only tans. And from the first day in the sun. This kid has got skin on him right out of Bible times."

Because of a damaged eardrum, our drawing card—as it pleases Herbie to call himself, particularly into the teeth of my mother's disapproval—is with us throughout the Second World War. Ongoing discussion from the rocking chairs and the card tables as to whether the disability is congenital or self-inflicted. The suggestion that something other than Mother Nature might have rendered Herbie unfit to fight Tojo, Mussolini, and Hitler—well, I am outraged, personally mortified by the very idea. Yet, how tantalizing to imagine Herbie taking a hatpin or a toothpick in his own hands—taking an ice pick!—and deliberately mutilating himself in order to outfox his draft board.

"I wouldn't put it past him," says guest A-owitz; "I wouldn't put anything past that operator. What a pistol he is!" "Come on, he did no such thing. That kid is a patriotic kid like anybody else. I'll tell you how he went half deaf like that, and ask the doctor here if I'm not right: from banging on those drums," says guest B-owitz. "Oh, can that kid play drums," says C-owitz; "you could put him on the stage of the Roxy right now—and I think the only reason he ain't is that, like you say, he doesn't hear right from the drums themselves." "Still," says D-owitz, "he don't say definitely yes or no whether he did it with some instrument or something." "But that's the showman in him, keeping you hanging by suspense. His whole stock-in-trade is that he's crazy enough for anything—that's his whole *act*." "Still, even to kid around about it don't strike me right. The Jewish people have got their hands full as it is." "Please, a kid who dresses like that right down to the key chain, and with a build like that that he works on day and night, plus those drums, you think he is gonna do himself serious physical damage just out of spite to the war effort?" "I agree, one hundred percent. Gin, by the way." "Oh, you caught me with my pants down, you s.o.b. What the hell am I holding these jacks for, will somebody tell me? Look, you know what you don't find? You don't find a kid who is good-looking like this one, who is funny like he is too. To take that kind of looks, and to be funny, and to go crazy like that with the drums, that to me is something special in the annals of show business." "And what about at the pool? How about on the diving board? If Billy Rose laid eyes on him, clowning around in the water like that, he'd be in the Aquacade tomorrow." "And what about that voice on him?" "If only he wouldn't kid *around* with it—if only he would sing *serious.*" "If that kid sang serious he could be in the Metropolitan Opera." "If he sang serious, he could be a cantor, for Christ sakes, with no problem. He could break your heart. Just imagine for yourself what he would look like in a white tallis with that tan!" And here at last I am spotted, working on a model R.A.F. Spitfire down at the end of the veranda rail. "Hey, little Kepesh, come here, you little eavesdropper. Who do you want to be like when you grow up? Listen to this—stop shuffling the cards a minute. Who's your hero, Kepaleh?"

I don't have to think twice, or at all. "Herbie," I reply, much to the amusement of the men in the congregation. Only the mothers look a little dismayed.

Yet, ladies, who else could it be? Who else is so richly endowed as to be able to mimic Cugie's accent, the shofar blowing, and, at my request, a fighter plane nose-diving over Berchtesgaden—*and* the Fuehrer going crazy underneath? Herbie's enthusiasm and virtuosity are such that my father must sometimes caution him to keep certain of his imitations to himself, unique though they may be. "But," protests Herbie, "my fart is perfect." "Could be, for all I know," replies the boss, "but not in front of a mixed crowd." "But I've been working on it for months. Listen!" "Oh, spare me, Bratasky, please. It just ain't exactly what a nice tired guest wants to hear in a casino after his dinner. You can appreciate that, can't you? Or can't you? I don't get you sometimes, where your brain is. Don't you realize that these are people who keep kosher? Don't you got it about women and children? My friend, it's simple—the shofar is for the High Holidays and the other stuff is for the toilet. Period, Herbie. Finished."

So he comes to imitate for me, his awestruck acolyte, the toots and the tattoos that are forbidden him in public by my Mosaic dad. It turns out that not only can he simulate the panoply of sounds—ranging from the faintest springtime sough to the twenty-one-gun salute—with which mankind emits its gases, but he can also "do diarrhea." Not, he is quick to inform me, some poor shlimazel in its throes—that he had already mastered back in high school—but the full Wagnerian strains of fecal *Sturm und Drang.* "I could be in Ripley's," he tells me. "You read Ripley's, don't you—then judge for yourself!" I hear the rasp of a zipper being undone. Then a most enviable stream belting an enamel bowl. Next the whoosh of the flush, followed by the gargle and hiccup of a reluctant tap commencing to percolate. And all of it emanating from Herbie's mouth.

I could fall down and worship at his feet.

"And catch *this!*" This is two hands soaping one another—but seemingly in Herbie's mouth. "All winter long I would go into the toilet at the Automat and just sit there and listen." "You would?" "Sure. I listen even to my own self every single time I go to the can." "You do?" "But your old man, he's the expert, and to him it's only one thing—dirty! 'Period!'" adds Herbie, and in a voice exactly like my old man's!

And he means every word he says. How come, I wonder. How can Herbie know so much and care so passionately about the tintinnabulations of the can? And why do tone-deaf philistines like my father care so little?

So it seems in summer, while I am under the demon drummer's spell. Then Yom Kippur comes and Bratasky goes, and what good does it do me to have learned what someone like that has to teach a growing boy? Our -witzes, -bergs, and -steins are dispersed overnight to regions as remote to me as Babylon—Hanging Gardens called Pelham and Queens and Hackensack—and the local terrain is reclaimed by the natives who till the fields, milk the cows, keep the stores, and work year round for the county and the state. I am one of two Jewish children in a class of twenty-five, and a feel for the rules and preferences of society (as ingrained in me, it seems, as susceptibility to the feverish, the flamboyant, the bizarre) dictates that, regardless of how tempted I may be to light my fuse and show these hicks a few of Herbie's fireworks, I do not distinguish myself from my schoolmates by anything other than grades. To do otherwise, I realize—and without my father even having to remind me—will get me nowhere. And nowhere is not where I am expected to go.

So, like a boy on a calendar illustration, I trudge nearly two miles through billowing snowdrifts down our mountain road to the school where I spend my winters excelling, while far to the south, in that biggest of cities, where anything goes, Herbie (who sells linoleum for an uncle during the day and plays with a Latin American combo on weekends) strives to perfect the last of his lavatory impressions. He writes of his progress in a letter that I carry hidden

away in the button-down back pocket of my knickers and reread
every chance I get; aside from birthday cards and stamp "ap-
provals," it is the only piece of mail I have ever received. Of course
I am terrified that if I should drown while ice skating or break my
neck while sledding, the envelope postmarked BROOKLYN, NY will be
found by one of my schoolmates, and they will all stand around my
corpse holding their noses. My mother and father will be shamed
forever. The Hungarian Royale will lose its good name and go
bankrupt. Probably I will not be allowed to be buried within the
cemetery walls with the other Jews. And all because of what Herbie dares to write down on a piece of paper and then mail through
a government post office to a nine-year-old child, who is imagined
by his world (and thus by himself) to be pure. Does Bratasky really
fail to understand how decent people feel about such things?
Doesn't he know that even sending a letter like this he is probably
breaking a law, and making of me an accomplice? But if so, why do
I persist in carrying the incriminating document around with me all
day long? It is in my pocket even while I am on my feet battling for
first place in the weekly spelling bee against the other finalist, my
curly-haired co-religionist and the concert-pianist-to-be, brilliant
Madeline Levine; it is in my pajama pocket at night, to be read by
flashlight beneath the covers, and then to sleep with, next to my
heart. "I am really getting down to a science how it sounds when
you pull the paper off the roller. Which about gives me the whole
shmeer, kid. Herbert L. Bratasky *and nobody else in the world* can
now do taking a leak, taking a crap, diarrhea—*and* unrolling the
paper itself. That leaves me just one mountain to climb—wiping!"

By the time I am eighteen and a freshman at Syracuse, my penchant for mimicry very nearly equals my mentor's, only instead of
imitations à la Bratasky, I do Bratasky, the guests, and the characters on the staff. I impersonate our tuxedoed Rumanian headwaiter
putting on the dog in the dining room—"This way, please, Mon-
sieur Kornfeld . . . Madame, more derma?"—then, back in the
kitchen, threatening in the coarsest Yiddish to strangle the drunken
chef. I impersonate our Gentiles, the gawky handyman George,
shyly observing the ladies' poolside rumba class, and Big Bud, the
aging muscular lifeguard (and grounds attendant) who smoothly
hustles the vacationing housewife, and then, if he can, her nubile
offspring sunning her new nose job. I even do a long dialogue
(tragical-comical-historical-pastoral) of my exhausted parents

undressing for bed the night after the close of the season. To find that the most ordinary events out of my former life are considered by others to be so *entertaining* somewhat astonishes me—also I am startled at first to discover that not everybody seems to have enjoyed formative years so densely populated with vivid types. Nor had I begun to imagine that I was quite so vivid myself.

In my first few semesters at college I am awarded leading roles in university productions of plays by Giraudoux, Sophocles, and Congreve. I appear in a musical comedy, singing, and even dancing, in my fashion. There seems to be nothing I cannot do on a stage—there would seem to be nothing that can keep me *off* the stage. At the beginning of my sophomore year, my parents visit school to see me play Tiresias—older, as I interpret the role, than the two of them together—and afterward, at the opening-night party, they watch uneasily as I respond to a request from the cast to entertain with an imitation of the princely rabbi with the perfect diction who annually comes "all the way" from Poughkeepsie to conduct High Holiday services in the casino of the hotel. The following morning I show them around the campus. On the path to the library several students compliment me on my staggering rendition of old age the night before. Impressed—but reminding me also, with a touch of her irony, that not so long ago the stage star's diapers were hers to change and wash—my mother says, "Everybody knows you already, you're famous," while my father, struggling with disappointment, asks yet again, "And medical school is out?" Whereupon I tell him for the tenth time—*telling* him it's the tenth time—"I want to act," and believe as much myself, until that day when all at once performing, in my fashion, seems to me the most pointless, ephemeral, and pathetically self-aggrandizing of pursuits. Savagely I turn upon myself for allowing everyone, indeed, to know me already, to glimpse the depths of mindless vanity that the confines of the nest and the strictures of the sticks had previously prevented me from exposing, even to myself. I am so humiliated by the nakedness of what I have been up to that I consider transferring to another school, where I can start out afresh, untainted in the eyes of others by egomaniacal cravings for spotlight and applause.

Months follow in which I adopt a penitential new goal for myself every other week. I *will* go to medical school—and train to be a surgeon. Though perhaps as a psychiatrist I can do even more good

for mankind. I will become a lawyer . . . a diplomat . . . why *not* a
rabbi, one who is studious, contemplative, *deep* . . . I read *I and
Thou* and the Hasidic tales, and home on vacation question my parents about the family's history in the old country. But as it is over
fifty years since my grandparents emigrated to America, and as
they are dead and their children by and large without any but the
most sentimental interest in our origins in mid-Europe, in time I
give up the inquiry, and the rabbinical fantasy with it. Though not
the effort to ground myself in what is substantial. It is still with the
utmost self-disgust that I remember my decrepitude in *Oedipus
Rex*, my impish charm in *Finian's Rainbow*—all that cloying *acting!*
Enough frivolity and manic showing off! At twenty I must stop
impersonating others and Become Myself, or at least begin to impersonate the self I believe I ought now to be.

He—the next me—turns out to be a sober, solitary, rather refined
young man devoted to European literature and languages. My fellow actors are amused by the way in which I abandon the stage
and retreat into a rooming house, taking with me as companions
those great writers whom I choose to call, as an undergraduate,
"the architects of my mind." "Yes, David has left the world," my
drama society rival is reported to be saying, "to become a man of
the cloth." Well, I have my airs, and the power, apparently, to
dramatize myself and my choices, but above all it is that I am an
absolutist—a *young* absolutist—and know no way to shed a skin
other than by inserting the scalpel and lacerating myself from end
to end. I am one thing or I am the other. Thus, at twenty, do I set
out to undo the contradictions and overleap the uncertainties.

During my remaining years at college I live somewhat as I had
during my boyhood winters, when the hotel was shut down and I
read hundreds of library books through hundreds of snowstorms.
The work of repairing and refurbishing goes on daily throughout
the Arctic months—I hear the sound of the tire chains nicking at the
plowed roadways, I hear planks dropping off the pickup truck into
the snow, and the simple inspiring noises of the hammer and the
saw. Beyond the snow-caked sill I see George driving down with
Big Bud to fix the cabanas by the covered pool. I wave my arm,
George blows the horn . . . and to me it is as though the Kepeshes
are now three animals in cozy, fortified hibernation, Mamma, Papa,
and Baby safely tucked away in Family Paradise.

Instead of the vivid guests themselves, we have with us in winter their letters, read aloud and with no deficiency of vividness or volume by my father at the dinner table. *Selling himself* is the man's specialty, as he sees it; likewise, *showing people a good time,* and, no matter how ill-mannered they themselves may be, *treating them like human beings.* In the off-season, however, the balance of power shifts a little, and it is the clientele, nostalgic for the stuffed cabbage and the sunshine and the laughs, who divest themselves of their exacting imperiousness—"They sign the register," says my mother, "and every *ballagula* and his *shtunk* of a wife is suddenly the Duke and the Duchess of Windsor"—and begin to treat my father as though he too were a paid-up member of the species, rather than the target for their discontent, and straight man for their ridiculous royal routines. When the snow is deepest, there are sometimes as many as four and five newsy letters a week—an engagement in Jackson Heights, moving to Miami because of health, opening a second store in White Plains . . . Oh, how he loves getting news of the best and the worst that is happening to them. That proves something to him about what the Hungarian Royale means to people—that proves everything, in fact, and not only about the meaning of his hotel.

After reading the letters, he clears a place at the end of the table, and beside a plate full of my mother's *rugalech,* and in his sprawling longhand, composes his replies. I correct the spelling and insert punctuation where he has drawn the dashes that separate his single run-on paragraph into irregular chunks of philosophizing, reminiscence, prophecy, sagacity, political analysis, condolence, and congratulation. Then my mother types each letter on Hungarian Royale stationery—below the inscription that reads, *"Old Country Hospitality In A Beautiful Mountain Setting. Dietary Laws Strictly Observed. Your Proprietors, Abe and Belle Kepesh"*—and adds the P.S. confirming reservations for the summer ahead and requesting a small deposit.

Before she met my father on a vacation in these very hills—he was then twenty-one, and without a calling, spending the summer as a short-order cook—she worked for her first three years out of high school as a legal secretary. As legend has it, she had been a meticulous, conscientious young woman of astounding competence, who all but lived to serve the patrician Wall Street lawyers who employed her, men whose stature—moral *and* physical—she will in fact speak of reverentially until she dies. Her Mr. Clark, a grandson of the firm's founder, continues sending her birthday greetings by telegram even after he retires to Arizona, and every year, with the telegram in her hand, she says dreamily to my balding father and to little me, "Oh, he was such a tall and handsome man. And so dignified. I can still remember how he stood up at his desk when I came into his office to be interviewed for the job. I don't think I'll ever forget that posture of his." But, as it happened, it was a burly, hirsute man, with a strong prominent cask of a chest, Popeye's biceps, and no class credentials, who saw her leaning on a piano singing "Amapola" with a group of vacationers up from the city, and promptly said to himself, "I'm going to marry that girl." Her hair and her eyes were so dark, and her legs and bosom so round and "well developed" that he thought at first she might actually be Spanish. And the besetting passion for impeccability that had endeared her so to the junior Mr. Clark only caused her to be all the more alluring to the energetic young go-getter with not a little of the slave driver in his own driven, slavish soul.

Unfortunately, once she marries, the qualities that had made her the austere Gentile boss's treasure bring her very nearly to the brink of nervous collapse by the end of each summer—for even in a small family-run hotel like ours there is always a complaint to be investigated, an employee to be watched, linens to be counted, food to be tasted, accounts to be tallied . . . on and on and on it goes, and, alas, she can never leave a job to the person supposed to be doing it, not when she discovers that it is not being Done Right. Only in the winter, when my father and I assume the unlikely roles of Clark *père* and *fils*, and she sits in perfect typing posture at the big black Remington Noiseless precisely indenting his garrulous replies, do I get a glimpse of the demure and happy little *señorita* with whom he had fallen in love at first sight.

Sometimes after dinner she even invites me, a grade-school child, to pretend that I am an executive and to dictate a letter to her so that she can show me the magic of her shorthand. "You own a shipping company," she tells me, though in fact I have only just been allowed to buy my first penknife, "go ahead." Regularly enough she reminds me of the distinction between an ordinary office secretary and what she had been, which was a *legal* secretary. My father proudly confirms that she had indeed been the most flawless legal secretary ever to work for the firm—Mr. Clark had written as much to him in a letter of congratulation on the occasion of their engage-

ment. Then one winter, when apparently I am of age, she teaches
me to type. No one, before or since, has ever taught me anything
with so much innocence and conviction.

But that is winter, the secret season. In summer, surrounded, her
dark eyes dart frantically, and she yelps and yipes like a sheep dog
whose survival depends upon driving his master's unruly flock to
market. A single little lamb drifting a few feet away sends her full-
speed down the rugged slope—a baa from elsewhere, and she is off
in the opposite direction. And it does not stop until the High Holidays are over, and even then it doesn't stop. For when the last
guest has departed, inventory-taking must begin—must! that minute! What has been broken, torn, stained, chipped, smashed, bent,
cracked, pilfered, what is to be repaired, replaced, repainted,
thrown out entirely, "a total loss." To this simple and tidy little
woman who loves nothing in the world so much as the sight of a
perfect, unsmudged carbon copy falls the job of going from room to
room to record in her ledger the extent of the violence that has been
wreaked upon our mountain stronghold by the vandal hordes my
father persists in maintaining—over her vehement opposition—are
only other human beings.

Just as the raging Catskill winters transform each of us back into
a sweeter, saner, innocent, more sentimental sort of Kepesh, so in
my room in Syracuse solitude goes to work on me and gradually I
feel the lightweight and the show-off blessedly taking his leave. Not
that, for all my reading, underlining, and note-taking, I become *entirely* selfless. A dictum attributed to no less notable an egotist than
Lord Byron impresses me with its mellifluous wisdom and resolves
in only six words what was beginning to seem a dilemma of in-
superable moral proportions. With a certain strategic daring, I
begin quoting it aloud to the coeds who resist me by arguing that
I'm too smart for such things. "Studious by day," I inform them,
"dissolute by night." For "dissolute" I soon find it best to substitute
"desirous"—I am not in a palazzo in Venice, after all, but in upstate
New York, on a college campus, and I can't afford to unsettle these
girls any more than I apparently do already with my "vocabulary"
and my growing reputation as a "loner." Reading Macaulay for
English 203, I come upon his description of Addison's collaborator
Steele, and, "Eureka!" I cry, for here is yet *another* bit of presti-
gious justification for my high grades and my base desires. "A rake
among scholars, a scholar among rakes." Perfect! I tack it to my

bulletin board, along with the line from Byron, and directly above the names of the girls whom I have set my mind to *seduce,* a word whose deepest resonances come to me, neither from pornography nor pulp magazines, but from my agonized reading in Kierkegaard's *Either/Or.*

I have only one male friend I see regularly, a nervous, awkward, and homely philosophy major named Louis Jelinek, who in fact is my Kierkegaard mentor. Like me, Louis rents a room in a private house in town rather than live in the college dormitory with boys whose rituals of camaraderie he too considers contemptible. He is working his way through school at a hamburger joint (rather than accept money from the Scarsdale parents he despises) and carries its perfume wherever he goes. When I happen to touch him, either accidentally or simply out of high spirits or fellow feeling, he leaps away as though in fear of having his stinking rags contaminated. "Hands off," he snarls. "What are you, Kepesh, still running for some fucking office?" Am I? It hadn't occurred to me. Which one?

Oddly, whatever Louis says of me, even in pique or in a tirade, seems significant for the solemn undertaking I call "understanding myself." Because he is not interested, as far as I can see, in pleasing anyone—family, faculty, landlady, shopkeepers, and certainly least of all, those "bourgeois barbarians," our fellow students—I imagine him to be more profoundly in touch with "reality" than I am. I am one of those tall, wavy-haired boys with a cleft in his chin who has developed winning ways in high school, and now I cannot seem to shake them, hard as I try. Especially alongside Louis do I feel pitifully banal: so neat, so clean, so *charming* when the need arises, and despite all my disclaimers to the contrary, not quite unconcerned as yet with appearances and reputation. Why can't I be more of a Jelinek, reeking of fried onions and looking down on the entire world? Behold the refuse bin wherein he dwells! Crusts and cores and peelings and wrappings—the perfect mess! Just look upon the clotted Kleenex beside his ravaged bed, Kleenex *clinging* to his tattered carpet slippers. Only seconds after orgasm, and even in the privacy of my locked room, I automatically toss into a wastebasket the telltale evidence of self-abuse, whereas Jelinek—eccentric, contemptuous, unaffiliated, and unassailable Jelinek—seems not to care at all what the world knows or thinks of his copious ejaculations.

I am stunned, can't grasp it, for weeks afterward won't believe it when a student in the philosophy program says in passing one day

that "of course" my friend is a "practicing" homosexual. *My* friend?
It cannot be. "Sissies," of course, I am familiar with. Each summer
we would have a few famous ones at the hotel, little Jewish pashas
on holiday, first brought to my attention by Herbie B. With fascination I used to watch them being carried out of the sunlight and into
the shade, even as they dizzily imbibed sweet chocolate drinks
through a pair of straws, and their brows and cheeks were cleansed
and dried by the handkerchiefs of galley slaves called Grandma,
Mamma, and Auntie. And then there were the few unfortunates at
school, boys born with their arms screwed on like girls, who
couldn't throw a ball right no matter how many private hours of
patient instruction you gave them. But as for a practicing homosexual? Never, never, in all my nineteen years. Except, of course, that
time right after my bar mitzvah, when I took a bus by myself to a
stamp collectors' fair in Albany, and in the Greyhound terminal
there was approached at the urinal by a middle-aged man in a
business suit who whispered to me over my shoulder, "Hey, kid,
want me to blow you?" "No, no, thank you," I replied, and quickly
as I could (though without giving offense, I hoped) moved out of
the men's room, out of the terminal, and made for a nearby department store, where I could be gathered up in the crowd of hetero-
sexual shoppers. In the intervening years, however, no homosexual
had ever spoken to me again, at least none that I knew of.

Till Louis.

Oh, God, does this explain why I am told to keep my hands to
myself when our shirtsleeves so much as brush against each other?
Is it because for him being touched by a boy carries with it the
most serious implications? But, if so, wouldn't a person as forthright
and unconventional as Jelinek come right out and say so? Or could
it be that while my shameful secret with Louis is that under it all I
am altogether ordinary and respectable, a closet Joe College, his
with me is that he's queer? As though to prove how very ordinary
and respectable I really am, I never ask. Instead, I wait in fear for
the day when something Jelinek says or does will reveal the truth
about him. Or has his truth been with me all along? Of course!
Those globs of Kleenex tossed about his room like so many little
posies . . . are they not intended to divulge? to *invite*? . . . is it so
unlikely that some night soon this brainy hawk-nosed creature, who
disdains, on principle, the use of underarm deodorant and is already losing his hair, will jump forth in his ungainly way from

behind the desk where he is lecturing on Dostoevsky and try to catch me in an embrace? Will he tell me he loves me and stick his tongue in my mouth? And what will I say in response, exactly what the innocent, tempting girls say to me? "No, no, please don't! Oh, Louis, you're too smart for this! Why can't we just talk about books?"

But precisely because the idea frightens me so—because I am afraid that I may well be the "hillbilly" and "hayseed" that he delights in calling me when we disagree about the deep meaning of some masterpiece—I continue to visit him in his odoriferous room and sit across the litter from him there talking loudly for hours about the most maddening and vexatious ideas, and praying that he will not make a pass.

Before he can, Louis is dismissed from the university, first for failing to show up at a single class during an entire semester, and then for not even deigning to acknowledge the notes from his adviser asking him to come talk over the problem. Snaps Louis indignantly, sardonically, disgustedly, "*What* problem?" and darts and cranes his head as though the "problem," for all he knows, might be somewhere in the air above us. Though all agree that Louis's is an extraordinary mind, he is refused enrollment for the second semester of his junior year. Overnight he disappears from Syracuse (no goodbyes, needless to say) and almost immediately is drafted. So I learn when an F.B.I. agent with an undeflectable gaze comes around to question me after Louis deserts basic training and (as I picture it) goes to hide out from the Korean War in a slum somewhere with his Kierkegaard and his Kleenex.

Agent McCormack asks, "What about his homosexual record, Dave?" Flushing, I reply, "I don't know about that." McCormack says, "But they tell me you were his closest buddy." "They? I don't know who you mean." "The kids over on the campus." "That's a vicious rumor about him—it's totally untrue." "That you were his buddy?" "No, sir," I say, heat again rising unbidden to my forehead, "that he had a 'homosexual record.' They say those things because he was difficult to get along with. He was an unusual person, particularly for around here." "But you got along with him, didn't you?" "Yes. Why shouldn't I?" "No one said you shouldn't. Listen, they tell me you're quite the Casanova." "Oh, yes?" "Yeah. That you really go after the girls. Is that so?" "I suppose," turning from his gaze, and from the implication I sense in his remark that the

girls are only a front. "That wasn't the case with Louis, though,"
says the agent ambiguously. "What do you mean?" "Dave, tell me
something. Level with me. Where do you think he is?" "I don't
know." "But you'd let me in on it, if you did, I'm sure." "Yes, sir."
"Good. Here's my card, if you should happen to find out." "Yes, sir;
thank you, sir." And after he leaves I am appalled by the way I
have conducted myself: my terror of prison, my Lord Fauntleroy
manners, my collaborationist instincts—and my shame over just
about everything.

The girls that I go after.

Usually I pick them up (or at least *out*) in the reading room of
the library, a place comparable to the runway of a burlesque house
in its power to stimulate and focus my desire. Whatever is imper-
fectly suppressed in these neatly dressed, properly bred middle-
class American girls is immediately apparent (or more often than
not, immediately imagined) in this all-pervasive atmosphere of academic propriety. I watch transfixed the girl who plays with the
ends of her hair while ostensibly she is studying her History—while
I am ostensibly studying mine. Another girl, wholly bland tucked in
her classroom chair just the day before, will begin to swing her leg
beneath the library table where she idly leafs through a *Look* magazine, and my craving knows no bounds. A third girl leans forward
over her notebook, and with a muffled groan, as though I am being
impaled, I observe the breasts beneath her blouse push softly into
her folded arms. How I wish I were those arms! Yes, almost nothing is necessary to set me in pursuit of a perfect stranger, nothing,
say, but the knowledge that while taking notes from the encyclopedia with her right hand, she cannot keep the index finger of her
left hand from tracing circles on her lips. I refuse—out of an inca-
pacity that I elevate to a principle—to resist whatever I find irresistible, regardless of how unsubstantial and quirky, or childish and
perverse, the source of the appeal might strike anyone else. Of
course this leads me to seek out girls I might otherwise find commonplace or silly or dull, but I for one am convinced that dullness
isn't their whole story, and that because my desire *is desire,* it is not
to be belittled or despised.

"Please," they plead, "why don't you just talk and be nice? You
can be so nice, if you want to be." "Yes, so they tell me." "But don't
you see, this is only my body. I don't want to relate to you on that
level." "You're out of luck. Nothing can be done about it. Your

body is sensational." "Oh, don't start saying that again." "Your ass is sensational." "Please don't be crude. You don't talk that way in class. I love listening to you, but not when you insult me like this." "Insult? It's high praise. Your ass is marvelous. It's perfect. You should be thrilled to have it." "It's only what I sit on, David." "The hell it is. Ask a girl who doesn't own one quite that shape if she'd like to swap. That should bring you to your senses." "Please stop making fun of me and being sarcastic. *Please.*" "I'm not making fun of you. I'm taking you as seriously as anybody has ever taken you in your life. Your ass is a masterpiece."

No wonder that by my senior year I have acquired a "terrible" reputation among the sorority girls whose sisters I have attempted to seduce with my brand of aggressive candor. Given the reputation, you would think that I had already reduced a hundred coeds to whoredom, when in fact in four years' time I actually succeed in achieving full penetration on but two occasions, and something vaguely resembling penetration on two more. More often than not, where physical rapture should be, there logical (and illogical) discourse is instead: I argue, if I must, that I have never tried to mislead anyone about my desire or her desirability, that far from being "exploitive," I am just one of the few honest people around. In a burst of calculated sincerity—miscalculated sincerity, it turns out—I tell one of the girls how the sight of her breasts pressing against her arms had led me to wish I were those arms. And is this so different, I ask, pushing on with the charm, from Romeo, beneath Juliet's balcony, whispering, "See! how she leans her cheek upon her hand:/ O! that I were a glove upon that hand,/ That I might touch that cheek." Apparently it is quite different. During my last year at college there are times when the phone actually goes dead at the other end after I announce who is calling, and the few nice girls who are still willing to take their chances and go out alone with me are, I am told (by the nice girls themselves), considered nearly suicidal.

I also continue to earn the amused disdain of my high-minded friends in the drama society. Now the satirists among them have it that I have given up holy orders to take on our cheerleading squad; and a far cry, that, from enacting the sexual angst of Strindberg and O'Neill. Well, so they think.

In fact, there is only one cheerleader in my life to bring to me the unadulterated agonies of a supreme frustration and render ridiculous my rakish dreams, a certain Marcella "silky" Walsh, from Plattsburg, New York. Doomed longing begins when I attend a basketball game one night to watch her perform, having met her in the university cafeteria line that afternoon and gotten a glimpse up close of that bounteous cushion, that most irresistible of bonbons, her lower lip. There is a cheer wherein each of the girls on the squad places one fist on her hip and with the other rhythmically pumps away at the air, all the while arching farther and farther back from the waist. To the seven other girls in brief, white, pleated skirts and bulky white sweaters the sequence of movements seems only so much peppy gymnastic display, to be executed with unsparing energy and at the edge of hilarity. Only in the slowly up-turning belly of Marcella Walsh is there the smoldering suggestion (inescapable to me) of an offering, of an invitation, of a lust that is eager and unconscious and so clearly (to my eyes) begging to be satisfied. Yes, she alone seems (to me, to me) to sense that the tame and harnessed vehemence of this insipid cheer is but the thinnest disguise for the raw chant to be uttered while a penis propels into ecstasy that rising pelvis of hers. Oh, God, how can my coveting that pelvis thrust so provocatively toward the mouth of the howling mob, how can coveting those hard and tiny fists which speak to me of the pleasantest of all struggles, how can coveting those long and strong tomboyish legs that quiver ever so slightly as the arc is made and her silky hair (from which derives her pet name) sweeps back against the gymnasium floor—how can coveting the minutest pulsa-tions of her being be "meaningless" or "trivial," "beneath" either me *or* her, while passionately rooting for Syracuse to win the NCAA basketball championship makes sense?

This is the line of reasoning that I take with Silky herself, and with which in time (oh, the time! the hours of debate that might have been spent cheering one another on to oceanic orgasms!) I hope to clear the way for those piercing erotic pleasures I have yet to know. Instead, I have to put aside logic, wit, candor, yes, and lit-erary scholarship too, to put aside every reasonable attempt at per-suasion—and at last all dignity as well—I have finally to turn as piti-ful and craven as a waif in a famine before Silky, who has probably never seen anyone quite so miserable before, will allow me to shower kisses on her bare midriff. Since she really is the sweetest and most well-meaning of girls, hardly cruel enough or cold enough to reduce even a dirty-minded Romeo, a dean's list Bluebeard, a

budding Don Giovanni and Johannes the Seducer to abject sup-
pliance, I may kiss the belly about which I have spoken so "obses-
sively," but no more. "No higher and no lower," she whispers, from
where I have her bent backward over a sink in the pitch-black
laundry room of her dormitory basement. "David, no lower, I said.
How can you even want to *do* a thing like that?"

So, between the yearnings and the myriad objects of desire, my
world interposes its arguments and obstructions. My father doesn't
understand me, the F.B.I. doesn't understand me, Silky Walsh
doesn't understand me, neither the sorority girls nor the bohemians
understand me—not even Louis Jelinek ever really understood me,
and, unlikely as it sounds, this alleged homosexual (wanted by the
police) has been my closest friend. No, nobody understands me, not
even I myself.

I arrive in London to begin my fellowship year in literature after
six days on a ship, a train ride up from Southampton, and a long
ride on the Underground out to a district called Tooting Bec. Here,
on an endless street of mock Tudor houses, and not in Bloomsbury,
as I had requested, the King's College accommodations office has
arranged lodgings for me in a private home. After I am shown to
my grim little attic room by the retired army captain and his wife
whose tidy, airless house this is—and with whom, I learn, I will be
taking my evening meals—I look at the iron bedstead on which I
am to spend the next three hundred nights or so, and in an instant
am bereft of the high spirits with which I had crossed the Atlantic,
the pure joy with which I had fled from all the constraining rituals
of undergraduate life, and from the wearisome concern of the
mother and father whom I believe have ceased to nourish me. But
Tooting Bec? This tiny room? My meals across from the captain's
hairline mustache? And for what, to study Arthurian legends and
Icelandic sagas? Why all this punishment just for being smart!

My misery is raw and colossal. In my wallet is the phone number
of a teacher of paleography at King's given me by his friend, one of
my Syracuse professors. But how can I phone this distinguished
scholar and tell him within an hour of my arrival that I want to
hand in my Fulbright and go home? "They chose the wrong appli-
cant—I'm not serious enough to suffer like this!" With the captain's
stout and kindly wife assisting—convinced by my coloring that I am
Armenian, she mumbles to me all the while something about new

carpets for the parlor—I find the phone in the hallway and dial. I
am only inches from tears (I am really only inches from phoning
collect to the Catskills), but scared and miserable as I am, it turns
out that I am even more scared of confessing to being scared and
miserable, for when the professor answers, I hang up.

Four or five hours later—night having fallen over Western
Europe, and my first English meal of tinned spaghetti on toast having been more or less digested—I make for a London courtyard that
I had learned about during the crossing. It is called Shepherd Market, and it provides me with an experience that alters considerably
my attitude toward being a Fulbright fellow. Yes, even before I attend my first lectures on the epic and the romance, I begin to understand that for an unknown lad to have traveled to an unknown
land may not have been a mistake after all. Terrified I am of course
of dying like Maupassant; nonetheless, only minutes after peering
timidly into the notorious alleyway, I have had a prostitute—the first
whore of my life, and what is more, the first of my three sexual
partners to date to have been born outside the continental United
States (outside the state of New York, to be exact) and in a year
prior to my own birth. Indeed, when she is astride me and is suddenly gravity's to do with as it wishes, I realize with an odd, repulsive sort of thrill that this woman whose breasts collide above my
head like caldrons—whom I chose from among her competitors on
the basis of these behemoth breasts and a no less capacious behind
—was probably born prior to the outbreak of World War I. Imagine
that, before the publication of *Ulysses,* before . . . but even as I am
trying to place her in the century, I find that rather more quickly
than I had planned—as though, in fact, one or the other of us is rac-
ing to make a train—I am being urged on to my big finale with the
unbidden assistance of a sure, swift, unsentimental hand.

I discover Soho on my own the next night. I also discover in the
Columbia Encyclopedia that I have lugged across the sea, along
with Baugh's *Literary History of England* and the three paperback
volumes of Trevelyan, that the final stages of *his* venereal disease
finished Maupassant off at forty-three. Nonetheless, I still cannot
think of anywhere I would rather be, following my dinner with the
captain and the captain's wife, than in a room with a whore who
will do whatever I wish—no, not after dreaming about paying for
this privilege ever since I was twelve and had my allowance of a
dollar a week to save up for anything I wanted. Of course if I chose

whores less whorish-looking my chances of dying of VD rather than of old age might appreciably diminish. But what sense is there in having a whore who doesn't look and talk and behave like one? I am not in search of a girl friend, after all, not quite yet. And when I am ready for her it isn't to Soho that I take myself, but to lunch on a herring at a restaurant near Harrods called the Midnight Sun.

The mythology of the Swedish girl and her sexual freedom is, during these years, in its first effulgence, and despite the natural skepticism aroused in me by the stories of insatiable appetite and odd proclivities that I hear around the college, I happily play hooky from my ancient Norse studies in order to find out for myself just how much truth there may be in all this titillating schoolboy speculation. Off then to the Midnight Sun, where the waitresses are said to be sex-crazed young Scandinavian goddesses who serve you their native dishes while dressed in colorful folk costumes, painted wooden clogs that display their golden legs to great advantage, and peasant bodices that cross-lace up the front and press into view the enticing swell of their breasts.

It is here that I meet Elisabeth Elverskog—and poor Elisabeth meets me. Elisabeth has taken a year off from the University of Lund in order to improve her English, and is living with another Swede, the daughter of friends of her family, who had left the University of Uppsala two years earlier to improve *her* English, and has not gotten around yet to going back. Birgitta, who entered England as a student and supposedly is taking courses at London University, works in Green Park collecting the penny rental for a deck chair, and, unbeknownst to Elisabeth's family, collecting such adventures as come her way. The basement flat Elisabeth shares with Birgitta is in a rooming house off Earl's Court Road inhabited mostly by students several tones darker than the girls. Elisabeth confesses to me that she is not too crazy about the place—the Indians, against whom she has no racial prejudice, distress her by cooking curried dishes in their rooms all hours of the night, and the Africans, against whom she has no racial prejudice either, sometimes reach out and touch her hair when they pass in the corridor, and though she understands why, and realizes they mean her no harm, it still makes her tremble a little each time it happens. However, in her compliant and good-natured way, Elisabeth has decided to accept the minor indignities of the hallway—and the general squalor of the neighborhood—as part of the adventure of living abroad until June, when she will return to spend the summer with her family at their vacation house in the Stockholm archipelago.

I describe for Elisabeth my own monkish accommodations and do an imitation that amuses her enormously of the captain and his wife telling me that they do not permit cohabitation on the premises, not even between themselves. And when I do an imitation of her own singsong English, she laughs still more.

For the first few weeks, small, dark-haired, and (to my mind) fetchingly buck-toothed Birgitta pretends to be asleep when Elisabeth and I arrive in their basement room and pretend not to be making love. I don't think the excitement I experience when we three suddenly give up the pretense is any greater than it was while we all held our breath and pretended that nothing out of the ordinary was going on. I am so dizzily elated over the change that has taken place in my life since I thought to have lunch at the Midnight Sun—indeed, since I subdued my fears and stepped into Shepherd Market to seek out the whoriest of whores—I am in such an egoistical frenzy over this improbable thing that is happening to me, not just with one but with two Swedish (or, if you will, *European*) girls, that I do not see Elisabeth slowly going to pieces from the effort of being a fully participating sinner in our intercontinental ménage, a half of what can only be called my harem.

Maybe I don't see it because she is in something of a frenzy of her own—a drowning frenzy, a wild thrashing about in order to stay afloat—and as a result seems often to be *enjoying* herself so much; that is, I take the excitement for pleasurable excitement, certainly so when we three go off with a picnic lunch and a tennis ball to spend a Sunday on Hampstead Heath. I teach the girls "running bases"—and could Elisabeth be more delighted by anything than to be caught in a screaming, hilarious rundown between Birgitta and myself?—and they teach me *brännboll*, bits and pieces of fly-catcher-up and stickball, which combine into a game they played in Stockholm as schoolchildren. When it rains we play cards together, gin or canasta. The old king, Gustav V, was a passionate gin-rummy player, I am told, as are Birgitta's mother and father and brother and sister. Elisabeth, whose circle of Gymnasium friends had apparently idled away hundreds of afternoons at canasta, picks up gin rummy after just half an hour of watching a few games between Birgitta and me. She is captivated by the patter I deliver during the game, and takes immediately to using it herself—as did I at eight or so, back when I learned it all at the feet of Klotzer the Soda Water King (said by my mother to be the heaviest guest in Hungarian Royale history—when Mr. Klotzer lowered his behind onto our wicker, she had sometimes to cover her eyes—and a marathon monologuist and sufferer at the card table). Says Elisabeth, sadly arranging and rearranging the cards that Birgitta has dealt her, "I got a hand like a foot," and when she lays down her melds in triumph, it pleases her no end—it pleases *me* no end—to hear her ask of her opponent, "What's the name of the game, Sport?" Oh, and when she calls the wild card in canasta the "yoker"—well, that just slays me. How on earth can she be going to pieces? *I'm* not! And what about our serious and maddening discussions of World War II, during which I try to explain—and not always in a soft voice either—to explain to these two self-righteous neutralists just what was going on in Europe when we were all growing up? Isn't it Elisabeth who is in fact more vehement (and innocently simpleminded) than Birgitta, who insists, even when I practically threaten to *slap* some sense into her, that the war was "everybody's fault"? How then can I tell that she is not only going to pieces but also thinking from morning to night about how to do herself in?

After the "accident"—so we describe in the telegram to her parents the broken arm and the mild concussion Elisabeth sustains by walking in front of a truck sixteen days after I move from Tooting Bec into the girls' basement—I continue to hang my tweed jacket in her closet and to sleep, or to try to, in her bed. And I actually believe that I am staying on there because in my state of shock I am simply *unable* to move out as yet. Night after night, under Birgitta's nose, I write letters to Stockholm in which I set out to explain myself to Elisabeth, rather, I sit down at my typewriter to begin the paper I must soon deliver in my Icelandic Saga tutorial on the decline of skaldic poetry through the overuse of the kenning, and wind up telling Elisabeth that I had not realized she was trying only to please me, but altogether innocently—"altogether unforgivably"—had believed that, like Birgitta and like myself, she had been pleasing herself first of all. Again and again—on the Underground, in the pub, during a lecture—I take her very first letter, written from her bedroom the day she had arrived back home, and uncrumple it to reread those primary-school sentences that have the Sacco and Vanzetti effect every time—what an idiot I have been, how callous, how blind! *"Älskade David!"* she begins, and then, in her English, goes on to explain that she had fallen in love with me, not with Gittan, and had gone to bed with the two of us only because I wanted her to and she would have done anything I wanted her to do . . . and, she adds in the tiniest script, she is afraid she would again if she were to return to London—

I am not a strong girl as Gittan. I am just a weak one Bettan, and I can't do anything about it. It was like being in hell. I was in love with someone and what I did had nothing to do with love. It was like I no more was human being. I am so stupid and my english is strange when I write, I am sorry for that. But I know I must never again do what we three did as long as I live. So the silly girl have learned something.

Din Bettan

And, below this, Bettan's forgiving afterthought: *"Tusen pussar och kramar"*—a thousand kisses and hugs.

In my own letters I confess again and again that I had been blind to the nature of her real feeling for me—blind to the depth of my feelings for *her!* I call that unforgivable too, and "sad," and "strange," and when the contemplation of this ignorance of mine brings me nearly to tears, I call it "terrifying"—and mean it. And this in turn leads me to try to give both of us some hope by telling her that I have found a room for myself (in only a matter of days I do intend to inquire about one) in a university residence hall, and that henceforth she should write to me there—if she should ever want to write to me again—rather than at the old address, in care of Birgitta . . . And in the midst of composing these earnest apologias and petitions for pardon, I am overcome with the most unruly and contradictory emotions—a sense of unworthiness, of loathsomeness, of genuine shame and remorse, and simultaneously as strong a sense that I am not guilty of anything, that it is as much the fault of those Indians cooking curried rice at 2 a.m. as it is mine that innocent, undefended Elisabeth stepped in the path of that truck. And what *about* Birgitta, who was supposed to have been Elisabeth's protector, and who now merely lies on the bed across the room from me, studying her English grammar, unmoved utterly—or so she pretends—by my drama of self-disgust? As though, since it was Elisabeth's arm, rather than neck, that was broken by the truck, *she* is entirely in the clear! As though Elisabeth's behavior with us is for Elisabeth's conscience alone to reckon with . . . and not hers . . . and not mine. But surely, *surely*, Birgitta is no less guilty than I am of misusing Elisabeth's pliable nature. Or is she? Wasn't it Birgitta rather than me to whom Elisabeth would instinctively turn for affection whenever she needed it most? When, depleted, we lay together on the threadbare rug—for it was the floor, not the bed, we used mostly as our sacrificial altar—when we would be lying there, dead limbs amid the little undergarments, groggy, sated, and confused, it was invariably Birgitta who held Elisabeth's head and gently stroked her face and whispered lullaby words like the kindest of mothers. My arms, my hands, my words didn't seem to be of any use to anyone at that point. The way it worked, my arms, hands, and words meant everything—until I came, and then the two girls huddled up together like playmates off in a tree house, or in a tent where there is just no room for another . . .

Leaving my letter half-written, I go barging out into the street and walk halfway across London (in the direction of Soho generally) to bring myself under control. I try, on these Raskolnikovian sojourns (Raskolnikov, admittedly, as played by Pudd'nhead Wilson), to "think things through." That is, I should like, if I can, to be able to deal with this unexpected turn of events the way Birgitta does. And since I don't seem able to arrive at that kind of equanimity spontaneously—or marshal that kind of strength, if strength it is—how about if I try to *reason* my way into her shoes? Yes, use my Fulbright fellow's brain—it's got to be good for something over here! Think it through, damn it! It's not that difficult. You didn't roll around on these two girls so as to set yourself up in business as a saint! Far from it! You didn't think up the things you all did so as to please the old folks at home! Far from it! Either go back and play patty-cake with Silky Walsh, or stay where you are and want what you want! Birgitta is human too, you know! Strong and clearheaded is human too (if strong and clearheaded it is), and blubbering is not becoming, over the age of four! Nor is the naughty-boy bit! Elisabeth is perfectly right: Gittan is Gittan, Bettan is Bettan, and now it is about time you were you!

Well, "thinking things through" in this manner, it is never too long before I wind up recollecting that night when Birgitta and I kept asking and asking Elisabeth—hounding and hounding Elisabeth—about what we had already cross-examined one another: what was it she secretly wanted most, what was it that she only dared to think about herself and never in her life had had the courage to do or to have done to her? "What is it you've never been able to admit to anyone, Elisabeth, not even to yourself?" Clinging with ten fingers to the blanket dragged from the bed to cover us all on the floor, Elisabeth began softly to weep, and in that charming, musical English admitted she wanted to be had from behind while bending over a chair.

I found no satisfaction in her reply. Only after I had pressed her further, only after I had demanded, "But what else—what more? That's nothing!"—only then did she at last break down and "confess" that she wanted me to do it to her like that while her hands and feet were tied down. And maybe she did and maybe she didn't . . .

Passing through Piccadilly, I compose yet another paragraph of moral speculation for the latest letter intended to educate my innocent victim—and me. In truth, I am trying with what wisdom—and what prose resources and literary models—is mine to understand if in fact I have been what the Christians call wicked and what I would call inhuman. "And even if you had *actually* wanted what you told us you wanted, what law says that whatever secret longing one is asked to satisfy must be satisfied forthwith? . . ." We had used the belt from my trousers and a strap from Birgitta's knapsack to bind Elisabeth to a straight-backed chair. Once again the tears came rolling down her face, causing Birgitta to touch her cheek and to ask her, "Bettan, you want to stop now?" But Elisabeth's long trailing locks, that child's length of amber hair, whipped across her bare back, so vehemently did she shake her head in defiance. Defiance of whom, I wonder. Of what? Why, I don't begin to know a thing about her! "No," Elisabeth whispered. The only word she spoke from start to finish. "No stop?" I asked. "Or no go on? Elisabeth, do you understand me—? Ask her in Swedish, ask her—" But "no" is all she will answer; "no," and "no," and "no" again. And so it was that I proceeded as I sort of believed I was being directed to. Elisabeth weeps, Birgitta watches, and suddenly I am so excited by it all—by the panting, dog-like sounds the three of us are making, by what the three of us are *doing*—that all traces

of reluctance drop away, and I know that I could do *anything*, and
that I want to, and that I will! Why not four girls, why not five—
". . . who but the wicked would hold that whatever longing one is
asked to satisfy must be satisfied forthwith? Yet, dearest, sweetest,
precious girl, that appeared to be the very law under which we
three had decided—had *agreed*—to live!" And by now I am in a
hallway on Greek Street, where at last I stop thinking about what
next to write to Elisabeth on the unfathomable subject of my iniq-
uity, and thinking too about this unfathomable Birgitta—*has* she no
remorse? no shame? no loyalty? no limits?—who must by now have
read the half-written letter left by me in my Olivetti (and which
surely will impress her with just how *deep* a sultan I am).

In a little room above a Chinese laundry, I try my luck with a
thirty-shilling whore, a fading Cockney milkmaid called Terry the
Tart who thinks me "a sexy bah-stard" and whose plucky lewdness
had, once upon a time, a most startling effect upon the detonation
of my seed. Now Terry's skills go for nought. She gives me her extraordinary collection of dirty pictures to look at; she describes,
with no less imagination than Mrs. Browning, the ways in which
she will love me; indeed, she praises to the skies the breadth and
height of my member and its depth of penetration when last seen
erect; but the fifteen minutes of hard labor she then puts in over
the recumbent lump is without significant result. Taking such com-
fort as I can from the tender way Terry puts it—"Sorry, Yank, 'c
seems a bit sleepy tonight"—I head back across London to our basement, finishing up as I go with that day's inquiry into the evil I may
or may not have done.

As it turns out, I would have been better off applying all this concentration to the excessive use of the kenning in the latter half of
the twelfth century in Iceland. That, in time, is something I could
have made some sense of. Instead, I seem to get nowhere near the
truth, or even the feel of the truth, in the prolix letters I regularly
address to Stockholm, while the scholarly essay I finally read before
my tutorial group prompts the tutor to invite me back to his office
after class, to sit me down in a chair, and to ask, with only the
faintest trace of sarcasm, "Tell me, Mr. Kepesh, are you sure you
are serious about Icelandic poetry?"

A teacher taking me to task! As unimaginable, this, as my sixteen
days in one room with two girls! As Elisabeth Elverskog's attempt
at suicide! I am so stunned and humiliated by this chastisement

(especially coming in the wake of the accusations that I have been leveling at myself in my capacity as Elisabeth's family's attorney) that I cannot find the courage to return to the tutorial ever again; like Louis Jelinek I do not even respond to the notes asking me to come talk to my tutor about my disappearance. Can it be? I am on my way to failing a course. *In God's name, what next?*

This.

One night Birgitta tells me that while I have been lying gloomily on Elisabeth's bed playing the "fallen priest" she has been doing something "a little perverse." Actually it goes back some time, to when she had first arrived in London two years ago and had gone to see a doctor about a digestive problem. The doctor had told her that to make a diagnosis he would need a vaginal smear. He asked her to disrobe and arrange herself on the examination table, and then with either his hand or an instrument—she had been so startled at the time she still wasn't sure—had begun to massage between her legs. "Please, what is it that you are doing?" she had asked him. According to Birgitta, he'd had the nerve to say in response, "Look, do you think I like this? I've a bad back, my dear, and this posture doesn't help it any. But I must have a specimen and this is the only way I can get it." "Did you let him?" "I didn't know what else to do. How do I tell him to stop? I had just arrived three days here. I was frightened a little, you know, and I wasn't sure I understood his English. And he looked like a doctor. Tall and nice-looking and kind. And very nice clothes. And I thought maybe this is the way they do it here. He kept saying, 'Are you getting cramps yet, my dear?' At first I didn't know what that means—then I got my clothes on and I left. There were people in the waiting room, there was a nurse . . . He sent a bill for two guineas." "He did? And you paid it?" I ask. "No." "And?" I ask, wavering between incredulity and excitement. "Last month," says Birgitta, her English emerging even more deliberately than usual, "I go to him again. I started to think all the time of it. That's what I think of when you are writing all your letters to Bettan." Is that true, I wonder—is any of it true? "And?" I say. "Now once a week I go to his office. For my lunch hour." "And he masturbates you? You let him masturbate you?" "Yes." "Is this the truth, Gittan?" "I close my eyes and he does it to me with his hand." "And—then?" "I get dressed. I go back to the park." I am craving for more—and more lurid even than this—but there is none. He masturbates her, and he lets her go. Can this be true? Do such things happen? "What's his name? Where is his office?" To my surprise, without any reluctance, Birgitta tells me.

Some hours later, having failed to comprehend a single paragraph of *Arthurian Tradition and Chrétien de Troyes* (an invaluable source, I have been told, for the paper now due in my other tutorial), I rush out to a telephone kiosk at the end of our street and search the directory for the doctor's name—and find it, and at the Brompton Road address! Tomorrow morning first thing I will call him up—I will say (perhaps even in my Swedish accent), "Dr. Leigh, you had better watch out, you had better leave your hands off foreign young girls or you are going to get yourself in a lot of trouble." But it seems that I do not really want to reform the lascivious doctor so much as to find out (inasmuch as I can) whether Birgitta's story is true. Not that I know for sure even yet whether I want it to be true or not. Wouldn't I be better off if it weren't?

When I get back to the flat I undress her. And she submits. With what self-possession does she submit—she and submission are thick as thieves! We are both panting and greatly worked up. I am clothed and she is naked. I call her a little whore. She begs me to pull her hair. How hard she wants it pulled I am not sure—no one has ever asked such a thing of me before. God, how far I have come from kissing Silky's navel in the dormitory laundry room just last spring! "I want to know you're here," she cries—"do it more!" "Like this?" "Yes!" "Like this, my whore? my filthy little Birgitta whore!" "Ah, yes! Ah, yes, yes!"

An hour earlier I had been fearful that it might be decades before I was potent again, that my punishment, if such it was, might even last *forever*. Now I spend a night overcome by a passion whose harsh energies I have never allowed myself to begin to know before; or maybe it is that I have never before known a girl of roughly my own age to whom such forcefulness would have been anything other than an outrage. I have been so steeped in cajoling and wheedling and begging my way toward pleasure that I had not known I was actually capable of such a *besiegement* of another, or that I wished to be besieged and assaulted in turn. Straddling her head with my legs, I force my member into her mouth as though it were at once the lifeline that will prevent her suffocation and the instrument upon which she will strangle. And, as though I am her saddle, she plants herself upon my face and rides and rides and rides. "Tell me things!" cries Birgitta, "I like to be told things! Tell me all kind of things!" And in the morning there is no remorse for anything said or done—far from it. "We appear to be two of a kind," I say. She laughs and says, "I know that a long time." "That's why I stayed, you know." "Yes," she replies, "I know that."

Yet I continue writing to Elisabeth (though no longer in Birgitta's presence). In care of a university residence hall—an American friend has arranged to receive my mail in his box there, and forward it to me—Elisabeth sends a photograph showing that her arm is no longer in a cast. On the back of the photograph she has printed, "Me." I write immediately to thank her for the picture of herself healed and healthy again. I tell her that I am making progress in my Swedish grammar book, that I pick up a *Svenska Dagbladet* on Charing Cross Road each week and try at least to read the front-page stories with the aid of the English-Swedish pocket dictionary she gave me. And though in fact it is Birgitta's newspaper that I take a stab at translating—during the time previously reserved for sweating over my Eddas—while I am writing to Elisabeth I believe I am doing it for her, for our future, so that I can marry her and settle down in her homeland, eventually to teach American literature there. Yes, I believe I could yet fall in love with this girl who wears around her neck a locket with her father's picture in it . . . indeed, that I should have already. Her face *alone* is so lovable! Look at it, I tell myself—look, you idiot! Teeth that couldn't be whiter, the ripe curve of her cheeks, enormous blue eyes, and the reddish-amber hair that I once told her—it was the night I received the little dictionary inscribed "From me to you"—was best described in English by "tresses," a poetical word out of fairy stories. "Common" is the English word which she tells me (after looking in the dictionary) best describes her nose. "It is a farm girl's nose," she says, "it is like the thing you plant in the garden to grow tulips." "Not quite." "How do you say that?" "Tulip bulb." "Yes. When I am forty I will look horrible because of this tulip bulb." But the nose is just the nose of millions and millions, and, on Elisabeth, actually touching in its utter lack of pride or pretension. Oh, what a sweet face, so full of the happiness of her childhood! the frothiness of her laugh! her innocent heart! This is the girl who knocked me out just by saying "I got a hand like a foot!" Oh, how incredibly moving a thing it is, a person's innocence! How it catches me off guard each time, that unguarded trusting look!

Yet, work myself up as I will over her photograph, it is with slender little Birgitta, a girl a good deal less innocent and vulnerable—a girl who confronts the world with a narrow foxy face, a nose delicately pointed and an upper lip ever so slightly protruding, a mouth ready, if need be, to answer a charge or utter a challenge—that I continue to live out my year as a visiting fellow in erotic daredevilry.

Of course, strolling around Green Park renting out deck chairs to passers-by, Birgitta is tendered invitations almost daily by men visiting London as tourists, or men out prowling on their lunch hour, or men on their way home to wives and children at the end of the day. Because of the opportunities for pleasure and excitement afforded by these meetings, she had decided against returning to Uppsala after her year's leave of absence and had given up her courses in London, too. "I think I get a better English education this way," says Birgitta.

One March afternoon when suddenly the sun appears, out of the blue, over dreary London, I take the Underground to the park and, sitting under a tree, I watch her, some hundred yards away, engaged in conversation with a gentleman nearly three times my age who is reclining in one of the deck chairs. It is almost an hour before the conversation ends, the gentleman rises, makes a formal bow in her direction, and departs. Could it be somebody she knows? Somebody from home? Could it be Dr. Leigh from the Brompton Road? Without telling her, I travel to the park every afternoon for almost a week and, keeping back in the shadows of the trees, spy upon her at work. I am surprised at first to find myself so enormously excited each time I see Birgitta standing over a deck chair in which a man is seated. Of course, all they ever do is talk. That is all I ever see. Never once do I see either a man touching Birgitta or Birgitta touching a man. And I am almost certain she does not make assignations and go off with any of them after work. But what excites me is that she might, that she could . . . that if I proposed such a thing to her, she probably would do it. "What a day," she says at dinner one evening. "The whole Portuguese navy is here. Feee! What men!" But if I were to say . . .

Only a few weeks later she startles me one evening by saying, "Do you know who came to see me today? Mr. Elverskog." "Who?" "Bettan's father." I think: They have found my letters! Oh, why did I put in writing that stuff about tying her hands to the chair! It's me they're after, the *two* families!" "He came to see you here?" "He knows where I work," says Birgitta, "so he came there." Is Birgitta lying to me, is she doing something "a little perverse" again? But how can she possibly know that all along I have been terrified of Elisabeth breaking down and turning us in, and of her father coming after me, with a Scotland Yard detective, or with his whip . . . "What's he doing in London, Gittan?" "Oh, his business—I don't know. He just came to the park to say hello." *And did you go off to his hotel room with him, Gittan? Would you like to make love with Elisabeth's father? Wasn't he the tall, distinguished-looking gentleman who bowed farewell to you that sunny day in March? Isn't he the old man I saw you listening to so avidly several months ago? Or was that the doctor who likes to play doctor with you in his office? What was he saying to you, that man, just what was he proposing that held your attention so?*

I don't know what to think, and so I think everything.

In bed later, when she wants to be excited by hearing "all kinds of things," I come to the very brink of saying to her, "Would you do it with Mr. Elverskog? Would you do it with a sailor, if I told you to? Would you do it with him for money?" I don't, not simply for fear that she will say yes (as she might, if only for the thrill of saying it), but because I might reply, "Then go ahead, my little whore."

At the end of the term Birgitta and I take a hitchhiking trip on the Continent, looking at museums and cathedrals during the day, and then after dark, in cafés and *caves* and tavernas, training our sights on girls. About leading Birgitta back into this, I have no such scruples as I had in London about tempting her to visit Mr. Elverskog in his hotel. "Another girl" is one of those "things" with which we have aroused one another continually during the months since Elisabeth's departure. To find other girls is, in fact, one of the reasons we are on this holiday. And we are not bad at it, not at all. To be sure, alone neither Birgitta nor I is ever quite so cunning or brave, but together it seems that we strongly reenforce one another's waywardness and, as the nights go by, become more and more adroit at charming perfect strangers. Yet, no matter how skillfully, how *professionally*, we come to maneuver as a team, I still go a little weak and dizzy when it appears that we have actually succeeded in finding a willing third and all of us get up as one to go find a quieter place to talk. Birgitta reports similar symptoms in herself—though out on the street wins my admiration by daring to reach out and push away from her face the hair of the game young student who is daring to see what develops. Yes, seeing my partner so plucky and confident, I recover my faculties—and my balance—and give each of the girls an arm, and, now, without so much as a quiver in my voice, with my worldly mix of irony and bonhomie, say, "Let's go, friends—come along!" And all the while I am thinking what I have been thinking now for months: *Is this happening? This, too?* For in my wallet along with Elisabeth's picture is a photo of her family's seaside house, sent to me just before I received my lamentable grades and boarded the boat-train with Birgitta. I have been invited to visit her on tiny Trångholmen and to stay on the island as long as I wish. And why don't I? And marry her there! Her father knows nothing, and he never will. The whip, the detective, the scenes of vengeful murderous rage, the secret plot to make me pay for what I have done to his daughter—that is all my imagination running wild. Why not let my imagination run another way? Why not imagine Elisabeth and myself rowing past the rocky shore and the tall pine trees, all the way down the length of the island to where the Waxholms ferry docks each day? Why not imagine her family beaming and waving at us when we return in the boat with the milk and the mail? Why not imagine this sweet Elisabeth on the porch of the Elverskogs' pretty barn-red house, pregnant with the first of our Swedish-Jewish children? Yes, there is Elisabeth's unfathomable and wonderful love and there is Birgitta's unfathomable and wonderful daring, *and whichever I want I can have*. Now isn't *that* unfathomable! Either the furnace or the hearth! Ah, this must be what is meant by the possibilities of youth.

More youthful possibilities. In Paris, in a bar not far from the Bastille, where the infamous marquis had himself been punished for his vile and audacious crimes, a prostitute sits in a corner with us and, while she jokes with me in French about my crew cut, is busy stroking Birgitta beneath the table. In the midst of our excitement—for I also have a hand moving under the table—a man looms up, berating me for the indignities that I am making my young wife submit to. I rise with a throbbing heart to explain that we happen not to be husband and wife, that we are students, that what we do is our business—but, despite my excellent pronunciation and perfect grammatical constructions, he pulls a hammer out of his overalls, and raises it into the air. "*Salaud!*" he cries. "*Espèce de con!*" Hand in hand with Birgitta, and for the first time ever, I run for my life.

We do not discuss what will happen when the month is over. Rather, each thinks: Given what has been, what else can be? That is, I assume that I will return to America alone in order to resume my education, this time *seriously*, and Birgitta assumes that when I leave she will pack her knapsack and come with me. Birgitta's parents have already been told that she is thinking of going to study next in America for a year, and apparently that is all right with them. Even if it weren't, Birgitta would probably still do as she pleased.

When I rehearse the difficult conversation that must take place sooner or later, I hear myself sounding very limp and whiny indeed. Nothing I can say comes out right, nothing she can say sounds wrong—and yet it is I, of course, who invent the dialogue. "I am going to Stanford. I am going back to get my degree." "So?" "I have terrible dreams about school, Gittan. Nothing like this has ever happened to me before. I fucked up my Fulbright but good." "Yes?" "And, as for the two of us—" "Yes?" "Well, I don't see that we have any future. Do *you*? I mean we would never be able to go back to ordinary sex. That can never work for us—we've upped the ante much too high. We've gone too far to go back." "We have?" "I think so, yes." "But it wasn't my idea alone, you know." "I didn't say that it was." "So then we stop going too far." "But *we* can't. Oh, come on, you know that." "But I do whatever you want." "That's not possible any longer. Or are you saying that I've had you in my power all along, that you're another Elisabeth I've corrupted?" She smiles her fetching buck-toothed smile. "Who then is the other Elisabeth?" she asks. "*You?* Oh, but that is not so. You say so yourself. You are a whoremaster by nature, you are a polygamist by nature, there is even the rapist in you—" "Well, maybe I've changed my mind about all that; maybe I was foolish to say such things." "But how can you change your mind about what is your nature?" she asks.

In reality, going home to resume my serious education hardly requires that I fight my way, a little helplessly, a little foolishly, through this thicket of flattering objections. No, no challenging debate about my "nature" is necessary for me to be free of her and our fantastical life of thrilling pleasures—at least not right then and there. We are undressing for bed in a room we have rented for the night in a town in the Seine Valley, some thirty kilometers from Rouen, where I intend the next day to visit Flaubert's birthplace, when Birgitta begins to reminisce about the silly dreams that used to be awakened in her as a teenager by the name California: convertible cars, millionaires, James Dean— I interrupt: "I'm going to California by myself. I'm going by myself—on my own."

Minutes later she is dressed again and her knapsack is ready for the road. My God, she is bolder even than I imagined! How many such girls can there be in the world? She dares to do everything, and yet she is as sane as I am. Sane, clever, courageous, self-possessed—and wildly lascivious! Just what I've always wanted. Why am I running away, then? In the name of what? More Arthurian legends and Icelandic sagas? Look, if I were to empty my pockets of Elisabeth's letters and Elisabeth's photographs—and empty my imagination of Elisabeth's father—if I were to give myself completely over to what I have, to whom I am with, to what may actually *be* my nature—"Don't be ridiculous," I say, "where can you find a room at this hour? Oh, damn it, Gittan, I *have* to go to California alone! I've got to go back to school!"

In response, no tears, no anger, and no real scorn to speak of. Though not too much admiration for me as a shameless carnal force. She says from the door, "Why did I like you so much? You are such a boy," and that is all there is to the discussion of my character, all, apparently, that her dignity requires or permits. Not the masterful young master of mistresses and whores, not the precocious dramatist of the satyric and the lewd, and something of a fledgling rapist too—no, merely "a boy." And then gently, so very gently (for despite being a girl who moans when her hair is pulled and cries for more when her flesh is made to smart with a little pain, despite her Amazonian confidence in the darkest dives and the nerves of iron that she can display in the chancy hitchhiking world, aside from the stunning sense of inalienable right with which she does whatever she likes, that total immunity from remorse or self-doubt that mesmerizes me as much as anything, she is also courteous, respectful, and friendly, the perfectly brought-up child of a Stockholm physician and his wife), she closes the door after her so as not to awaken the family from whom we have rented our room.

Yes, easily as that do young Birgitta Svanström and young David Kepesh rid themselves of each other. Ridding himself of what he is

by nature may be a more difficult task, however, since young
Kepesh does not appear to be that clear, quite yet, as to what his
nature is, exactly. He is awake all night wondering what he will do
if Birgitta should steal back into the room before dawn; he wonders
if he oughtn't to get up and lock the door. Then when dawn arrives,
when noon arrives, and she is nowhere to be found, neither in the
town of Les Andelys nor in Rouen—not at the Grosse Horloge; not
at the Cathedral; not at the birthplace of Flaubert or the spot
where Joan of Arc went up in flames—he wonders if he will ever
see the likes of her and their adventure again.

Helen Baird appears some years later, when I am in the final
stretch of graduate studies in comparative literature and feeling
triumphant about the determination I have mustered to complete
the job. Out of boredom, restlessness, impatience, and a growing
embarrassment that naggingly informs me I am too old to be sitting
at a desk still being tested on what I know, I have come near to
quitting the program just about every semester along the way. But
now, with the end in sight, I utter my praises aloud while shower-
ing at the end of the day, thrilling myself with simple statements
like "I did it" and "I stuck it out," as though it is the Matterhorn I
have had to climb in order to qualify for my orals. Following the
year with Birgitta, I have come to realize that in order to achieve
anything lasting, I am going to have to restrain a side of myself
strongly susceptible to the most bewildering and debilitating sort of
temptations, temptations that as long ago as that night outside
Rouen I already recognized as inimical to my overall interests. For,
far as I had gone with Birgitta, I knew how very easy it would have
been for me to have gone further still—more than once, I remember
the thrill it had given me imagining her with men other than myself, imagining her taking money to bring home in her pocket . . .
But *could* I have gone on to that so easily? Actually have become
Birgitta's pimp? Well, whatever my talent may have been for that
profession, graduate school has not exactly encouraged its development . . . Yes, when the battle appears to have been won, I am
truly relieved by my ability to harness my good sense in behalf of a
serious vocation—and not a little touched by my virtue. Then Helen
appears to tell me, by example and in so many words, that I am
sadly deluded and mistaken. Is it so as never to forget the charge
that I marry her?

Hers is a different brand of heroism from what, at that time, I take mine to be—indeed, it strikes me as its antithesis. A year of U.S.C. at eighteen, and then she had run off with a journalist twice her age to Hong Kong, where he was already living with a wife and three children. Armed with startling good looks, a brave front, and a strongly romantic temperament, she had walked away from her homework and her boy friend and her weekly allowance and, without a word of apology or explanation to her stunned and mortified family (who thought for a week she had been kidnapped or killed), taken off after a destiny more exhilarating than sophomore year in the sorority house. A destiny that she had found—and only recently abandoned.

Just six months earlier, I learn, she had given up everyone and everything that she had gone in search of eight years before—all the pleasure and excitement of roaming among the antiquities and imbibing the exotica of gorgeous places alluringly unknown—to come back to California and begin life anew. "I hope I never again have to live through a year like this last one" is nearly the first thing she says to me the night we meet at a party given by the wealthy young sponsors of a new San Francisco magazine "of the arts." I find Helen ready to tell her story without a trace of shyness; but then I had not been shy myself, once we'd been introduced, about meandering away from the girl I'd arrived with, and hunting her down through the hundreds of people milling around in the town house. "Why?" I ask her—the first of the whys and whens and hows she will be obliged to answer for me—"What's the year been like for you? What went wrong?" "Well, for one thing, I haven't been anywhere for six months at a stretch since I did my time as a coed." "Why did you come back, then?" "Men. Love. It all got out of hand." Instantly I am ready to attribute her "candor" to a popular-magazine mentality—and a predilection for promiscuity, pure and simple. Oh, God, I think, so beautiful, and so corny. It seems from the stories she goes on to tell me that she has been in fifty passionate affairs already—aboard fifty schooners already, sailing the China Sea with men who ply her with antique jewelry and are married to somebody else. "Look," she says, having sized up how I seem to have sized up such an existence, "what do you have against passion anyway? Why the studied detachment, Mr. Kepesh? You want to know who I am—well, I'm telling you." "It's quite a saga," I say. She asks, with a smile, "Why shouldn't it be? Better a 'saga' than a lot of other things I can think of. Come now, what do you have against passion anyway? What harm has it ever done you? Or should I ask, what good?" "The question right now is what it has or hasn't done for you." "Fine things. Wonderful things. God knows, nothing I'm ashamed of." "Then why are you here and not there, being impassioned?" "Because," Helen answers, and without any irony at all for protection—which may be what makes me begin to surrender some of my own, and to see that she is not only stunning-looking, she is also real, and here with me, and maybe even mine if I should want her—"Because," she tells me, "I'm getting on."

At twenty-six, getting on. Whereas the twenty-four-year-old Ph.D. candidate who is my date for the evening—and who eventually leaves the party in a huff, without me—had been saying on the way over that, sorting her index cards in the library just that afternoon, she had been wondering if and when her life would ever get underway.

I ask Helen what it was like to come back. We have left the party by now and are across from one another in a nearby bar. Less passively than I, she has given the slip to the companion with whom she started the evening. If I want her . . . but do I? *Should* I? Let me hear first what it had been like coming back from running away. For me, of course, there had been far more relief than let-down, and I had been adrift for only a year. "Oh, I signed an armistice with my poor mother, and my kid sisters followed me around like a movie star. The rest of the family gaped. Nice Republican girls didn't do what I did. Except that seems to be all I ever met everywhere I went, from Nepal to Singapore. There's a small army of us out there, you know. I'd say half the girls who fly out of Rangoon on that crate that goes to Mandalay are generally from Shaker Heights." "And now what do you do?" "Well, first I have to figure out some way to stop crying. I cried every day I was back for the first few months. Now that seems to be over, but, frankly, from the way I feel when I wake up in the morning I might as *well* be in tears. It's that it was all so beautiful. Living in all that loveliness—it was overwhelming. I never stopped being thrilled. I got to Angkor every single spring, and in Thailand we would fly from Bangkok up to Chiengmai with a prince who owned elephants. You should have seen him with all his elephants. A nut-colored little old man moving like a spider in a herd of the most enormous animals. You could have wrapped him twice around in one of their ears. They were all screaming at one another, but he just walked along, unfazed. You probably think seeing that is, well, seeing only that. Well, that isn't what I thought. I thought, 'This is what it is.' I used to go down in the sailboat—this is in Hong Kong—to get my friend from work at the end of the day. He sailed with the boat boy to work in the morning and then at night we sailed home together, right down between the junks and the U.S. destroyers." "The good colonial life. It isn't for nothing they hate giving up those empires. But I still don't understand precisely why you gave up yours."

And in the weeks that follow I continue to find it hard to believe —despite the tiny ivory Buddhas, the jade carvings, and the row of rooster-shaped opium weights that are arranged by her bedside table—that this way of life ever really was hers. Chiengmai, Rangoon, Singapore, Mandalay . . . why not Jupiter, why not Mars? To be sure, I know these places exist beyond the Rand McNally map on which I trace the course of her adventures (as once I traced down an adventure of Birgitta's in the London phone directory), and the novels of Conrad where I first encountered them—and so, of course, do I know that "characters" live and breathe who choose to make their destiny in the stranger cities of the world . . . What then fails to persuade me completely that living, breathing Helen is one of them? My being with her? Is the unbelievable character Helen in her diamond-stud earrings or is it the dutiful graduate teaching assistant in his wash-and-dry seersucker suit?

I even become somewhat suspicious and critical of her serene, womanly beauty, or rather, of the regard in which she seems to hold her eyes, her nose, her throat, her breasts, her hips, her legs— why, even her feet would seem to her to have charming little glories to be extolled. How does she come by this regal bearing anyway, this aristocratic sense of herself that seems to derive almost entirely from the smoothness of skin, the length of limb, the breadth of mouth and span of eyes, and the fluting at the very tip of what she describes, without batting an eyelid (shadowed in the subtlest green), as her "Flemish" nose? I am not at all accustomed to someone who bears her beauty with such a sense of attainment and self-worth. My experience—running from the Syracuse undergraduates who did not want to "relate" to me "on that level," to Birgitta Svanström, for whom flesh was very much there to be investigated for every last thrill—has been of young women who make no great fuss about their looks, or believe at least that it is not

seemly to show that they do. True, Birgitta knew well enough that
her hair cut short and carelessly nicely enhanced her charming fur-
tiveness, but otherwise how she framed her unpainted face was not
a subject to which she appeared to give much thought from one
morning to the next. And Elisabeth, with an abundance of hair no
less praiseworthy than Helen's, simply brushed it straight down her
back, letting it hang there as it had since she was six. To Helen,
however, all that marvelous hair—closest in shading to the Irish set-
ter—seems to be in the nature of a crown, or a spire, or a halo, there
not simply to adorn or embellish but to express, to symbolize. Perhaps it is only a measure of how narrow and cloistered my life has
become—or perhaps it is in fact the true measure of a courtesan like
power that emanates from Helen's sense of herself as an idolized
object that might just as well have been carved of one hundred
pounds of jade—but when she twists her hair up into a soft knot at
the back of her head, and draws a black line above her lashes—
above eyes in themselves no larger and no bluer than Elisabeth's—
when she dons a dozen bracelets and ties a fringed silk scarf
around her hips like Carmen to go out to buy some oranges for
breakfast, the effect is not lost upon me. Far from it. I have from
the start been overcome by physical beauty in women, but by
Helen I am not just intrigued and aroused, I am also alarmed, and
made deeply, deeply uncertain—utterly subjugated by the authority
with which she claims and confirms and makes singular her loveliness, yet as suspicious as I can be of the prerogatives, of the *place*,
thereby bestowed upon her in her own imagination. Hers seems to
me sometimes such a banalized conception of self and experience,
and yet, all the same, enthralling and full of fascination. *For all I
know, maybe she is right.*

"How come," I ask—still asking, still apparently very much hoping to expose what is fiction in this fabulous character she calls herself and in the Asiatic romance she claims for a past—"how come
you gave up the good colonial life, Helen?" "I had to." "Because
the inheritance money had made you independent?" "It's six thousand lousy dollars a year, David. Why, I believe even ascetic college teachers make that much." "I only meant that you might have
decided youth and beauty weren't going to get you through
indefinitely." "Look, I was a kid, and school meant nothing to me,
and my family was just like everyone else's—sweet and boring and
proper, and living lo these many years under a sheet of ice at 18

Fern Hill Manor Road. The only excitement came at mealtime. Every night when we got to dessert my father said, 'Is that it?' and my mother burst into tears. And so at the age of eighteen I met a grown man, and he was marvelous-looking, and he knew how to talk, and he could teach me plenty, and he knew what I was all about, which nobody else seemed to know at all, and he had wonderful elegant ways, and wasn't really a brutal tyrant, as tyrants go; and I fell in love with him—yes, in two weeks; it happens and not just to schoolgirls, either—and he said, 'Why don't you come back with me?' and I said yes—and I went." "In a 'crate'?" "Not that time. Paté over the Pacific and fellatio in the first-class john. Let me tell you, the first six months weren't a picnic. I'm not in mourning over that. You see, I was just a nicely brought-up kid from Pasadena, that's all, really, in her tartan skirt and her loafers—my friend's *children* were nearly as old as I was. Oh, splendidly neurotic, but practically my age. I couldn't even learn to eat with chopsticks, I was so scared. I remember one night, my first big opium party, I somehow wound up in a limousine with four of the wildest pansies—four Englishmen, dressed in gowns and gold slippers. I couldn't stop laughing. 'It's surreal,' I kept saying, 'it's surreal,' until the plumpest of them looked down his lorgnette at me and said, 'Of course it's surreal, dear, you're nineteen.'" "But you came back. Why?" "I can't go into that." "Who was the man?" "Oh, you are becoming a *cum laude* student of real life, David." "Wrong. Learned it all at Tolstoy's feet."

I give her *Anna Karenina* to read. She says, "Not bad—only it wasn't a Vronsky, thank God. Vronskys are a dime a dozen, friend, and bore you to tears. It was a man—very much a Karenin, in fact. Though not at all pathetic, I hasten to add." *That* stops me for a moment: what an original way to see the famous triangle! "Another husband," I say. "Only the half of it." "Sounds mysterious; sounds like high drama. Maybe you ought to write it all down." "And perhaps you ought to lay off reading what all has been written down." "And do what instead with my spare time?" "Dip a foot back into the stuff itself." "And there's a book about that, you know. Called *The Ambassadors*." I think: And there's also a book about you. It's called *The Sun Also Rises* and her name is Brett and she's about as shallow. So is her whole crew—so, it seems, was yours. "I'll bet there's a book about it," says Helen, gladly rising, with her confident smile, to the bait. "I'll bet there are thousands of books about it. I used to see them all lined up in alphabetical order in the library. Look, so there is no confusion, let me only mildly overstate the case: I hate libraries, I hate books, and I hate schools. As I remember, they tend to turn everything about life into something slightly other than it is—'slightly' at best. It's those poor innocent theoretical bookworms who do the teaching who turn it all into something worse. Something ghastly, when you think about it." "What do you see in me, then?" "Oh, you really hate them a little too. For what they've done to you." "Which is?" "Turned you into something—" "Ghastly?" I say, laughing (for we are having this little duel beneath a sheet in the bed beside the little bronze opium weights). "No, not quite. Into something slightly other, slightly . . . wrong. Everything about you is just a little bit of a lie—except your eyes. They're still you. I can't even look into them very long. It's like trying to put your hand into a bowl of hot water to pull out the plug." "You put things vividly. You're a vivid creature. I've noticed your eyes too." "You're misusing yourself, David. You're hopelessly intent on being what you're not. I get the sense that you may be riding for a very bad fall. Your first mistake was to give up that spunky Swede with the knapsack. She sounds a little like a guttersnipe, and—I have to say it—from the snapshot looks to me a little squirrely around the mouth, but at least she was fun to be with. But of course that's a word you just despise, correct? Like 'crate' for beat-up airplane. Every time I say 'fun' I see you positively wincing with pain. God, they've really done a job on you. You're so damn smug, and yet I think secretly you know you lost your nerve." "Oh, don't simplify me *too* much. And don't romanticize my 'nerve' either—okay? I like to have a good time now and then. I have a good time sleeping with you by the way." "By the way, you have more than a good time sleeping with me. You have the best time you've ever had with anybody. And, dear friend," she adds, "don't simplify me either."

"Oh, God," says Helen, stretching languorously when morning comes, "fucking is such a lovely thing to do."

True, true, true, true, true. The passion is frenzied, inexhaustible, and in my experience, singularly replenishing. Looking back to Birgitta, it seems to me, from my new vantage point, that we were, among other things, helping each other at age twenty-two to turn into something faintly corrupt, each the other's slave and slaveholder, each the arsonist and the inflamed. Exercising such strong sexual power over each other, *and* over total strangers, we had created a richly hypnotic atmosphere, but one which permeated the inexperienced *mind* first of all: I was intrigued and exhilarated at least as much by the idea of what we were engaged in as by the sensations, what I felt and what I saw. Not so with Helen. To be sure, I must first accustom myself to what strikes me at the height of my skepticism as so much theatrical display; but soon, as understanding grows, as familiarity grows, and feeling with it, I begin at last to relinquish some of my suspiciousness, to lay off a little with my interrogations, and to see these passionate performances as arising out of the very fearlessness that so draws me to her, out of that determined abandon with which she will give herself to whatever strongly beckons, and regardless of how likely it is to bring in the end as much pain as pleasure. I have been dead wrong, I tell myself, trying to dismiss hers as a corny and banalized mentality deriving from *Screen Romance*—rather, she is *without* fantasy, there is no *room* for fantasy, so total is her concentration, and the ingenuity with which she sounds her desire. Now, in the aftermath of orgasm, I find myself weak with gratitude and the profoundest feelings of self-surrender. I am the least guarded, if not the simplest, organism on earth. I don't even know what to say at such moments. Helen does, however. Yes, there are the things that this girl knows and knows and knows. "I love you," she tells me. Well, if something has to be said, what makes more sense? So we begin to tell each other that we are lovers who are in love, even while my conviction that we are on widely divergent paths is revived from one conversation to the next. Convinced as I would like to be that a kinship, rare and valuable, underlies and nourishes our passionate rapport, I still cannot wish away the grand uneasiness Helen continues to arouse. Why else can't we stop—can't *I* stop—the fencing and the parrying?

Finally she agrees to tell me why she gave up all she'd had in the Far East: tells me either to address my suspiciousness directly or to enrich the mystique I cannot seem to resist.

Her lover, the last of her Karenins, had begun to talk about arranging for his wife to be killed in an "accident." "Who was he?" "A very well-known and important man" is all she is willing to say. I swallow that as best I can and ask: "Where is he now?" "Still there." "Hasn't he tried to see you?" "He came here for a week." "And did you sleep with him?" "Of course I slept with him. How

could I resist sleeping with him? But in the end I sent him back. It
nearly did me in. It was hideous, seeing him go for good." "Well,
maybe he'll go ahead and have his wife killed anyway, as an en-
ticement—" "Why must you make fun of him? Is it so impossible
for you to understand that he's as human as you?" "Helen, there
are ways of dealing with a mate you want to be rid of, short of
homicide. You can just walk out the door, for one thing." "Can you,
'just'? Is that the way they do it in the Comparative Literature Department? I wonder what it will be like," she says, "when you can't
have something you want." "Will I blow somebody's brains out to
get it? Will I push somebody down the elevator shaft? What do you
think?" "Look, I'm the one who gave up everything and nearly died
of it—because I couldn't bear to hear the idea even spoken. It
terrified me to know that he could even have such a thought. Or
maybe it was so excrutiatingly tempting that that's why I went running. Because all I had to say was yes; that's all he was waiting for.
He was desperate, David, and he was serious. And do you know
how easy it would have been to say what he wanted to hear? It's
only a word, it takes just a split second: yes." "Only maybe he
asked because he was so sure you'd say no." "He couldn't be sure. I
wasn't sure." "But such a well-known and important man could certainly have gone ahead then and had the thing done on his own,
could he not—and without your knowing he was behind it? Surely
such a well-known and important man has all kinds of means at his
disposal to get a measly wife out of the way: limousines that crash,
boats that sink, airplanes that explode in mid-air. Had he done it on
his own to begin with, what you thought about it all would never
even have come up. If he asked your opinion, maybe it was to hear
no." "Oh, this is interesting. Go on. I say no, and what does he
gain?" "What he has: the wife and you. He gets to keep it all, and
to cut a very grand figure into the bargain. That you ran, that the
whole idea took on reality for you, had moral consequences for you
—well, he probably hadn't figured on getting that kind of rise out of
a beautiful, adventurous, American runaway." "Very clever, indeed.
A plus, especially the part about 'moral consequences.' All that's
wrong is that you haven't the faintest understanding of what there
was between us. Just because he's someone with power, you think
he has no feelings. But there are men, you know, who have both.
We met two times a week for two years. Sometimes more—but
never less. And it never changed. It was never anything but perfect.

You don't believe such things happen, do you? Or even if they do, you don't want to believe they matter. But this happened, and to me and to him it mattered more than anything." "But so has coming back happened. So did sending him away happen. So did your terror happen and your revulsion. This guy's machinations are beside the point. It mattered to you, Helen, that your limit had been reached." "Maybe I was mistaken and that was only so much sentimentality about myself. Or some childish kind of hope. Maybe I should have stayed, gone beyond my limit—and learned that it wasn't beyond me at all." "You couldn't," I say, "and you didn't."

And who, oh, who is being the sentimentalist now?

It appears then that the capacity for pain-filled renunciation joined to the gift for sensual abandon is what makes her appeal inescapable. That we never entirely get along, that I am never entirely *sure*, that she somehow lacks depth, that her vanity is so enormous, well, all that is nothing—isn't it?—beside the esteem that I come to have for this beautiful and dramatic young heroine, who has risked and won and lost so much already, squarely facing up to appetite. And then there is the beauty itself. Is she not the single most desirable creature I have ever known? With a woman so physically captivating, a woman whom I cannot take my eyes from even if she is only drinking her coffee or dialing the phone, surely with someone whose smallest bodily movement has such a powerful sensuous hold upon me, I need hardly worry ever again about imagination tempting me to renewed adventures in the base and the bewildering. Is not Helen the enchantress whom I had already begun searching for in college, when Silky Walsh's lower lip stirred me to pursue her from the university cafeteria to the university gymnasium and on to the dormitory laundry room—that creature to me *so* beautiful that upon her, and her alone, I can focus all my yearning, all my adoration, all my curiosity, all my lust? If not Helen, who then? Who ever will intrigue me more? And, alas, I still so need to be intrigued.

Only if we marry . . . well, the contentious side of the affair will simply dwindle away of itself, will it not, an ever-deepening intimacy, the assurance of permanence, dissolving whatever impulse remains, on either side, for smugness and self-defense? Of course it would not be quite such a gamble if Helen were just a little more like this and a little less like that; but, as I am quick to remind myself—imagining that I am taking the *mature* position—that is not how we are bestowed upon each other in the world this side of dreams. Besides, what I call her "vanity" and her "lack of depth" is just what makes her so interesting! So then, I can only hope that mere differences of "opinion" (which, I readily admit—if that will help—I am often the first to point up and to dramatize) will come to be altogether beside the point of the passionate attachment that has, so far, remained undiminished in spite of our abrasive, rather evangelical dialogues. I can only hope that just as I have been mistaken about her motives before, I am wrong again when I suspect that what she secretly hopes to gain by marriage is an end to her love affair with that unpathetic Karenin in Hong Kong. I can only hope that it is in fact I whom she will marry and not the barrier I may seem to be against the past whose loss had very nearly killed her. I can only hope (for I can never know) that it is I with whom she goes to bed, and not with memories of the mouth and the hands and the member of that most perfect of all lovers, he who would murder his wife in order to make his mistress his own.

Doubting and hoping then, wanting and fearing (anticipating the pleasantest sort of lively future one moment, the worst in the next), I marry Helen Baird—after, that is, nearly three full years devoted to doubting-hoping-wanting-and-fearing. There are some, like my own father, who have only to see a woman standing over a piano singing "Amapola" to decide in a flash, "There—there is my wife," and there are others who sigh, "Yes, it is she," only after an interminable drama of vacillation that has led them to the ineluctable conclusion that they ought never to see the woman again. I marry Helen when the weight of experience required to reach the monumental decision to give her up for good turns out to be so enormous and so moving that I cannot possibly imagine life without her. Only when I finally know *for sure* that *this must end now*, do I discover how deeply wed I already am by my thousand days of indecision, by all the scrutinizing appraisal of possibilities that has somehow made an affair of three years' duration seem as dense with human event as a marriage half a century long. I marry Helen then—and she marries me—at the moment of impasse and exhaustion that must finally come to all those who spend years and years and years in these clearly demarcated and maze-like arrangements that involve separate apartments and joint vacations, assumptions of devotion and designated nights apart, affairs terminated with relief every five or six months, and happily forgotten for seventy-two hours, and then resumed, oftentimes with a delicious, if effervescent, sexual frenzy, following a half-fortuitous meeting at the local supermarket; or begun anew after an evening phone call intended solely to apprise the relinquished companion of a noteworthy documentary to be rerun on television at ten; or following attendance at a dinner party to which the couple had committed themselves so long ago it would have been unseemly not to go ahead and, together, meet this last mutual social obligation. To be sure, one or the other might have answered the obligation by going off to the party alone, but alone there would have been no accomplice across the table with whom to exchange signs of boredom and amusement, nor afterward, driving home, would there have been anyone of like mind with whom to review the charms and deficiencies of the other guests; nor, undressing for bed, would there have been an eager, smiling friend lying unclothed atop the bed sheet to whom one allows that the only truly engaging person present at the table happened to have been one's own previously underrated mate manqué.

We marry, and, as I should have known and couldn't have known and probably always knew, mutual criticism and disapproval continue to poison our lives, evidence not only of the deep temperamental divide that has been there from the start, but also of the sense I continue to have that another man still holds the claim upon her deepest feelings, and that, however she may attempt to hide this sad fact and to attend to me and our life, she knows as well as I do that she is my wife only because there was no way short of homicide (or so they say) for her to be the wife of that very important and well-known lover of hers. At our best, at our bravest and most sensible and most devoted, we do try very hard to hate what divides us rather than each other. If only that past of hers weren't so vivid, so grandiose, so operatic—if somehow one or the other of us could forget it! If I could close this absurd gap of trust that exists between us still! Or ignore it! Live *beyond* it! At our best we make resolutions, we make apologies, we make amends, we make love. But at our worst . . . well, our worst is just about as bad as anybody's, I would think.

What do we struggle over mostly? In the beginning—as anyone will have guessed who, after three years of procrastination, has thrown himself headlong and half convinced into the matrimonial flames—in the beginning we struggle over the toast. Why, I wonder, can't the toast go in while the eggs are cooking, rather than before? This way we can get to eat our bread warm rather than cold. "I don't believe I am having this discussion," she says. "Life isn't toast!" she finally screams. "It is!" I hear myself maintaining. "When you sit down to eat toast, life is toast. And when you take out the garbage, life is garbage. You can't leave the garbage halfway down the stairs, Helen. It belongs in the can in the yard. Covered." "I forgot it." "How can you forget it when it's already in your hand?" "Perhaps, dear, because it's garbage—and what difference does it make anyway!" She forgets to affix her signature to the checks she writes and to stamp the letters she mails, while the letters I give her to mail for me and the household turn up with a certain regularity in the pockets of raincoats and slacks months after she has gone off to deposit them in the mailbox. "What do you think about between Here and There? What makes you so forgetful, Helen? Yearnings for old Mandalay? Memories of the 'crate' and the lagoons and the elephants, of the dawn coming up like thunder—" "I can't think about your letters, damn it, every inch of the way." "But why is it you think you've gone outside with the letter in your hand to *begin* with?" "For some air, that's why! To see some sky! To breathe!"

Soon enough, instead of pointing out her errors and oversights, or retracing her steps, or picking up the pieces, or restraining myself (and then going off to curse her out behind the bathroom door), I make the toast, I make the eggs, I take out the garbage, I pay the bills, and I mail the letters. Even when she says, graciously (trying, at *her* end, to bridge the awful gap), "I'm going out shopping, want me to drop these—" experience, if not wisdom, directs me to say, "No—no, thanks." The day she loses her wallet after making a withdrawal from the savings account, I take over the transactions at the bank. The day she leaves the fish to rot under the car's front seat after going out in the morning to get the salmon steaks for dinner, I take over the marketing. The day she has the wool shirt that was to have been dry-cleaned laundered by mistake, I take over going to the cleaners. With the result that before a year is out I am occupied —and glad of it—some sixteen hours a day with teaching my classes and rewriting into a book my thesis on romantic disillusionment in the stories of Anton Chekhov (a subject I'd chosen before even meeting my wife), and Helen has taken increasingly to drink and to dope.

Her days begin in jasmine-scented waters. With olive oil in her hair to make it glossy after washing, and her face anointed with vitamin creams, she reclines in the tub for twenty minutes each morning, eyes closed and the precious skull at rest against a small inflated pillow; the woman moves only to rub gently with her pumice stone the rough skin on her feet. Three times a week the bath is followed by her facial sauna: in her midnight-blue silk kimono, embroidered with pink and red poppies and yellow birds never seen on land or sea, she sits at the counter of our tiny kitchenette, her turbaned head tilted over a bowl of steaming water sprinkled with rosemary and camomile and elder flower. Then, steamed and painted and coiffed, she is ready to dress for her exercise class—and wherever else it is she goes while I am at school: a close-fitting Chinese dress of navy-blue silk, high at the collar and slit to the thigh; the diamond-stud earrings; bracelets of jade and of gold; her jade ring; her sandals; her straw bag.

When she returns later in the day—after Yoga, she decided to go into San Francisco "to look around": she talks (has talked for years) of plans to open a Far East antique shop there—she is already a little high, and by dinnertime she is all smiles: mellow, blotto, wry. "Life is toast," she observes, sipping four fingers of rum while I season the lamb chops. "Life is leftovers. Life is leather soles and rubber heels. Life is carrying forward the balance into the new checkbook. Life is writing the correct amount to be paid out onto each of the stubs. *And* the correct day, month, and year." "That is all true," I say. "Ah," she says, watching me as I go about setting the table, "if only his wife didn't forget what she puts in to broil and leave everything to burn; if only his wife could remember that when David had dinner in Arcadia, his mother always set the fork on the left and the spoon on the right and never never both on the same side. Oh, if only his wife could bake and butter his potato the way Mamma did in the wintertime."

By the time we are into our thirties we have so exacerbated our antipathies that each of us has been reduced to precisely what the other had been so leery of at the outset, the professorial "smugness" and "prissiness" for which Helen detests me with all her heart— "You've actually done it, David—you are a full-fledged young fogy" —no less in evidence than her "utter mindlessness," "idiotic wastefulness," "adolescent dreaminess," etc. Yet I can never leave her, nor she me, not, that is, until outright disaster makes it simply ludi-

48 THE PROFESSOR OF DESIRE

crous to go on waiting for the miraculous conversion of the other. As much to our wonderment as to everyone else's, we remain married nearly as long as we had been together as lovers, perhaps because of the opportunity this marriage now provides for each of us to assault head-on what each takes to be his demon (and had seemed at first to be the other's salvation!). The months go by and we remain together, wondering if a child would somehow resolve this crazy deadlock . . . or an antique shop of her own for Helen . . . or a jewelry shop . . . or psychotherapy for us both. Again and again we hear ourselves described as a strikingly "attractive" couple: well dressed, traveled, intelligent, worldly (especially as young academic couples go), a combined income of twelve thousand dollars a year . . . and life is simply awful.

What little spirit smolders on in me during the last months of the marriage is visible only in class; otherwise, I am so affectless and withdrawn that a rumor among the junior faculty members has me "under sedation." Ever since the approval of my dissertation I have been teaching, along with the freshman course "Introduction to Fiction," two sections of the sophomore survey in "general" literature. During the weeks near the end of the term when we study Chekhov's stories, I find, while reading aloud to my students passages which I particularly want them to take note of, that each and every sentence seems to me to allude to my own plight above all, as though by now every single syllable I think or utter must first trickle down through my troubles. And then there are my classroom daydreams, as plentiful suddenly as they are irrepressible, and so obviously inspired by longings for miraculous salvation—reentry into lives I lost long ago, reincarnation as a being wholly unlike myself—that I am even somewhat grateful to be depressed and without anything like the will power to set even the mildest fantasy in motion.

"I realized that when you love you must either, in your reasoning about that love, start from what is higher, more important than happiness or unhappiness, sin or virtue in their usual meaning, or you must not reason at all." I ask my students what's meant by these lines, and while they tell me, notice that in a far corner of the room the poised, soft-spoken girl who is my most intelligent, my prettiest—and my most bored and arrogant—student is finishing off a candy bar and a Coke for lunch. "Oh, don't eat junk," I say to her, silently, and see the two of us on the terrace of the Gritti, squinting through the shimmer over the Grand Canal across to the ocher façade of the perfect little palazzo where we have taken a shuttered room . . . we are having our midday meal, creamy pasta followed by tender bits of lemoned veal . . . and at the very table where Birgitta and I, arrogant, nervy youngsters not much older than these boys and girls, sat down to eat on the afternoon we pooled much of our wealth to celebrate our arrival in Byron's Italy . . .

Meanwhile, my other bright student is explaining what the land-owner Alyohin means at the conclusion of "About Love" when he speaks of "what is higher . . . than happiness or unhappiness, sin or virtue in their usual meaning." The boy says, "He regrets that he didn't yield to his feeling and run off with the woman he fell in love with. Now that she's going away, he's miserable for having allowed conscience and scruples, and his own timidity, to forbid him confessing his love to her just because she is already married and a mother." I nod, but clearly without comprehension, and the clever boy looks dismayed. "Am I wrong?" he asks, turning scarlet. "No, no," I say, but all the while I am thinking, "What are you doing, Miss Rodgers, dining on Peanut Chews? We should be sipping white wine . . ." And then it occurs to me that, as an under-graduate at U.S.C., Helen probably looked rather like my bored Miss Rodgers in the months before that older man—a man of about my age!—plucked her out of the classroom and into a life of roman-tic adventure . . .

Later in the hour, I look up from reading aloud out of "Lady with a Lapdog" directly into the innocent and uncorrupted gaze of the plump, earnest, tenderhearted Jewish girl from Beverly Hills who has sat in the front row all year long writing down everything I say. I read to the class the story's final paragraph, in which the adulterous couple, shaken to find how deeply they love one an-other, try vainly "to understand why he should have a wife and she a husband." "And it seemed to them that in only a few more min-utes a solution would be found and a new, beautiful life would begin; but both of them knew very well that the end was still a long, long way away and that the most complicated and difficult part was only just beginning." I hear myself speaking of the moving transparency of the ending—no false mysteries, only the harsh facts directly stated. I speak of the amount of human history that Che-khov can incorporate in fifteen pages, of how ridicule and irony gradually give way, even within so short a space, to sorrow and pathos, of his feel for the disillusioning moment and for those processes wherein actuality seemingly pounces upon even our most harmless illusions, not to mention the grand dreams of fulfillment and adventure. I speak of his pessimism about what he calls "this business of personal happiness," and all the while I want to ask the chubby girl in the front row, who is rapidly recording my words in her notebook, to become my daughter. I want to look after her and see that she is safe and happy. I want to pay for her clothes and her doctor bills and for her to come and put her arms around me when she is feeling lonely or sad. If only it were Helen and I who had raised her to be so sweet! But how could we two raise anything?

And later that day, when I happen to run into her walking toward me on the campus, I feel impelled yet again to say to someone who is probably no more than ten or twelve years my junior that I want to adopt her, want her to forget her own parents, about whom I know nothing, and let me father and protect her. "Hi, Mr. Kepesh," she says, with a little wave of the hand, and that affectionate gesture does it, apparently. I feel as though I am growing lighter and lighter, I sense an emotion coming my way that will pick me up and turn me over and deposit me I know not where. Am I going to have my nervous collapse right here on the walk in front of the library? I take one of her hands in mine—I am saying, through a throat clogged with feeling, "You're a good girl, Kathie." She ducks her head, her forehead colors. "Well," she says, "I'm glad somebody around here likes me." "You're a good girl," I repeat, and release the soft hand I am holding and go home to see if childless Helen is sober enough to prepare dinner for two.

About this time we are visited by an English investment banker named Donald Garland, the first of Helen's Hong Kong friends ever to be invited to dine with us in our apartment. To be sure, she has on occasion made herself spectacularly beautiful so as to go into San Francisco to have lunch with somebody or other out of paradise lost, but never before have I seen her approach such a meeting in this mood of happy, almost childlike anticipation. Indeed, in the past there have been times when, having spent hours getting made up for the luncheon engagement, she would emerge from the bathroom in her drabbest robe, announcing herself unable to leave the house to see anyone. "I look hideous." "You don't at all." "I do," and with that she returns to bed for the day.

Donald Garland, she tells me now, is "the kindest man" she has ever known. "I was taken to lunch at his house my first week in Hong Kong, and we were the best of friends from then on. We just adored each other. The center of the table was strewn with orchids he'd picked from his garden—in my honor, he said—and the patio where we ate looked out over the crescent of Repulse Bay. I was eighteen years old. He must have been about fifty-five. My God. Donald is probably seventy! I could never believe he was over forty; he was always so happy, so youthful, so thrilled with everything. He lived with the most easy-going and good-natured American boy. Chips must have been about twenty-six or -seven then. On the phone this afternoon Donald told the most terrible news—one morning two months ago Chips died of an aneurysm at breakfast; just keeled over dead. Donald took the body back to Wilmington, Delaware, and buried it, and then he couldn't leave. He kept booking plane tickets and canceling. Now, finally, he's on his way home."

Chips, Donald, Edgar, Brian, Colin . . . I have no response to make, no interrogations or cross-examination, nothing faintly resembling sympathy, curiosity, or interest. Or patience. I had long ago heard all I could stand about the doings of the wealthy Hong Kong circle of English homosexuals who had "adored" her. I exhibit only a churlish sort of surprise to find that I am to be a party to this very special reunion. She shuts her eyes tightly, as though she must obliterate me momentarily from sight just in order to survive. "Don't talk to me like that. Don't take that terrible tone. He was my dearest friend. He saved my life a hundred times." *And why did you risk it a hundred times?* But the interrogatory accusation, and the terrible tone that goes with it, I manage to squelch, for by now even I know that I am being diminished far more by my anger at everything she does and did than by those ways of hers I ought to have learned to disregard, or to have accepted with a certain grace, long, long ago . . . Only as the evening wears on, and Garland becomes increasingly spirited in his reminiscences, do I wonder if she has invited him to the apartment so that I might learn at first hand just how very far from the apex she has fallen by insanely joining her fate to this fogy's. Whether or not that is her intention, it is something like the result. In their company I am no easygoing, good-natured Chips, but entirely the Victorian schoolmaster whose heart stirs only to the crack of the whip and the swish of the cane.

In a vain attempt to force this pious, sour, censorious little prig out
of my skin, I try hard to believe that Helen is simply showing this
man who has meant so much to her and been so kind to her, and
who has himself just suffered a terrible blow, that all is well in her
life, that she and her husband live comfortably and amicably, and
that her protector hasn't to worry about her any longer. Yes, Helen
is only acting as would any devoted daughter who wished to spare
a doting father some harsh truth . . . In short: simple as the explanation for Garland's presence might have seemed to someone else,
it is wholly beyond my grasp, as though now that living with Helen
has ceased to make the least bit of sense, I cannot discover the
truth about anything.

At seventy, delicate, small-boned Garland still does have a youthful sort of charm, and a way about him at once worldly and boyish.
His forehead is so fragile-looking it seems it could be cracked with
the tap of a spoon, and his cheeks are the small, round, glazed
cheeks of an alabaster Cupid. Above the open shirt a pale silk scarf
is tied around his neck, almost completely hiding from view the
throat whose creases are the only sign of his age. In that strangely
youthful face all there is to speak of sorrow are the eyes, soft,
brown, and awash with feeling even while his crisp accent refuses
to betray the faintest hint of grief.

"Poor Derek was killed, you know." Helen did not know. She
puts her hand to her mouth. "But *how*? Derek," she says, turning to
me, "was an associate in Donald's firm. A very silly man sometimes,
very muddled and so on, but such a good heart, really—" My dead
expression sends her quickly back to Garland. "Yes," he says, "he
was a very kind person, and I was devoted to him. Oh, he could
talk and go on, but then you just had to tell him, 'Derek, that's
enough now,' and he'd shut up. Well, two Chinese boys thought
that he hadn't given them enough money, so they kicked him down
a flight of stairs. Broke Derek's neck." "How terrible. How awful.
Poor, poor man. And what," asks Helen, "has happened to all his
animals?" "The birds are gone. Some sort of virus wiped them out
the week after he was killed. The rest Madge adopted. Madge
adopted them and Patricia looks after them. Otherwise, those two
won't have anything to do with each other." "Again?" "Oh yes. She
can be a good bitch, that Madge, when she wants to be. Chips did
her house over for her a year ago. She nearly drove the poor boy
crazy with her upstairs bath." Helen tries yet again to bring me into

the company of the living: she explains that Madge and Patricia, who own houses down along the bay from Donald, were stars of the British cinema in the forties. Donald rattles off the names of the movies they made. I nod and nod, just like an agreeable person, but the smile I make a stab at presenting him does not begin to come off. The look Helen has for me does, however, quite effectively. "And how does Madge look?" Helen asks him. "Well, when she makes up, she still looks wonderful. She ought never to wear a bikini, of course." I say, "Why?" but no one seems to hear me. The evening ends with Garland, by now a little drunk, holding Helen's hand and telling me about a famous masquerade party held in a jungle clearing on a small island in the Gulf of Siam owned by a Thai friend of his, half a mile out to sea from the southern finger of Thailand. Chips, who designed Helen's costume, had put her all in white, like Prince Ivan in *The Firebird*. "She was ravishing. A silk Cossack shirt and full silk trousers gathered into soft silver kid boots, and a silver turban with a diamond clasp. And around her waist a jeweled belt of emeralds." Emeralds? Bought by whom? Obviously by Karenin. Where's the belt now, I wonder? What do you have to return and what do you get to keep? You certainly get to keep the memories, that's for sure. "A little Thai princess burst into tears at the very sight of her. Poor little thing. She'd come wearing everything but the kitchen stove and expected people to swoon. But the one who looked like royalty that night was this dear girl. Oh, it was quite a to-do. Hasn't Helen ever shown you the photographs? Don't you have photographs, dear?" "No," she says, "not any more." "Oh, I wish I'd brought mine. But I never thought I'd see you—I didn't even know who I was when I left home. And remember the little boys?" he says, after a long sip from his brandy glass. "Chips, of course, got all the little native boys stripped down, with just a little coconut shell around their how-dee-dos, and Christmas tinsel streaming down around their necks. What a sight they were when the wind blew! Well, the boat landed, and there were these little chaps to greet the guests and to lead us up a torch-lined path to the clearing where we had the banquet. Oh, my goodness, yes—Madge came in the dress that Derek wore for his fortieth birthday party. Never would spend money, if she could help it. Always angry about something, but mostly it's the money everyone's stealing from her. She said, 'You can't just go to one of these things, you have to have something wonderful to wear.' So I said to her, only as a joke, mind you, 'Why don't you come in Derek's dress? It's white chiffon covered with Diamonte and with a long train. And cut very low in the back. You'll look lovely in it, darling.' And Madge said, 'How could it be cut low in the back, Donald? How in the world could Derek have worn it? What about the hair on his back, and all that disgusting rubbish?' And I said, 'Oh, darling, he only shaves once every three years.' You see," Garland says to me, "Derek was rather the old Guards officer type— slim, elegant, very pink-complexioned, altogether the most extraordinarily hairless person. Oh, there's a photograph of Helen you must see, David. I must send it to you. It's Helen being led from the boat by these enchanting little native boys streaming Christmas tinsel. With her long legs and all that silk clinging to her, oh, she was absolute perfection. And her face—her face in that photograph is classic. I must send it to you; you must have it. She was the most ravishing thing. Patricia said about Helen, the first moment she laid eyes on her—that was at lunch at my house, and the darling girl still had the most ordinary little clothes—but Patricia said then she had star quality, that without a doubt she could be a film star. And she could have been. She still has it. She always will." "I know," replies the schoolmaster, silently swishing his cane.

After he leaves, Helen says, "Well, there's no need to ask what you thought of him, is there?" "It's as you said: he adores you." "Really, just what has empowered you to sit in judgment of other people's passions? Haven't you heard? It's a wide, wide world; room for everybody to do whatever he likes. Even you once did what you liked, David. Or so the legend goes." "I sit in judgment of nothing. What I sit in judgment of, you wouldn't believe." "Ah, yourself. Hardest on yourself. Momentarily I forgot." "I sat, Helen, and I listened and I don't remember saying anything about the passions or preferences or private parts of anybody from here to Nepal." "Donald Garland is probably the kindest man alive." "Fine with me." "He was always there when I needed someone. There were weeks when I went to live in his house. He protected me from some terrible people." *Why didn't you just protect yourself by staying away from them?* "Good," I say; "you were lucky and that was great." "He likes to gossip and to tell tales, and of course he got a little maudlin tonight—look what he's just been through. But he happens to know what people are, just how much and just how little—and he is devoted to his friends, even the fools. The loyalty of those kind of men is quite wonderful, and not to be disparaged by anyone. And don't you be misled. When he is feeling himself he can be like iron. He can be unmovable, and marvelous." "I am sure he was a wonderful friend to you." "He still is!" "Look, what are you trying to tell me? I don't always get the gist of things these days. Rumor has it my students are going to give *me* the final exam, to see if they've been able to get anything through my skull. What are we talking about now?" "About the fact that I am still a person of consequence to quite a few people, even if to you and the learned professors and their peppy, dowdy little wives I am beneath contempt. It's true I'm not clever enough to bake banana bread and carrot bread and raise my own bean sprouts and 'audit' seminars and 'head up' committees to outlaw war for all time, but people still look at me, David, wherever I go. I could have married the kind of men who *run* the world! I wouldn't have had to look far, either. I hate to have to say such a vulgar, trashy thing about myself, but it's what you're reduced to saying to someone who finds you repulsive." "I don't find you repulsive. I'm still awestruck that you chose me over the president of ITT. How can someone unable even to finish a little pamphlet on Anton Chekhov feel anything but gratitude to be living with the runner-up for Queen of Tibet? I'm honored to have been chosen to be your hair shirt." "It's debatable who is the hair shirt around here. I am repugnant to you, Donald is repugnant to you—" "Helen, I neither liked the man nor disliked the man. I did my level fucking best. Look, my best friend as long ago as college was practically the only queer *there*. I had a queer for a friend in 1950—before they even existed! I didn't know what one was, but I had one. I don't care *who* wears *whose* dress—oh, fuck it, forget it, I quit."

Then on a Saturday morning late in the spring, just as I have sat down at my desk to begin marking exams, I hear the front door of our apartment open and shut—and finally the dissolution of this hopeless misalliance has begun. Helen is gone. Several days pass—hideous days, involving two visits to the San Francisco morgue, one with Helen's demure, bewildered mother, who insists on flying up from Pasadena and bravely coming along with me to look at the broken body of a drowned "Caucasian" woman, age thirty to thirty-five—before I learn her whereabouts.

The first telephone call—informing me that my mate is in a Hong Kong jail—is from the State Department. The second call is from

Garland, who adds certain lurid and clarifying details: she had gone from the Hong Kong airport directly by taxi to the well-known ex-lover's mansion in Kowloon. He is the English Onassis, I am told, son and heir of the founder of the MacDonald-Metcalf Line, and king of the cargo routes from the Cape of Good Hope to Manila Bay. At Jimmy Metcalf's home, she had not even been allowed past the servant posted at the door, not after her name had been announced to Metcalf's wife. And when, some hours later, she left her hotel to tell the police of the plan made some years earlier by the president of MacDonald-Metcalf to have this wife run down by a car, the officer on duty at the police station made a telephone call and subsequently a packet of cocaine was found in her purse.

"What happens now?" I ask him. "My God, Donald, now what?"

"I get her out," says Garland.

"Can that be done?"

"It can."

"How?"

"How would you think?"

Money? Blackmail? Girls? Boys? I don't know, I don't care, I won't ask again. *Whatever works, do it.*

"The question is," says Garland, "what happens when Helen is free? I can, of course, make her quite comfortable right here. I can provide her with all she needs to pull herself together again, and to go on. I want to know what you think is for the best. She cannot afford to be caught in between again."

"In between what? Donald, this is all a little confusing. I have no idea what's best, frankly. Tell me, please, why didn't she go to you when she got there?"

"Because she got it in her head to see Jimmy. She knew that if she'd come first to me I would never have let her go anywhere near him. I know the man, better than she does."

"And you knew she was coming?"

"Yes, of course."

"The night you were here for dinner."

"No, no, my dear boy. Only a week ago. But she was to have cabled. I would have been at the airport to meet her. But she did it Helen's way."

"She shouldn't have," I say dumbly.

"The question is, does she come back to you or stay with me? I'd like you to tell me which you think is best."

"You're sure she's getting out of jail, you're sure the charges will be dropped—"

"I wouldn't have phoned to say what I'm saying otherwise."

"What happens then . . . well, it's up to Helen, isn't it? That is, I'd have to talk to her."

"But you can't. I'm lucky I could. We're lucky she isn't in irons already and halfway to Malaysia. Our police chief is not the most charitable of men, except on his own behalf. And your rival is not Albert Schweitzer."

"That is apparent."

"She used to tell me, 'It's so difficult to go shopping with Jimmy. If I see something I like, he buys me twelve.' She used to say to him, 'But, Jimmy, I can only wear one at a time.' But Jimmy never understood, Mr. Kepesh. He does everything by twelves."

"Okay, I believe that."

"I don't want anything further to go wrong for Helen—ever," says Garland. "I want to know exactly where Helen stands, and I want to know now. She has been through years of hell. She was a marvelous, dazzling creature, and life has treated her hideously. I won't allow either one of you to torture her again."

But I can't tell him where she stands—I don't know where I stand. First, I say, I must reach Helen's family and calm their fears. He will hear from me.

Will he? Why?

As though I have just reported that her daughter has been detained by a club meeting after school, Helen's mother says, politely, "And when will she be home?"

"I don't know."

But this does not appear to faze the adventuress's mother. "I do hope you'll keep me informed," she says, brightly.

"I will."

"Well, thank you for calling, David."

What else can the mother of an adventuress do but thank people for calling and keeping her informed?

And what does the husband of an adventuress do while his wife is in jail in the Far East? Well, at dinnertime I prepare an omelette, make it very carefully, at just the right heat, and serve it to myself with a little chopped parsley, a glass of wine, and a slice of but-

tered toast. Then I take a long hot shower. He doesn't want me to
torture her; all right, I won't torture her—but best of all, I won't torture myself. After the shower I decide to get into my pajamas and
to do my night's reading in bed, all by myself. No girls, not yet.
That will come in its own sweet time. Everything will. Can it be? I
am back where I was six years ago, the night before I ditched my
sensible date and took Hong Kong Helen home from that party. Except that now I have my job, I have my book to complete, and I
seem to have this comfortable apartment, so charmingly and taste-
fully decorated, all to myself. What is Mauriac's phrase? "To revel
in the pleasures of the unshared bed."

For some hours my happiness is complete. Have I ever heard or
read of something like this happening, of a person being catapulted
out of his misery *directly* into bliss? The common wisdom has it
that it works the other way around. Well, I am here to say that on
rare occasions it seems to work this way too. My God, I do feel
good. I will not torture her, or myself, ever again. Fine with me.

Two hundred and forty minutes of this, more or less.

With a loan from Arthur Schonbrunn, a colleague who had been
my thesis adviser, I buy a round-trip ticket and fly off to Asia the
next day. (At the bank I discover that the entire balance in our savings account had been withdrawn by Helen the week before, for
her one-way air ticket, and to start her new life.) On the plane
there is time to think—and to think and to think and to think. It
must be that I want her back, that I can't give her up, that I am in
love with her whether I've known it or not, that she is my destiny—

Not one word of this stuff convinces me. Most are words I despise: Helen's kind of words, Helen's kind of thinking. I can't live
without this, he can't live without that, my woman, my man, my
destiny . . . Kid stuff! Movie stuff! *Screen Romance!*

Yet if this woman is not *my woman*, what am I doing here? If she
is not *my destiny*, why was I on the phone from 2 to 5 a.m.? Is it
just that pride won't permit me to abdicate in favor of her homosexual protector? No, that's not what's done it. Nor am I Acting Re-
sponsibly, or out of shame, or masochism, or vindictive glee . . .

Then that leaves love. Love! At this late date! Love! After all
that's been done to destroy it! More love, suddenly, than there was
anywhere along the way!

I spend the rest of my waking hours on that flight remembering
every single charming, sweet, beguiling word she has ever spoken.

Accompanied by Garland—grim, courteous, impeccably now the banker and businessman—a Hong Kong police detective, and the clean-cut young man from the American consulate who is also there to meet my airplane, I am taken to a jail to see my wife. As we leave the terminal for the car, I say to Garland, "I thought she was to be out by now." "The negotiations," he says, "seem to involve more interests than we had imagined." "Hong Kong," the young consulate officer informs me wryly, "is the birthplace of collective bargaining." Everybody in the car seems to know the score, except me.

I am searched and then allowed to sit with her in a tiny room whose door is dramatically locked behind us. The sound of the lock catching makes her reach wildly for my hand. Her face is blotchy, her lips are blistered, her eyes . . . her eyes I cannot look into without my innards crumbling. And Helen smells. And as for all that I felt for her up in the air, well, I simply cannot bring myself to love her like that down here on the ground. I have never loved her quite like that down on the ground before, and I'm not going to start in a jail. I am not that kind of an idiot. Which maybe makes me some other kind of idiot . . . but that I will have to determine later.

"They planted cocaine on me." "I know." "He can't get away with that," she says. "He won't. Donald is going to get you out of here." "*He has to!*" "He is, he's doing it. So you don't have to worry. You'll be out very soon now." "I have to tell you something terrible. All our cash is gone. The police stole it. He told them what to do to me—and they did it. They laughed at me. They touched me." "Helen, tell me the truth now. I have to know. We all have to know. When you get out of here, do you want to stay on with Donald in his house? He says he will look after you, he—" "But I can't! No! Oh, don't leave me here, please! Jimmy will kill me!"

On the return flight Helen drinks until the stewardess says she cannot serve her another. "I'll bet you were even faithful to me," she says, oddly "chatty" suddenly. "Yes, I'll bet you were," she says, serene in a dopey sort of way now that the whiskey has somewhat dimmed the horrors of incarceration and she is beyond the nightmare of Jimmy Metcalf's revenge. I don't bother to answer one way or the other. Of the two meaningless copulations of the last year there is nothing to say; she would only laugh if I were to tell her who her rivals had been. Nor could I expect much sympathy were I to try to explain to her how unsatisfying it had been to deceive her with women who hadn't a hundredth of her appeal to me—who hadn't a hundredth of her character, let alone her love-liness—and whose faces I could have spit into when I realized how much of *their* satisfaction derived from putting Helen Kepesh in her place. Quickly enough—*almost* quickly enough—I had seen that deceiving a wife as disliked as Helen was by other women just wasn't going to be possible without humiliating myself in the process. I hadn't a Jimmy Metcalf's gift for coldly rearing back and delivering the grand and fatal blow to my opponent; no, vengeance was his style and contentious melancholia was mine . . . Helen's speech is badly slurred by liquor and fatigue, but now that she has had a bath, and a meal, and a change of clothes, and a chance to make up her face, she intends to have a conversation, her first in days and days. She intends now to resume her place in the world, and not as the vanquished, but as herself. "Well," she says, "you didn't have to be *such* a good boy, you know. You could have had your affairs, if that would have made you any happier. I could have taken it." "Good to know that," I say. "It's you, David, who wouldn't have survived in one piece. You see, I've been faithful to you, whether you believe it or not. The only man I've been faithful to in my life." Do I believe that? Can I? And if I should? Where does *that* leave me? I say nothing. "You don't know yet where I used to go sometimes after my exercise class." "No, I don't." "You don't know why I went out in the morning wearing my favorite dress." "I had my ideas." "Well, they were wrong. I had no lover. Never, never with you. Because it would have been too hideous. You couldn't have taken it—and so I didn't do it. You would have been crushed, you would have forgiven me, and you would never have been yourself again. You would have gone around bleeding forever." "I went around bleeding anyway. We both went around bleeding. Where did you go all dressed up?" "I went out to the air-port." "And?" "And I sat in the Pan Am waiting room. I had my passport in my handbag. And my jewelry. I sat there reading the paper until somebody asked if I wanted to have a drink in the first-class lounge." "And I'll bet somebody always did." "Always—that's right. And I'd go there and have a drink. We would talk . . . and then they would ask me to go away with them. To South America, to Africa, everywhere. A man even asked me to come with him on a business trip to Hong Kong. But I never did it. Never. Instead, I came back home and you started in on me about the checkbook stubs." "You did this how often?" "Often enough," she replies. "Enough for what—to see if you still had the power?" "No, you idiot, to see if *you* still had the power." She begins to sob. "Will it startle you," she asks, "to hear that I think we should have had that baby?" "I wouldn't have risked it, not with you." My words knock the wind out of her, what wind is left. "Oh, you shit, that was unnecessary, there are less cruel ways . . ." she says. "Oh, why didn't I let Jimmy kill her when he wanted to!" she cries. "Quiet down, Helen." "You should see her now—she stood there, ten feet inside the hallway, glaring out at me. You should see her—she looks like a whale! That beautiful man goes to bed with a whale." "I said quiet down." "He told them to plant cocaine on me—on me, the person he loves! He let them take my purse and steal my money! And how I loved that man! I only left him to save him from committing a murder! And now he hates me for being too decent, and you despise me for being indecent, and the truth of it is that I'm better and stronger and braver than both of you. At least I was—and I was when I was only twenty years old! *You* wouldn't risk a baby with *me?* What about someone like *you?* Did it ever occur to you that about a baby it may have been the other way around? No? Yes? Answer me! Oh, I can't wait to see the little sparrow you do take the risk with. If only you had taken it into your hands long ago, years ago—at the beginning! I should have had nothing to say about it!" "Helen, you're exhausted and you're loaded and you don't know what you're saying. A lot you cared about having a baby." "A lot I did, you fool, you dope! Oh, why did I come on this airplane with you! I could have stayed with Donald! He needs someone as much as I do. I should have stayed with him in his house, and told *you* to go on home. Oh, why did I lose my nerve in that jail!" "You lost it because of your Jimmy. You thought when you got out he'd kill you." "But he wouldn't—that was crazy! He only did what he did because he loves me so, and I loved him! Oh, I waited and I waited and I waited—I've waited for you for six years! Why didn't you take me into your world like a man!" "Maybe you mean why didn't I take you out of yours. I couldn't. The only kind to take *you* out is the kind who took you in. Sure, I know about my terrible tone, and the scornful looks I can give, but I never went and got a hit-man in about the toast, you know. Next time you want to be saved from a tyrant, find another tyrant to do the job. I admit defeat." "Oh, God, oh, Jesus God, why must they be either brutes or choirboys? Stewardess," she says, grabbing the girl's arm as she passes in the aisle, "I don't want a drink, I've had enough. I only want to ask a question of you. Don't be frightened. Why are they either brutes or choirboys, do you know?" "Who, madam?" "Don't you find that in your travels from one continent to the other? They're even afraid, you know, of a sweet little thing like you. That's why you have to go around grinning like that. Just look the bastards right in the eye and they're either at your knees or at your throat."

When at last Helen has fallen asleep—her face rolling familiarly on my shoulder—I take the final exams out of my briefcase and begin where I had had to leave off a hundred or so hours ago. Yes, I have taken my schoolwork with me—and a good thing too. I cannot imagine how I could get through the million remaining hours of the flight without these examination papers to hang on to. "Without this . . ." and see myself strangling Helen with the coil of her waist-long hair. Who strangles his lover with her hair? Isn't it somebody somewhere in Browning? Oh, who cares!

"The search for intimacy, not because it necessarily makes for happiness, but because it is necessary, is one of Chekhov's recurrent themes."

The paper I have chosen to begin with—to begin again with—is by Kathie Steiner, the girl I had dreamed of adopting. "Good," I write in the margin alongside her opening sentence; then I reread it and after "necessary" make an insertion mark and write, "for survival(?)." And all the while I am thinking, "And miles below are the beaches of Polynesia. Well, dear, dazzling creature, a lot of good that does us! Hong Kong! The whole damn thing could have taken place in Cincinnati! A hotel room, a police station, an airport. A vengeful megalomaniac and some crooked cops! And a would-be Cleopatra! Our savings gone on this trashy Grade-B thriller! Oh, this voyage is the marriage itself—traversing four thousand miles of the exotic globe twice over, and for no good reason at all!"

Struggling to fix my attention once again on the task at hand—and not on whether Helen and I should have had a child, or who is to blame because we didn't; refusing to charge myself yet again with all I could have done that I didn't do, and all I did that I shouldn't have—I return to Kathie Steiner's final exam. Jimmy Metcalf instructs the police: "Kick her ass a little, gentlemen, it'll do the whore some good," while I subdue my emotions by reading carefully through each of Kathie's pages, correcting every last comma fault, reminding her about her dangling-modifier problem, and dutifully filling the margin with my commentary and questions. Me and my "finals"; my marking pen and my paper clips. How the Emperor Metcalf would enjoy the spectacle—likewise Donald Garland and his uncharitable chief of police. I suppose I ought to laugh a little myself; but as I am a literature professor and not a policeman, as I am someone who long ago squeezed out what little of the tyrant was ever in him—from the look of things, maybe squeezed out just a bit too much—instead of laughing it all off, I come to Kathie's concluding sentence, and am undone. The hold I have had on myself since Helen's disappearance dissolves like that, and I must turn my face and press it into the darkened window of the humming airship that is carrying us back home to complete, in orderly and legal fashion, the disentanglement of our two wrecked lives. I cry for myself, I cry for Helen, and finally I seem to cry hardest of all with the realization that somehow not every last thing *has* been destroyed, that despite my consuming obsession with my marital unhappiness and my dreamy desire to call out to my young students for their help, I have somehow gotten a sweet, chubby, unharmed and as yet unhorrified daughter of Beverly Hills to end her sophomore year of college by composing this grim and beautiful lament summarizing what she calls "Anton Chekhov's overall philosophy of life." But can Professor Kepesh have taught her this? How? *How?* I am only just beginning to learn it on this flight! "We are born innocent," the girl has written, "we suffer terrible disillusionment before we can gain knowledge, and then we fear death— and we are granted only fragmentary happiness to offset the pain."

I am finally extracted from the rubble of my divorce by a job offer from Arthur Schonbrunn, who has left Stanford to become chairman of the comparative literature program at the State University of New York on Long Island. I have already begun seeing a psychoanalyst in San Francisco—only shortly after I began seeing the lawyer—and it is he who recommends that when I return East to teach I continue therapy with a Dr. Frederick Klinger, whom he knows and can recommend as someone who is not afraid to speak up with his patients, "a solid, reasonable man," as he is described to me, "a specialist," I am told, "in common sense." But are reason and common sense what I need? Some would say that I have ruined things by far too narrow a devotion to exactly these attributes.

Frederick Klinger is solid, all right: a hearty, round-faced fellow, full of life, who, with my permission, smokes cigars throughout the sessions. I don't much like the aroma myself, but allow it because smoking seems even further to concentrate the keenness with which Klinger attends to my despair. Not many years older than me, and sporting fewer gray hairs than I have lately begun to show, he exudes the contentment and confidence of a successful man in his middle years. I gather from the phone calls which, to my distress, he takes during my hour, that he is already a key figure in psychoanalytic circles, a member of the governing bodies of schools, publications, and research institutes, not to mention the last source of hope for any number of souls in disrepair. At first I find myself

somewhat put off by the sheer relish with which the doctor seems
to devour his responsibilities—put off, to be truthful, by nearly everything about him: the double-breasted chalk-stripe suit and the
floppy bow tie, the frayed Chesterfield coat growing tight over the
plumpening middle, the *two* bursting briefcases at the coat rack,
the photos of the smiling healthy children on the book-laden desk,
the tennis racket in the umbrella stand—put off even by the gym
bag pushed behind the big worn Eames chair from which, cigar in
hand, he addresses himself to my confusion. Can this snazzy, energetic conquistador possibly understand that there are mornings
when on the way from the bed to the toothbrush I have to struggle
to prevent myself from dropping down and curling up on the living-room floor? I don't entirely understand the depth of this plunge
myself. Having failed at being a husband to Helen—having failed at
figuring out how to make Helen a wife—it seems I would rather
sleep through my life now than live it.

How, for instance, have I come to be on such terrible terms with
sensuality? "You," he replies, "who married a *femme fatale?*" "But
only to de-fatalize her, to de-fang her, along the way. All that nag-
ging at her, at Helen, about the garbage and the laundry and the
toast. My mother couldn't have done a better job. About every last
detail!" "Too divine for details, was she? Look, she isn't the Helen
born of Leda and Zeus, you know. She's of the earth, Mr. Kepesh—a
middle-class Gentile girl from Pasadena, California, pretty enough
to get herself a free trip to Angkor Wat every year, but that's about
it, in the way of supernatural achievement. And cold toast is cold
toast, no matter how much jewelry the cook may have accumulated
over the years from rich married men with a taste for young girls."
"I was frightened of her." "Sure you were." His phone rings. No, he
cannot possibly be at the hospital before noon. Yes, he has seen the
husband. No, the gentleman does not seem willing to cooperate.
Yes, that is most unfortunate. Now back to this uncooperative gentleman. "Sure you were frightened," he says, "you couldn't trust
her." "I *wouldn't* trust her. And she *was* faithful to me. I believe
that." "Neither here nor there. Some game she was playing with
herself, that's all. What value did it have when the fact is that the
two of you had no real business together ever? From the sound of it
the only thing each of you did *totally* out of character was to marry
the other." "I was frightened of Birgitta, too." "My God," he exclaims, "who wouldn't have been?" "Look, either I'm not making

myself clear or you don't even want to begin to understand me. I'm saying that these were special creatures, full of daring and curiosity —and freedom. They were not ordinary young women." "Oh, I understand that." "Do you? I think sometimes that you'd prefer to assign them both to some very tawdry category of humankind. But what made them special is that they weren't tawdry, not to me, neither one of them. They were exceptional." "Granted." The phone rings. Yes, what is it? I am in session, yes. No, no, go ahead. Yes. Yes. Of course he understands. No, no, he's pretending, pay no attention. All right, increase the dosage to four a day. But no more. And call me if he continues crying. Call me anyway. Goodbye. "Granted," he says, "but what were you supposed to do, having *married* one of these 'special creatures'? Spend days as well as nights fondling her perfect breasts? Join her opium den? The other day you said the only thing you learned from six years with Helen was how to roll a joint." "I think saying that is what is known as courting the analyst's favor. I learned plenty." "The fact remains— you had your work to do." "The work is just a habit," I say, without disguising my irritation with his dogged "demythologizing." "Perhaps," I wearily suggest, "reading books is the opiate of the educated classes." "Is it? Are you thinking of becoming a flower child?" he says, lighting up a new cigar. "Once Helen and I were sunbathing in the nude on a beach in Oregon. We were on a vacation, driving north. After a while we spotted a guy watching us from off in some brush. We started to cover up, but he came toward us anyway and asked if we were nudists. When I said no he gave us a copy of his nudist newspaper in case we wanted to subscribe." Klinger laughs loudly. "Helen said to me that God Himself must have sent him because it had been, by that time, fully ninety minutes since I'd read anything." Again Klinger laughs with genuine amusement. "Look," I tell him, "you just don't know what it was like when I first met her. It's not to be so easily disparaged. You don't know what I was like, nor can you—nor can I, any more—seeing me in this shape. But I was a fearless sort of boy back in my early twenties. More daring than most, especially for that woebegone era in the history of pleasure. I actually did what the jerk-off artists dreamed about. Back when I started out on my own in the world, I was, if I may say so, something of a sexual prodigy." "And you want to be one again, in your thirties?" I don't even bother to answer, so narrow and wrongheaded does the common sense he's mastered strike me. "Why allow Helen," Klinger continues, "who has disfigured herself so in the frantic effort to be the high priestess of Eros—who very nearly destroyed you with her pronouncements and insinuations—why allow her judgment power over you still? How long do you intend to let her go on rebuking you where you feel weakest? How long do you intend to go on *feeling* weak over such utter foolishness? What was this 'daring' search of hers—?" The telephone. "Excuse me," he says. Yes, this is he. Yes, go ahead. Hello—yes, I can hear you very well. How is Madrid? What? Well, of course he's suspicious, what did you expect? But you just tell him that he is behaving stupidly and then forget it. No, of course you don't want to get into a fight. I understand. Just say it, and then try to have some courage. You can stand up to him. Go back up to the room and tell him. Come on now, you know very well you can. All right. Good luck. Have a good time. I said, then go out and have a good time. Goodbye. "What was this search of hers," he says, "but so much evasion, a childish flight from the real attainable projects of a life?" "Then, on the other hand," I say, "maybe the 'projects' are so much evasion of the search." "Please, you like to read and write about books. That, by your own testimony, gives you enormous satisfaction—did, at any rate, and will again, I assure you. Right now you're fed up with everything. But you like being a teacher, correct? And from what I gather you are not uninspired at it. I still don't know what alternative you have in mind. You want to move to the South Seas and teach great books to the girls in sarongs at the University of Tahiti? You want to have a go at a harem again? To be a fearless prodigy again, playing at Jack and Jill with your little Swedish daredevil in the working-class bars of Paris? You want a hammer over your head again—though maybe this time one that finds the mark?" "Burlesquing what I'm talking about doesn't do me any good, you know. It's obviously not going back to Birgitta that's on my mind. It's going ahead. I can't go *ahead*." "Perhaps going ahead, on that road anyway, is a delusion." "Dr. Klinger, I assure you that I am sufficiently imbued by now with the Chekhovian bias to suspect as much myself. I know what there is to know from 'The Duel' and other stories about those committed to the libidinous fallacy. I too have read and studied the great Western wisdom on the subject. I have even taught it. I have even practiced it. But, if I may, as Chekhov also had the ordinary good sense to write: in psychological matters, 'God preserve us from generalizations.'" "Thank you for the literature lesson. Tell me this, Mr. Kepesh: can you really be in the doldrums about what has befallen her—over what you seem to think you have 'done' to her—or are you just trying to prove to us that you are a man of feeling and conscience? If so, don't overdo it. Because *this* Helen was bound to spend a night in jail, sooner or later. Destined for it long before she met you. From the sound of it, it's how she landed on you—in the hope of being saved from the hoosegow, and the other inevitable humiliations. And that you know, as well as I do."

But whatever he may say, however he may bully, burlesque, or even try a smidgen of charm in order to get me to put the marriage and divorce behind me, I am, whether he believes it or not, never altogether immune from self-recrimination when stories reach me of the ailments that are said to be transforming the one-time Occidental princess of the Orient into a bitter hag. I learn of a debilitating case of rhinitis that cannot seem to be checked by drugs and necessitates that she live with a tissue continuously rubbing away at her nose—at the fluted nostrils that flare as though catching the wind when she achieves her pleasure. I hear tell of extensive skin eruptions, on the cunning fingers ("You like this? . . . this? . . . oh, you do like it, my darling!"), and on her wide, lovely lips ("What do you see first in a face? The eyes or the mouth? I like that you discovered my mouth first"). But then Helen's is not the only flesh slowly taking its revenge, or doing penance, or losing heart, or removing itself from the fray. Eating hardly anything, I have dropped since the divorce to scarecrow weight, and for the second time in my life I am bereft of my potency, even for an entertainment as unambitious as self-love. "I should never have come home from Europe," I tell Klinger, who has at my request put me on an anti-depressant drug, which pries me out of bed in the morning but then leaves me for the rest of the day with vague, other-worldly feelings of encapsulation, of vast unpassable reaches between myself and the flourishing hordes. "I should have gone all the way and become Birgitta's pimp. I'd be a happier, healthier member of society. Somebody else could teach the great masterworks of disillusionment and renunciation." "Yes? You would rather be a pimp than an associate professor?" "That's one way of putting it." "Put it your own way." "This something in me that I turned against," I say in a fit of hopelessness, "before I even understood it, or let it have a life . . . I throttled it to death . . . killed it, practically overnight. And why? Why on earth was *murder* required?"

In the weeks that follow I attempt, between phone calls, to describe and chronicle the history of this something that, in my hopeless and de-energized state, I continue to think of as "murdered." I speak at length now not just of Helen but of Birgitta as well. I go back to Louis Jelinek, even to Herbie Bratasky, speak of all that each meant to me, what each excited and alarmed, and of how each was dealt with, in my way. "Your rogues' gallery," Klinger calls them one day in the twentieth or thirtieth week of our debate. "Moral delinquency," he observes, "has its fascination for you." "Also," I say, "for the authors of *Macbeth* and *Crime and Punishment*. Sorry to have mentioned the names of two works of art, Doctor." "Quite all right. I hear all sorts of things here. I'm used to it." "I do seem to get the feeling that it's somehow against house rules for me to call upon my literary reserves in these skirmishes of ours, but the only point I'm trying to make is that 'moral delinquency' has been on the minds of serious people for a long time now. And why 'delinquents,' anyway? Won't 'independent spirits' do? It's no *less* accurate." "I only mean to suggest that they aren't wholly harmless types." "Wholly harmless types probably lead rather constricted lives, don't you think?" "On the other hand, one oughtn't to underestimate the pain, the isolation, the uncertainty, and everything else unpleasant that may accompany 'independence' of this kind. Look at Helen now." "Please, look at me now." "I am. I do. I suspect that she is worse off. You at least haven't put *all* your eggs in that basket." "I cannot maintain an erection, Dr. Klinger. I cannot maintain a smile, for that matter." Whereupon his phone rings.

Fastened to no one and to nothing, drifting, drifting, sometimes, frighteningly, sinking; and, with the relentlessly clever and commonsensical doctor, quarreling, bickering, and debating, arguing yet again the subject which had been the source of so much marital bitterness—only when I am supine it is generally I who wind up taking Helen's part, while he who sits up takes mine.

Each winter my parents come down to New York City to spend three or four days visiting family, friends, and favorite guests. In times gone by, we all used to stay on West End Avenue with my father's younger brother, Larry, a successful kosher caterer, and his wife, Sylvia, the Benvenuto Cellini of strudel, and, in childhood,

my favorite aunt. Until I was fourteen, I would, to my astonished
delight, be put to bed there in the same room with my cousin Lorraine. Sleeping beside a bed with a live girl in it—a "developing"
girl, at that—going out to dine at Moskowitz and Lupowitz (on
food described by my father as *nearly* as good as what is prepared
in the kitchen of the Hungarian Royale), waiting in subfreezing
temperatures to get in to see the Rockettes, sipping cocoa amid the
thick draperies and the imposing furniture sets of haberdashery
wholesalers and produce merchants whom I have known only in
their voluminous half-sleeve shirts and their drooping swim trunks,
and who are called by my father the Apple King and the Herring
King and the Pajama King—everything about these New York visits
hold a secret thrill for me, and invariably from "overexcitement" I
develop a "strep throat" on the drive home, and back on our moun-
taintop have to spend at least two or three days in bed recovering.
"We didn't visit Herbie," I say sullenly, only seconds before our
departure—to which my mother invariably responds, "A summer
isn't enough with him? We have to travel to Brooklyn to make a
special trip?" "Belle, he's teasing you," my father says, but on the
sly shakes a fist in my direction, as though for mentioning the Fart
King to my mother I deserve no less than a blow to the head.

Now that I am back East and my uncle and aunt live in Cedarhurst, Long Island, I respond by phone to a letter from my father
and invite my parents to stay in my apartment rather than at a
hotel when they come down for their annual winter visit. The two
rooms on West Seventy-fifth Street are not actually mine but,
through an ad in the *Times,* have been sublet, furnished, from a
young actor who has gone to try his luck in Hollywood. There is a
crimson damask on the bedroom walls, perfumes lined up on a
bathroom shelf, and, in boxes that I discover at the rear of the linen
closet, a half-dozen wigs. The night I find them I indulge my curiosity and try a couple on. I look like my mother's sister.

Near the beginning of my occupancy, the phone rings one night
and a man asks, "Where's Mark?" "He's in California. He'll be
there for two years." "Yeah, sure. Look, you just tell him Wally's
in town." "But he's not here. I have an address for him out there." I
begin to recite it, but the voice, grown gruff and agitated now, interrupts: "Then who are you?" "His tenant." "Is that what they call
it in the thee-yater? What do you look like, sweetpants? You got
big blue eyes too?" When the calls persist, I have the telephone

number changed, but then it is through the intercom that connects my apartment to the downstairs hallway of the brownstone that the repartee continues. "You just tell your little pal—" "Mark is in California, you can reach him out there." "Ha ha—that's a good one. What's your name, honey? Come to the doorway and we'll see whether I can reach you." "Come on, Wally, leave me alone. He's gone. Go away." "You like the rough stuff too?" "Oh, take off, will you?" "Take what off, sweetpants? What do you want me to take off?" So the flirtation goes.

Nights when I am at my loneliest, nights when I start talking to myself and to people who are not present, I sometimes have to suppress a powerful urge to call for help into the intercom. What holds me back isn't that it makes no sense but, rather, the fear that one of my neighbors or, what is worse, Patient Wally will be standing in the entryway just as my strident cry comes through; what I fear is the kind of help I might get—if not my homosexual suitor, the Bellevue emergency squad. So I go into the bathroom instead, close the door behind me, and leaning over the mirror to look at my own drawn face, I let it out. "I want somebody! I want somebody! I want somebody!" Sometimes I can go on like this for minutes at a time in an attempt to bring on a fit of weeping that will leave me limp and, for a while at least, empty of longing for another. I of course am not *so* far gone as to believe that screaming aloud in a closed-off room will make the somebody I want appear. Besides, who is it? If I knew I wouldn't have to holler into the mirror—I could write or phone. *I want somebody*, I cry—and it is my parents who arrive.

I carry their suitcases upstairs while my father lugs the Scotch cooler in which are packed some two-dozen round plastic containers of cabbage soup, matzoh-ball soup, kugel, and flanken, all frozen and neatly labeled. Inside the apartment my mother takes an envelope from her purse—"DAVID" is typed exactly at the center and underlined in red. The envelope contains instructions for me typewritten on hotel stationery: time required for the defrosting and heating of each dish, details as to seasoning. "Read it," she says, "and see if you have any questions." My father says, "How about if he reads it after you get out of your coat and sit down?" "I'm fine," she says. "You're tired," he tells her. "David, you have enough room in your freezer? I didn't know how big a freezer you had here." "Mamma, room to spare," I say lightly. But when I open the refrigerator she groans as though her throat has just been slit.

"One this and one that, and that's it?" she cries. "Look at that lemon, it looks older than I do. How do you eat?" "Out, mostly." "And your father told me I was overdoing it." "You've been tired," he says to her, "and you *were* overdoing." "I knew he wasn't taking care of himself," she says. "You're the one who has to take care of herself," he says. "What is it?" I ask, "what's the matter with you, Ma?" "I had a little pleurisy, and your father is making it into a production. I get a little pain when I knit for too long. That's the whole outcome of all the money thrown away on doctors and tests."

She does not know—nor do I, until my father comes with me the next morning to buy a paper and some things for breakfast and then to walk me gravely up toward where Larry and Sylvia used to put us all up on West End Avenue—that she is dying of cancer that has spread from the pancreas. This then explains his letter saying, "Maybe if we could stay with you this one time . . ." Does it also explain her request to visit landmarks she has not been to in decades? I almost believe she knows just what is happening and this display of exuberance is to spare *him* from knowing she knows. Each protecting the other from the horrible truth—my parents like two brave and helpless children . . . And what can I do about it? "But dying—*when?*" I ask him as we turn back, the two of us in tears, to my apartment. For several moments he cannot answer. "That's the worst of it," he manages finally to say. "Five weeks, five months, five years—five *minutes*. Every doctor tells me something different!"

And back at the apartment she asks me again, "Will you take us to Greenwich Village? Will you take us to the Metropolitan Museum of Art? When I worked for Mr. Clark one of the girls used to eat the most delicious green noodles at an Italian restaurant in Greenwich Village. I wish I could remember the name. It couldn't be Tony's, could it, Abe?" "Honeybunch," my father says, his voice already tinged with grief, "it wouldn't even be there after all this time." "We could look—and what if it was!" she says, turning with excitement to me. "Oh, David, how Mr. Clark loved the Museum of Art! Every Sunday when his sons were growing up he took them there to see the paintings."

I accompany them everywhere, to see the famous Rembrandts at the Metropolitan, to look for a Tony's that serves green noodles, to visit their oldest and dearest friends, some of whom I haven't seen

in over fifteen years but who kiss and embrace me as though I were
still a child, and then, because I am a professor, ask me serious
questions about the world situation; we go, as of old, to the zoo and
to the planetarium, and finally on a pilgrimage to the building
where she was once a legal secretary. Following lunch in Chinatown, we stand at the corner of Broad and Wall Streets on a chilly
Sunday afternoon, and, as always, with perfect innocence, she rem-
inisces about her days with the firm. And how different for her it
would have been, I think, had she stayed on to be one of Mr.
Clark's girls for life, one of those virgin spinsters who adore the fatherly boss and play auntie on holidays to the boss's children. Without the interminable demands of a family-run resort hotel, she
might actually have known some serenity, have lived in accordance
with her simple gifts for tidiness and order rather than at their
mercy. On the other hand, she would never have known my father
and me—*we* would never have been. If only, if only . . . If only
what? She has cancer.

They sleep in the double bed in the bedroom while I lie awake
under a blanket on the living-room sofa. My mother is about to
vanish—that's what it comes down to. And her last memory of her
only child will be of his meager, rootless existence—her last memory
will be of this lemon I live with! Oh, with what disgust and remorse
do I recall the series of mistakes—no, the one habitual and recurrent mistake—that has made these two rooms my home. Instead of
being enemies, of providing one another with the *ideal* enemy, why
couldn't Helen and I have put that effort into satisfying each other,
into steady, dedicated living? Would that have been so hard for
two such strong-willed people? *Should* I have said at the very outset, "Look, we're having a child"? Lying there listening to my
mother breathing her last, I try to infuse myself with new resolve: I
must, I *will*, end this purposeless, pointless . . . and into my thoughts
comes Elisabeth, of all people, with the locket around her neck and
her broken arm healed. How sweet, how welcoming she would be
to my widowed father! But without an Elisabeth, what can I do for
him? How ever will he survive up there on his own? Oh, why must
it be Helen and Birgitta at one extreme or life with a lemon at the
other?

As the sleepless minutes pass—or, rather, do not seem to pass at
all—all the thoughts that can possibly distress me seem to coalesce
into an unidentifiable nonsense word that will not let me be. To

free myself from its insipid thralldom, I begin to toss angrily from one side of the couch to the other. I feel half in, half out of deep anesthesia—immersed back in the claustrophobic agonies of the recovery room, which I last saw at the age of twelve, following my appendectomy—until the word resolves itself at last into nothing other than the line of keys, read from left to right, on which my mother taught me to rest the tips of my fingers when I learned typing from her on the hotel's Remington Noiseless. But now that I know the origin of this commonplace alphabetical scrambling, it is worse even than before. As though it *is* a word after all, and the one that holds within its unutterable syllables all the pain of her baffled energies and her frenetic life. And the pain of my own. I suddenly see myself struggling with my father over her epitaph, the two of us are hurling each other against enormous pieces of rock, while I insist to the stonecutter that ASDFGHJKL be carved beneath her name on the tombstone.

I cannot sleep. I wonder if it is possible that I will never be able to sleep again. All my thoughts are either simple or crazy, and after a while I cannot distinguish which is which. I want to go into the bedroom and get into their bed. I rehearse in my mind how I will do it. To ease them out of their initial timidity, I will just sit first at the edge of the bed and quietly talk to them about the best of the past. Looking down at their familiar faces side by side on the fresh pillowcases, at their two faces peering out at me from above the sheet drawn up to their chins, I will remind them of how very long it's been since last we all snuggled up together under a single blanket. Wasn't it in a tourist cabin just outside Lake Placid? Remember that little box of a room? Was it 1940 or '41? And, am I right, didn't it cost Dad just one dollar for the night? Mother thought that it would be good for me to see the Thousand Islands and Niagara Falls during my Easter vacation. That's where we were headed, in the Dodge. Remember, you told us how Mr. Clark took his little boys each summer to see the sights of Europe; remember all those things you told me that I had never heard before; God, remember me and the two of you and the little Dodge back before the war . . . and then, when they are smiling, I will take off my robe and crawl into the bed between them. And before she dies, we will all hold each other through one last night and morning. Who will ever know, aside from Klinger, and why should I care what he or anyone makes of it?

Near midnight the doorbell rings. At the intercom in the kitchenette I depress the lever and ask, "Who is it?"

"The plumber, sweetpants. Last time you were out. How's your leak, fixed yet?"

I don't respond. My father has come into the living room in his robe. "Somebody you know? At this hour?"

"Just some clown," I say, as the bell rings now to the rhythm of "Shave and a Haircut."

"What is it?" my mother calls from the bedroom.

"Nothing, Ma. Go to sleep."

I decide to speak into the intercom one more time. "Cut it out or I'm going to call the cops."

"Call 'em. Nothing I'm doing is actionable, kiddo. Why don't you just let me up? I'm not half bad, you know. I'm all bad."

My father, standing now at my elbow and listening, has gone a little white.

"Dad," I say, "go back to bed. It's just one of those things that happen in New York. It's nothing."

"He knows you?"

"No."

"Then how does he know to come here? Why does he talk like that?"

A pause, and the bell is ringing again.

Thoroughly irritated now, I say, "Because the fellow I sublet from is a homosexual—and, as best I can gather, this was a friend of his."

"A Jewish fellow?"

"Who I rented from? Yes."

"Jesus," snaps my father, "what the hell is the *matter* with a guy like that?"

"I think I'm going to have to go downstairs."

"By yourself?"

"I'll be all right."

"Don't be crazy—two is better than one. I'll come with you."

"Dad, that's not necessary."

From the bedroom my mother calls, "Now what?"

"Nothing," my father says. "The bell is stuck. We're going downstairs to fix it."

"At this hour?" she calls.

"We'll be right back," my father says to her. "Stay in bed." To me he whispers, "You got some kind of stick, a bat or something?"

"No, no—"

"What if he's armed? You got an umbrella, at least?"

In the meantime, the ringing has stopped. "Maybe he's gone," I say.

My father listens.

"He's gone," I say. "He left."

My father, however, has no intention of going back to bed now. Closing the door to the bedroom—"Shhhh," he whispers to my mother, "everything's fine, go to sleep"—he comes to sit across from the sofa. I can hear how heavily he is breathing as he prepares himself to speak. I am not all that relaxed myself. Propped stiffly up against the pillow, I wait for the bell to start ringing again.

"You're not involved"—he clears his throat—"with something you want to tell me about . . ."

"Don't be silly."

"Because you left us, Davey, when you were seventeen years old and since then there has been no interfering with the kind of influences you let yourself under."

"Dad, I'm not under any 'influences.'"

"I want to ask you a question. Outright."

"Go ahead."

"It's not about Helen. I never asked you about that, and I don't want to start now. I always treated her like a daughter-in-law. Didn't I, didn't your mother, always with respect—?"

"Yes, absolutely."

"I held my tongue. We didn't want her to turn against us. She can have nothing against us to this day. All things considered, I think we did excellent. I am a liberal person, son—and in my politics even more than liberal. Do you know that in 1924 I voted for Norman Thomas for the governor of New York with the first vote I ever cast? And in '48 I voted for Henry Wallace—which maybe was meaningless and a mistake, but the point is that I was probably the only hotel owner in the whole country who voted for somebody that everybody was calling a Communist. Which he wasn't—but the point is, I have never been a narrow man, never. You know—and if you don't, you should—it was never that the woman was a shiksa that bothered me. Shiksas are a fact of life, and they are not going to go away just because Jewish parents might like it better that way. And why should they? I am a believer in all the races and religions living together in harmony, and that you married a Gentile girl was never the point to your mother and me. I think we did excellent on that score. But that doesn't mean I could stomach the rest of her and her attitudes. The truth of the matter, if you want to know, is that I didn't have a good night's sleep in the three years you were married."

"Well, neither did I."

"Is that true? Then why the hell didn't you get out right off the bat? Why did you get in that damn mess to begin with?"

"You want me to go over that territory, do you?"

"No, no—you're right—the hell with it. As far as I'm concerned, if I never hear her name again, that won't be too soon. You are all I care about."

"What do you want to ask?"

"David, what is Tofranil, that I see it in the medicine chest, a big bottle full? What are you taking this drug for?"

"It's an anti-depressant. Tofranil."

He hisses. Disgust, frustration, disbelief, contempt. I must first have heard that sound out of him a hundred years ago, when he had to fire a waiter who wet his bed and stank up the attic where the help slept. "And *why* do you need that? Who told you to take a thing like that and put it in your bloodstream?"

"A psychiatrist."

"You go to a pychiatrist?"

"Yes."

"*Why?*" he cries.

"To keep me afloat. To figure things out. To have someone to talk to . . . confidentially."

"Why not a *wife* to talk to? That's what a wife is for! I mean this time a *real* wife, not somebody who it must have cost you your whole school salary just to pay the beauty parlors. All this is all *wrong*, son. It is no way to live! A psychiatrist, and being on strong drugs, and people showing up at all hours—people who aren't even people—"

"There is nothing to get worked up about."

"There is *everything* to get worked up about."

"No, no," I say, lowering my voice. "Dad, there is only Mother . . ."

He puts a hand over his eyes and quietly begins to cry. With his other hand he makes a fist which he waves at me. "This is what I have had to be all my life! *Without* psychiatrists, *without* happy pills! I am a man who has never said die!"

And once again, the downstairs doorbell.

"Forget it. Let it ring. Dad, he'll go away."

"And then come back? I'll crack his head open, and, believe me, then he'll go away for good!"

Here the bedroom door opens and my mother appears in her nightgown. "Who are you cracking in the head?"

"Some lousy stinking fairy who won't leave him alone!"

The bell again: two shorts, a long; two shorts, a long. Wally is drunk.

Her eyes tearful now, my tiny mother says, "And how often does this go on?"

"Not often."

"But—why don't you report him?"

"Because by the time the police come he'd be gone. You don't want the police for something like this."

"And you swear to me," says my father, "this is nobody you know?"

"I swear to you."

My mother comes into the living room and sits beside me. She takes my hand and clutches it. The three of us listen to the bell— mother, father, and son.

"You know what would fix the son of a bitch once and for all?" my father says. "Boiling water."

"*Abe!*" cries my mother.

"But it would teach him where he don't belong!"

"Dad, you mustn't make too much of it."

"And don't you make so little! Why do you hang *around* with such people?"

"But I don't."

"Then why do you live in a place like this, where they show up and make trouble for you? Do you need more trouble still?"

"Calm down, please," says my mother. "It isn't *his* fault some maniac rings his doorbell. This is New York. He told you. This is what happens."

"That doesn't mean you leave yourself unprotected, Belle!"

Jumping up from his chair, he rushes to the intercom. "Hey! You!" he shouts. "Cut it out! This is David's father—!"

Stroking her arm—already skeletal—I whisper, "It's okay, it's all right, he's not working the thing right anyway. Don't worry, Ma, please—the fellow can't even hear him."

"—you want third-degree burns, we'll give them to you! Do what you want to do in some gutter somewhere, but if you know what's good for you, don't come near my son!"

Two months later, in the hospital in Kingston, my mother dies. After the funeral guests have all left, my father urges me to take the food she has frozen for me only the month before, the last things cooked by her on this earth. I say, "And what are *you* going to eat?" "I was a short-order man before you were even born. Take it. Take what she made for you." "Dad, how are you going to live here by yourself? How are you possibly going to manage the season? Why did you shoo everybody away? Don't be so brave. You can't stay up here alone." "I can look after myself fine. Her going is not something we didn't expect. Please, take it. Take it all. She wanted you to. She said whenever she remembered the inside of your refrigerator, she saw red. She cooked for you," he says, his voice trembling, "and then she went away." He begins to sob. I put my arms around him. "Nobody understood her," he says, "the guests, never, *never*. She was a good person, Davey. When she was young, everything thrilled her, the littlest things even. She had a nervous nature only when the summer got hectic and out of control. So they made fun of her. But do you remember the winter? The peace and the quiet? The fun we had? Remember the letters at night?" Those words do it: for the first time since her death the morning before, I break down completely. "Of course I do, sure I do." "Oh, sonny, that's when she was herself. Only who knew it?" "We did," I tell him, but he repeats, with an angry sob, "And who knew it!"

He carries the frozen food in a shopping bag out to my car. "Here, please, in her memory." And so I return to New York with the half-dozen containers each bearing the same typewritten label: "Tongue with Grandma's famous raisin sauce—2 portions."

Within a week, I am driving back up to the country again, this time with my Uncle Larry, to take my father to Cedarhurst, where he will move in with his brother and sister-in-law. Though only temporarily, he says while we pack his suitcase in the car; just till he is over the shock. In a few days he is sure he will be himself. He has to be, that's all there is to it. "I've been working since I'm fourteen years old. You don't give in to a thing like this," he says. "You tighten your belt and you go on." Besides, it is winter, and there is always the risk up there of fire. Yes, the handyman and his wife will be living on the grounds, but that is no guarantee against the possibility of the hotel burning down in his absence.

It is true, of course, that dozens of mysterious fires have broken out in abandoned hotels and boardinghouses ever since the region began to pass out of fashion as a Jewish summer resort at about the time I was going off to college, but as he and my mother have been able, even in recent years, to hang on to a remnant of their aging clientele and to keep the main house open and the grounds respectable-looking, the arsonists had never before seemed to him a real threat. But now on the drive down the Thruway they are all he can think about. He names for my uncle and me the local hoodlums— "Men, thirty- and forty-year-old men!"—whom he has always suspected of setting the fires. "No, no," he says to my uncle, who has offered his standard analysis as to where the trouble begins, "not even anti-Semites. Too stupid even for that! Just plain demented no-good idiots, fit for the lunatic asylum. Just people who like to see flames! And when it is in ashes, you know who they will accuse? I've seen it a dozen times. Me! That I did it for the insurance money! Because my wife is gone and I want to get out! The blame will fall on my good name! And half the time you know who else I sometimes think that does it? The volunteer fire fighters themselves! Yes—so they can rush out in the fire engines in the middle of the night and ride up and down the mountain in their helmets and boots!"

Even after he is comfortably installed in what used to be Lorraine's bedroom, there is no calming his fears for the empire built of his sweat and his blood. Every night I call him on the phone and he tells me he cannot get to sleep for worrying about a fire. And he has other things to worry about now as well. "That fairy never came back, did he?" "No," I say, knowing it best to lie. "See—it paid to threaten him. Unfortunately that's all some people understand, is the fist," says my father, who has never struck another person in his life. "And how are Uncle Larry and Aunt Sylvia?" I ask. "Wonderful. They couldn't be kinder. Every other word is 'Stay.'" "Well, that sounds reassuring," I say. But no, another ten days, he tells me, and the worst of being without her will be over. Has to be. He has to get back up there while the damn place is still in one piece!

And then it is another five days, and then another, until at last, following an emotional Sunday car ride alone with me, he agrees to put the Hungarian Royale up for sale. His face in his hands, he says, "But I never said die in my life." "There's no shame in it, Dad. Things have just changed." "But I don't *give* up," he cries. "Nobody is going to see it that way," I say, and drive him back to his brother's.

And during this time hardly a night passes when I do not think about the girl I knew for barely two months back when I was a twenty-two-year-old sexual prodigy, the girl who wore a locket around her neck with her father's picture in it. I even think of writing to her, in care of her parents. I even get up out of bed and search through my papers, looking for the Stockholm address. But by now Elisabeth must certainly be married and a mother two or three times over, and assuredly she does not think of me. No woman alive thinks of me, certainly not with love.

Though my department chairman Arthur Schonbrunn is a handsome and exquisitely groomed middle-aged man of unflagging charm and punctiliousness—as adroit and gracious a social being as I have ever seen in action—his wife, Deborah, is someone for whom I have never been able to work up much enthusiasm, even when I was Arthur's favorite graduate student and she was frequently my affectionate and hospitable hostess. In those first years at Stanford, I used to spend a certain amount of my time, in fact, trying to figure out what bound a man so scrupulous about the amenities, so tirelessly concerned to oppose, from the highest principles, the burgeoning political assaults upon university curriculum—what bound such a man of conscience to a woman whose very favorite public performance was in the role of the dizzy dame whose beguiling charm is her reckless and impudent "candor"? The very first time I was invited by Arthur to have dinner with the two of them, I remember thinking at the end of the evening's conversation—conversation consisting largely of Deborah's coquettishly "outrageous" chatter—"This is surely the loneliest man alive." How pained and disenchanted I was at twenty-three by this first look into my fatherly professor's domestic life . . . only to be told by Arthur the

following day about his wife's "wonderful powers of observation"
and her "gift" for "getting right to the heart of the problem." And,
along these lines, I remember another night, years later, when
Arthur and I were working late in our offices—that is, Arthur was at
work, while I was immobile at my desk, hopeless as usual about the
loveless impasse Helen and I had reached and hadn't the strength
or the courage to resolve. When Arthur saw me apparently looking
even more benumbed than usual, he came in and, until 3 a.m., tried
his best to protect me from the crazier sort of solutions that might
enter the head of a dreadfully unhappy husband having trouble
getting himself to go home. Time and again he reminded me of the
fine piece of work my thesis had been. The important thing now
was to get back to revising it for book publication. Indeed, much
that Arthur said to me that night sounded very like what Dr.
Klinger was eventually to say to me about me, my work, and Helen.
And I, in turn, poured out my grievances, and at one point lowered
my face to my desk and wept. "I figured it was that bad," said
Arthur. "We both did. But much as we care for you, we never felt
it was our business to say anything. We've had enough experience
by now to know that always comes between friends, sooner or later.
But still there were days when I wanted to shake you for being such
a fool. You don't know how many times I talked to Debbie about
what could be done to get you to save yourself from all this unhappiness. Nothing was more upsetting for us than remembering what
you'd been like when you first got here, and then seeing what was
happening to you with her. But I couldn't do a thing, David, unless
you came to me—and that's not how you go about things. You're
someone who goes so far with people, and no further, and the result is that you're rather more alone with yourself than many people are. I'm not so unlike that myself."

Near the end of his vigil—and for the first time ever—Arthur
spoke about his own personal life almost as though we were men of
the same age and rank. In his twenties, when he was an instructor
at Minnesota, he too had been involved with "a wildly neurotic and
destructive woman." Scandalous public quarrels, two harrowing
abortions, despair so enormous that he had actually come to think
that suicide was the only way he might ever be able to extricate
himself from his confusion and pain. He showed me a small scar on
his hand, where this mad, pathetic little librarian, whom he could
not stand and yet could not leave, had once stabbed him with a

table fork at breakfast . . . And while Arthur tried to give me hope
(and guidance) by associating his own early misfortune—and sub-
sequent recovery—with what I was going through, I only wanted to
say, "But how dare you? What do you call what you have now?
Debbie is so *common;* her spontaneity so much guile-filled play-act-
ing; her candor so much tactless showing-off; capricious for the
company; devilish for Daddy—Arthur, none of it means a thing,
audacious behavior with nothing at stake! While Helen—my God,
Helen is a hundred times, Helen is a thousand times . . ." But of
course I rose to no such heights of virtuous indignation, uttered no
words so foolish as these about the falsity and shallowness of his
wife as against the integrity, intelligence, charm, beauty, and brav-
ery of mine—uxoriousness, after all, being his line, and certainly
that night, dreams of uxoricide being somewhat more like mine.

Is this chivalry of Arthur's to be pitied or envied? Is my former
mentor and current benefactor a little bit of a liar, a little bit of a
masochist, or is he just in love? Or is it that Debbie, with her
slightly shrill kittenishness and vaguely slatternly good looks, is the
touch of the disreputable that makes bearable an otherwise
stiflingly decorous life?

"Vizzied" is the diagnosis rendered by our resident poet, Ralph
Baumgarten: "vizzied" or "vizzified"—both adjectives deriving
from "vizzy," an uncommon noun of Baumgarten's strewn throughout his verse, rhyming with "fizzy" and "tizzy," closely related to
"fuzzy" and "buzz," and referring, of course, to the pudenda. The
vizz-ridden—to this class of husbands is Arthur Schonbrunn con-
signed by the unmarried poet—are those who slavishly conform to
standards of propriety and respectability which, as Baumgarten
sees it, have been laid down by generations of women to disarm
and domesticate men. Of which domestication the poet himself is
clearly having none. I tend to agree with Baumgarten that it is in
part because of his own decidedly undeferential attitude toward
the other gender—and his sexual predilections generally—that the
young literary roughneck is not to be reappointed when his con-
tract here runs out. However, if he has, by his manner, earned the
disdain of certain of our colleagues and their wives, it has not
caused him to be any less flagrant about what he likes and how he
likes it. For him flagrancy appears to be much of the fun. "Picked
up a girl at the Modern Museum, and on our way out we ran into
your pals, Kepesh. Debbie hustled the girl off to the ladies' room to

get the latest lowdown on me, and Arthur, in the course of his
pleasantries, asked how long Rita and I had been friends. I told
him about an hour and a half. I said we were leaving because the
museum seemed to afford no comfortable corner where we might
go down on each other. But what, I wondered, did Arthur make of
her plump little behind? Well, he wouldn't tell me. Gave me a lecture on compassion, instead."

No arguing that Baumgarten throws a rather large net out to
catch his little minnows in. When the two of us are walking on the
streets of Manhattan, hardly a woman under fifty or a girl over
fifteen passes by from whom he does not attempt to extract information that he manages to intimate is absolutely vital to his survival. "Gee, what a nice coat!" he says, flashing his grin at a young
woman in a ratty fur pushing a baby carriage. "Oh, thanks." "May
I ask what it's made of? What kind of an animal was that? I never
saw a coat quite like that before." "This? It's a fake." "*Really?*"
Within minutes he is barely this side of stupefaction (not all of it
feigned, either) at learning that this young woman in the fake fur is
already divorced, the mother of three small children, and a dropout
from the University of Two Thousand Miles Away. To me, standing
self-consciously off to the side, he calls, "Did you hear that, Dave?
This is Alice. Alice was born in Montana—yet here she is wheeling
a baby carriage in New York." And no less than Baumgarten, the
young mother herself now seems a little wonderstruck to have been
transported such a distance in a mere twenty-four years.

Success with strangers, Baumgarten informs me, resides in never
asking a question of them that can't be answered without thinking,
and then being wholly attentive to the reply, no matter how pedes-
trian. "You remember your James, Kepesh—'Dramatize, dramatize.'
Get these people to understand that who they are and where
they're from and what they wear is *interesting*. In a manner of
speaking, *momentous*. *That's* compassion. And, please, display no
irony, will you? Your problem is you scare 'em off with your wonderful feel for the complexity of things. My experience is that the
ordinary woman in the streets doesn't cotton to irony, really. It's
irony, really, that pisses her off. She wants attention. She wants ap-
preciation. She surely doesn't want to match wits with you, boy.
Save all that subtlety for your critical article. When you get out
there on the street, *open up*. That's what streets are *for*."

During my first months at the university I discover that when

Baumgarten's name comes up at faculty gatherings there is always someone around who cannot stand the sight of him, and is more than willing to say why. Debbie Schonbrunn holds that the "abomination-in-residence" would be comical were he not so—the word is a favorite of hers and Arthur's—"destructive." Of course in response I need say nothing: just drink my drink and start back to New York. "Oh, he's not so bad," I tell her. "In fact," I add, "I sort of like him." "And what is there to 'like' so?" Go home, Kepesh. That empty apartment is where you belong; between this predictable discussion and that faggy apartment, there is no doubt where you will be better off. "What is there to *dislike* so?" I reply. "Where do I begin?" asks Deborah; "his contempt for women, for one thing. He is a murderous, conscienceless womanizer. He hates women." "Looks to me as though he rather likes them." "David, you are being contrary and disingenuous, and just a little hostile, and I'm really not sure why. Ralph Baumgarten is an abomination and so is his poetry. I have never read anything so dehumanized in my life. Read that first book of his and see for yourself just how much he likes girls." "Well, I haven't read him yet"—a lie—"but we've had lunch a few times. He isn't so reprehensible, as far as I can see. Could be, Deborah, that the poetry isn't exactly the man." "Ah, but it *is:* mean and smug and overbearing and actually quite stupid. And what *about* 'the man'? That walk of his, that *glide;* those army clothes; that face—well, actually he hasn't got a face, has he? Just mean, flat eyes and that surly grin. The mystery is how any girl can even go near him." "Well, he must have something." "Or *they* lack something. Really, you have such innate elegance and he is a carrion vulture right down to his claws, and why you would want even to associate with him . . ." "I get along with him," I say, shrugging my shoulders, and *now* put down my drink and go on home.

Soon enough, news reaches me as to what Debbie's powers of observation have uncovered in our conversation. It is what I should have expected, certainly, and probably what I deserve. The only surprise, really, is my surprise—that, and the vulnerability.

It seems that at a dinner party at the Schonbrunns' the hostess had announced to all in attendance that Baumgarten has become David Kepesh's "alter ego," "acting out fantasies of aggression against women" David harbors as a consequence of his marriage and its "mortifying" ending. The mortifying ending in Hong Kong —the cocaine, the cops, the works—as well as mortifying tidbits from the beginning and the middle were then narrated for the edification of all. I am given these details by a nice enough man, a guest at the Schonbrunns', who is no part of this story, and who thought he was doing me a good turn.

A correspondence ensues. Initiated by me and, alas, perpetuated by me too.

Dear Debbie:

Word has reached me that at a dinner party last week you were talking a little freely about my private affairs—namely, my marriage, my "mortifications," and what you are said to have described as my "aggressive fantasies against women." How would you know about my fantasies, if I may ask? And why should Helen and I be the subject for dinner conversation among people most of whom I have never even met? For the sake of a friendship with Arthur which goes back some time now, and which we have only just had the chance to rekindle, I hope that you will refrain in the future from discussing with perfect strangers my aggressive fantasies and my mortifying history. Otherwise, it is going to be difficult for me to be myself with Arthur, and, of course, with you.

Sincerely,
David

Dear David:

I do apologize for blabbing to people who don't know you, and won't do it again. Although I would do anything if you'll tell me the name of the s.o.b. who spilled his and/or her guts. Just so they don't set their teeth in my rack of lamb again!

To salve your wounds, I want to add, first, that your name only came up in passing—alas, you weren't the subject of a whole night's conversation—and, second, I think you have every justification for resenting Helen as much as you do, and, third, it isn't really so strange or shameful that your anger with Helen should take the form for now of an association with a young man who punishes women the way that vulture does. But, if you view your frendship with him one way, and I see it another, that's certainly all right with me—as I think it should be with you.

Lastly, if I spoke thoughtlessly about Helen to my dinner guests, it is probably because back at Stanford she was, as you well know, rather ostentatious about herself, and consequently a prime topic of conversation among any number of people, including your friends. And you yourself were not averse to talking about her with us, whenever you came home with Arthur.

But, dear David, enough of this is enough. Will you come to have dinner with us—how is this Friday night? Come, by yourself or with somebody (other than the Visigoth) if you like. If you bring a girl I promise I won't breathe a word about your misogyny all the time you're here.

Love,
Debbie

P.S. I'd give anything to know the name of the skunk who turned me in.

Dear Debbie:

I can't say that your reply strikes me as satisfactory. You seem not at all to grasp how indiscreet you were with what you know, and think you know, about me. Surely that I shared certain confidences with Arthur, and he in turn shared them with you, cannot be offered to me as a mitigating factor. Do you understand why? Nor do I see how you can fail to realize that my marriage is still painful to me, and the pain is not lessened when I learn that it is being discussed like so much soap opera by people to whom I once unburdened myself of some of my troubles.

The spirit in which your letter was written only seems to have worsened the situation for me, and I don't see any way to accept your invitation.

David

Dear David:

I'm sorry you found my note unsatisfactory. Actually it was purposely superficial in tone—I rather thought it suited what you considered my crime.

Do you really see me as some harridan hell-bent on sullying your spotless reputation or invading your privacy by vicious, hurtful innuendo? Obviously you do, and that's monstrous, of course, but simply because you believe it to be so, doesn't make it so.

I apologized for speaking carelessly about you to strangers, because I know I do that sometimes. I assumed that what came back to you was just that—foolish and careless. I know I never said anything so awful it would cause you any pain. Remembering back to your own judgments of yourself with the ladies—stories of your student days, remember?—I never dreamt you saw yourself as being beyond reproach. I will admit I never saw you as a perfect angel in relation to women, but neither did I think that summed you up as a person. I did enjoy you and care for you as a friend.

I must say I would be very sorry to hear that you had flailed out at any of those others who were your friends in California just because they were "indiscreet" enough to mention you in conversation. And to mention you not out of unkindness, or viciousness or malice, but only because they happen to know all you have been through.

I am afraid that your letter tells me more about you than I care to know.

Debbie

Dear David:

Debbie is replying to your last letter, but now I feel compelled to mix in too.

It seems to me that Debbie made an effort, stopping short of abject prostration before you, to apologize for what she considered a just complaint. At the same time she tried to indicate by her joking tone that what she did was not as serious as you seem to feel. I agree with her from what I know about the situation, and it strikes me that your last letter, with its aggressive, exasperated, self-righteous tone, is more seriously hurtful than anything Deborah may have been guilty of. I have no idea, by the way, what you think Deborah may have said about you (a little documentation would have helped here), but I can assure you that it was little more than dinner-table conversation that lasted a few minutes and maligned you in no way. I suspect that you may have said a lot worse about her in passing conversations (though presumably not before strangers). It seems to me that friends ought to be more willing to forgive each other their occasional frailties.

Sincerely,
Arthur

Dear Arthur:

You can't have it both ways: that Debbie took "a joking tone" or, as she put it, a "purposely superficial . . . tone" because that best expressed her attitude toward what was bothering me, and that simultaneously she "made an effort short of abject prostration" before me. Debbie's indiscretion was of course forgivable, and I indicated as much in my first letter. But that she should continue, not only to be so obtuse, but to be so casual about all this, leads me to view her lapse as something other than an example of "occasional frailty" displayed by a friend.

David

Dear David:

I have hesitated about replying to your last letter because it left me with very little to say. I find it incredible you could even imagine Deborah ever meant you any harm. It is also somewhat incredible that you fail to see that in blowing up this situation as you have, you are arguing only too well for the truth of Deborah's observation about the aggressive nature of your attitude toward women these days. Rather than pressing on with the attack, why don't you stop and think for a moment why it was you refused to accept the apology she made for her tactlessness at the outset—why did you prefer instead to jeopardize our friendship in order to beat her over the head with her alleged misconduct?

Short of divorcing Debbie and sending her out in the street in rags, I don't know what I can do that would prove sufficient to restore friendly relations between you. I'd be grateful to hear any suggestions.

Sincerely,
Arthur

It is Klinger who mercifully utters the magic formula that puts an end to all this. I tell him what I intend to say in my next message to Arthur—already half typed in a second draft—about the Freudian noose that he would now like to tighten around my neck. And I am still a little wild about his request, two letters back (and tucked between parentheses), for "a little documentation." What does he think we are, student and teacher, still Ph.D. candidate and

dissertation adviser? Those letters weren't sent him for a grade! I
don't care how beholden I am supposed to be—I won't have them
saying I am something I am not! I will not be maligned and belittled by her reckless neurotic slander! Nor will I let Helen be slan-
dered either! "Aggressive fantasies"! All that means is I can't stand
her! And why the hell *doesn't* he throw her out into the street in
rags? It's a marvelous idea! I'd *respect* him for it! The whole com-
munity would!

When my day's tirade has run its course, Klinger says, "So she
gossips about you—who the hell pays any attention?"

Eleven words, but all at once I am, yes, mortified, and see *myself*
for the neurotic fool. So peevish! So purposeless still! Without
focus, without meaning—without a single friend! And making only
enemies! My angry letters to the Devoted Couple constitute the
whole of my critical writing since my return to the East, all I have
been able to marshal sufficient concentration, stamina, and wisdom
to get down on paper. Why, I spend entire evenings rewriting them
for brevity and tone . . . while my Chekhov book has all but been
abandoned. Imagine—drafts and drafts, and of what? Nothing! Oh,
something about the drift of things doesn't look right to me, Doctor.
Fending off Wally, fighting with Debbie, hanging on for dear life to
your apron strings—oh, where is the way of living that will make all
this nothingness *truly* nothing, instead of being all I have and all I
do?

Strangely, my run-in with the Schonbrunns serves to enliven a
friendship with Baumgarten that hadn't really amounted to much
before—or, not so strangely at all, given those old vested interests
contending for a say in my new and barely lived-in life. Following
what I take to be doctor's orders, I abandon the Schonbrunn correspondence—though indignant rejoinders, *clinching* rejoinders,
continue to provide lively company as I drive along the Expressway
to school each morning—and then late one afternoon, acting on
what I assume at the time to be a harmless impulse, I stop at
Baumgarten's office and ask him to join me for coffee. And the following Sunday evening, when I return from a visit to my father and
find that back in my apartment I am, on the scale of loneliness,
hovering near a hundred—right up there with my own dad—I turn
down the flame under the soup I am warming in my little spinster's

saucepan, and telephone Baumgarten to invite him to come share the very last container of food prepared and frozen by my mother.

Soon we are meeting once a week for dinner at a small Hungarian restaurant on upper Broadway, not far from where each of us lives. No more than Wally is Baumgarten the someone for whom I used to cry out before the bathroom mirror during my first months of mourning in New York (the mourning that preceded the mourning for the only one of us who actually died). But then that longed-for someone may very likely never turn up—because in fact she already did: was here, was mine, and has been lost, destroyed because of some terrible mechanism that causes me to challenge and challenge—finally to challenge to the death—what once I thought I wanted most. Yes, I miss Helen! Suddenly I *want* Helen! How meaningless and ridiculous all those arguments seem now! What a gorgeous, lively, passionate creature! Bright, funny, mysterious—and gone! Oh, why on earth did I do what I did? It all should have been so different! And when, if ever, will there be another?

So—little more than a decade of adult life behind me, and already I have the sense that all my chances have been used up; indeed, pondering my past over that pathetic little enameled saucepan, I invariably feel as though I have not simply been through a bad marriage but in fact through all the female sex, and that I am so constructed as to live harmoniously with no one.

Over cucumber salad and stuffed cabbage (not bad, but nothing to compare, I inform Baumgarten—and sounding not so unlike my father—to the Hungarian Royale in its heyday), I show him an old picture of Helen, as inviting and seductive a passport photo as may ever have passed through customs. I have unstapled it from her International Driver's License, which turned up only recently—to each his own discordances and incongruities—in a carton of Stanford papers, among my lecture notes on François Mauriac. I bring Helen's photograph to dinner with me, then wonder for half the meal whether to take it out of my wallet or, rather, wonder why I would. Some ten days earlier I had brought the picture to his office to show to Klinger, intending to prove to him that, blind as I may have been to certain dire consequences, I was by no means blind to everything.

"A real beauty," says Baumgarten when, with some of the anxiety of a student handing in a plagiarized paper, I pass the picture across the table. And then I am hanging on to his every word! "A queen bee, all right," he says. "Yes, sir, and followed aloft by the drones." He is a long time savoring it. Too long. "Makes me jealous," he informs me, and not to be polite either. He is reporting a genuine emotion.

Well, I think, at least *he* won't disparage her, or me . . . yet I am reluctant to go ahead now and try to puzzle out anything truly personal in Baumgarten's presence, as though any challenge he might offer to Klinger's perspective—and the willingness with which I now try to yield to it—might actually send me reeling, perhaps even all the way back to where I was when I would start off the day on my knees. It hardly pleases me, of course, to feel so susceptible still to this sort of confusion, or to feel so very thinly protected from the elements by my therapy, or to find that, at this moment, I seem to share Debbie Schonbrunn's sense of Baumgarten as a source of contamination. The fact is that I *do* look forward to our evening out together, that I *am* interested in listening to the stories he tells, stories, as with Helen, of someone on the friendliest of terms with the sources of his excitement, and confidently opposed to—in fact, rather amused by—all that stands in opposition. Yet it is also a fact that my attachment to Baumgarten is increasingly marked by uncertainty, by what amount at times almost to seizures of doubt, the stronger our friendship grows.

Baumgarten's family story is pretty much a story of pain and little else. The father, a baker, died only recently, destitute and alone on the ward of a V.A. hospital—he had deserted his family sometime during Baumgarten's adolescence ("later rather than sooner"), and only after years of horrific depressions that had all but turned family life into one long tearful wake. Baumgarten's mother had worked for thirty years stitching gloves in a loft near Penn Station, fearful of the boss, of the shop steward, of the subway platform and the third rail, then at home afraid of the cellar stairs, the gas oven, the fuse box, even of a hammer and a nail. She had suffered a disabling stroke when Ralph was at college, and since has been staring at the wall in a Jewish home for the aged and infirm in Woodside. Every Sunday morning when her youngest child pays his visit—wearing that cocky grin on his face, bearing the *Sunday News* under his arm, and in his hand carrying a little paper bag from the delicatessen with her bagel in it—the nurse precedes him into the room with a perky introduction intended to give a lift to the frail little woman sitting like a sack in her chair, safe at last from all the world's weaponry: "Guess who's here with the goodies, Mildred. Your professor!"

Aside from those expenses of the mother's care which are not covered by the government and which Baumgarten pays out of his university salary, there has also fallen to him a father's responsibilities to his older sister, who lives in New Jersey with three children and a husband who haplessly runs a dry-cleaning store there. The three kids Uncle Baumgarten describes as "dummies"; the sister he describes as "lost," raised from infancy on the mother's terrors and the father's gloom, and now, at about my age, alive to nothing but a welter of superstitions which, says Baumgarten, have come through untouched from the shtetl. Because of her looks, and her clothes, and the odd things she says to her children's schoolmates, she is known as the "gypsy lady" in the Paramus housing development where the family lives.

It surprises me, hearing tales of this mercilessly beaten-down clan from its inextinguishable survivor, that Baumgarten has never, to my knowledge, written a single line about the way in which his unhappy family is unlike any other, or about why he cannot turn his back on the wreckage, despite the disgust aroused in him by memories of his upbringing in this household of the dead. No, not a single word on that subject in his two books of verse, the first impudently titled, at twenty-four, *Baumgarten's Anatomy*, and the most recent, called after a line from an erotic poem of Donne's, *Behind, Before, Above, Between, Below*. I must admit to myself—if not to a Schonbrunn—that after a week of Baumgarten as bedtime reading, the interest I have long had in the fittings and fixtures of the other sex seems to me just about sated. Yet, narrow as his subject strikes me—or, rather, his means of exploration—I find in the blend of shameless erotomania, microscopic fetishism, and rather dazzling imperiousness a character at work whose unswerving sense of his own imperatives cannot but arouse my curiosity. But then at first even watching him eat his dinner arouses my curiosity —it is as hard at times for me to watch as it is to look away. Is it really the untamed animal in him that causes this carnivore to tear at the meat between his teeth with such stupendous muscle power, or does he not masticate his food genteelly simply because the rest of us agree to do it that way? Where *did* he first eat flesh, in Queens or in a cave? One night the sight of Baumgarten's incisors severing

the meat from the bone of his breaded veal chop sends me home
later to my bookshelves to take down the collection of Kafka's stories and to reread the final paragraph of "A Hunger Artist," the description of the young panther who is put into the sideshow cage to
replace the professional abstinent after he expires of starvation.
"The food he liked was brought without hesitation by the attend-
ants, he seemed not even to miss his freedom; his noble body,
furnished almost to the bursting point with all that it needed,
seemed to carry freedom around with it too; somewhere in its jaws
it seemed to lurk . . ."

Yes, and what "it" lurks in these strong jaws? Freedom also? Or
something more like the rapacity of one once very nearly buried
alive? Are his the jaws of the noble panther or of the starved rat?

I ask him, "How come you've never written about your family,
Ralph?" "Them?" he says, giving me his indulgent look. "Them," I
say, "and you." "Why? So I can read to a full house at the Y? Oh,
Kepesh"—five years my junior, he nonetheless enjoys talking to me
as though I am the kid and, too, something of an unredeemable
square—"spare me the subject of the Jewish family and its travails.
Can you actually get worked up over another son and another
daughter and another mother and another father driving each other
nuts? All that loving; all that hating; all those meals. And don't forget the *menschlichkeit*. And the baffled quest for dignity. Oh, and
the *goodness*. You can't write that stuff and leave out the goodness.
I understand somebody has just published a whole book on our
Jewish literature of goodness. I expect any day to read that an Irish
critic has come out with a work on conviviality in Joyce, Yeats, and
Synge. Or an article by some good old boy from Vanderbilt on hospitality in the Southern novel: 'Make Yourself at Home: The
Theme of Hospitality in Faulkner's "A Rose for Emily." ' "

"I just wondered if it might not give you access to other feelings."

He smiles. "Let the other guys have the other feelings, okay?
They're used to having them. They *like* having them. But virtue
isn't my bag. Too bo-ring." A favorite word, sung by Baumgarten
with the interval of a third between the two syllables. "Look," he
says, "I can't even take that much of Chekhov, that holy of holies.
Why isn't he ever implicated in the shit? You're an authority. Why
is the brute never Anton but some other slob?"

"That's a strange way to go at Chekhov, you know, expecting

Céline. Or Genet. Or you. But then maybe the brute isn't always
Baumgarten, either. It doesn't sound that way when you tell me
about those visits to Paramus, or to the old-age home. Sounds more
like Chekhov, actually. The family serf."

"Don't be too sure. Besides, besides, why bother to write that
kind of stuff down? Has it not been done—and done? Do they need
me too to scratch my name on the Wailing Wall? For me the books
count—my own included—where the writer incriminates *himself*.
Otherwise, why bother? To incriminate the other guy? Best leave
that to our betters, don't you think, and that cunning Yiddish theater they've evolved, called Literary Criticism. Ah, those noble middle-aged Jewish sons, with their rituals of rebellion and atonement!
Ever read them on the front of the Sunday *Times*? All the closet
cunt hunters coming on like old man Tolstoy. All that sympathy for
the humble of the earth, all that guarding of the sacred flame,
which, by the way, don't cost them a fucking dime. Look, all those
deeply suffering Jewish culture-bearers *need* a fallen Jewish ass to
atone for their sins on in public—so why not mine? Keeps their
wives in the dark; gives their girl friends someone sensitive to
suffering to suck off; and goes a very long way with the Brandeis
Kollege of Musical Knowledge. Every year I read in the papers
about the powers-that-be up there awarding them merit badges for
their neckerchiefs. Virtue, virtue, who's got the virtue? Biggest Jewish racket since Meyer Lansky in his prime."

Yes, he is steamed up now, and with no regard for the loudness
of his voice or the windmilling of his arms—and not without pleasure in his broadside biliousness—he goes on about the lascivi-
ousness (well known to all Manhattan, Baumgarten claims) of the
"esteemed professor" who demolished his second book of poems in
an omnibus review in the *Times*. "No 'culture,' no 'heart,' and what
is worse, no 'historical perspective.' As if the esteemed professor has
historical perspective when he is sticking it into some graduate assistant! No, they don't like it too much when you get down in there
and burrow away just for the sake of the fishy little vizzy in your
face. No, no, if you're a real man of letters in the humanist tradition
you have historical perspective while you're doing it."

Not till we down our tea and strudel does he finish (for the
night) with his investigation into the hypocrisies, pieties, and bo-
ring-ness generally of the literary world and the humanist tradition
(largely as it is embodied in the reviewers of his books and the

members of his department), and begin to speak, with a different
sort of relish, of his other chosen arena of assertion. Like so many
of his stories of the pleasant surprises that the hunt turns up, what
he narrates over the dregs of dessert touches upon certain old but
vivid recollections of my own. Indeed, there are times when, listening to him speak with such shamelessness of the wide range of his
satisfactions, I feel that I am in the presence of a parodied projec-
tion of myself. A parody—a possibility. Maybe Baumgarten feels
somewhat the same about me, and *this* explains the curiosity at either end. I am a Baumgarten locked in the Big House, caged in the
kennels, a Baumgarten Klingered and Schonbrunned into submission—while he is a Kepesh, oh, what a Kepesh! with his mouth froth-
ing and his long tongue lolling, leash slipped and running wild.

Why am I here with him? Passing time, sure, sure—and meanwhile, what is passing in and out of me? In the presence of the ap-
petitious Baumgarten, am I looking to be exposed ever so mildly to
the virulent strain, and thereby immunized for good? Or am I half
hoping to be reinfected? Have I taken the healing of myself into
my own hands at last, or is it rather that the convalescence is over,
and I am just about ready to begin to conspire *against* the doctor
and his bo-ring admonitions?

"One night last winter," he says, eyeing the round rear end of the
largish Hungarian waitress who is trundling in carpet slippers back
to the kitchen to make us some more tea, "I was browsing in Mar-
boro's—" And I can see him browsing already; I *have* seen it, a
dozen times at least. BAUMGARTEN: Hardy? GIRL: Why—yes.
BAUMGARTEN: *Tess of the d'Urbervilles,* is that what you've got
there? GIRL *(looking at the book jacket)*: That's right, it is—"—and I
started talking to this nice red-cheeked girl who told me she had
just come down on the train from visiting her family in West-
chester. Sitting a couple of seats in front of her there'd been a
fellow in a suit and tie and an overcoat who kept looking back at
her over his shoulder and jacking off under the coat. I asked her
what she did about it. 'What do you think I did?' she said. 'I looked
him right in the eye, and when we got into Grand Central, I went
up to him, and I said, "Hey, I think we should meet, I'd like to
meet you." ' Well, he took off, started running out of the station, but
the girl kept right on him, trying to explain to him that she was
serious—she liked the way he looked, she admired his courage, she
was terrifically flattered by what he had done, but the guy disap-

peared into a taxi before she could convince him that he was in for a good time. Anyway, we struck it off, you might say, and went back to her apartment. It was over on the East River, in one of those hi-rise villages. When we got there she showed me the view up the river, and the kitchen with all the cookbooks, and then she wanted me to take off her clothes and tie her to the bed. Well, I haven't played with a rope since Troop 35, but I managed. Did it with dental floss, Kepesh, twelve yards of it—got her spread-eagled, arms and legs, just the way she wanted. Took me forty-five minutes. And you should have heard the sounds coming out of that girl. You should have seen what she looked like, excited like that. Very stirring image. Makes you understand the creeps more. Anyway, she told me to go and get the poppers out of the medicine chest. Well, there weren't any, they were all gone. It seems one of her friends had stolen them. So I told her I had some coke at home, and I'd get it if she wanted me to. 'Go, get it, get it,' she said. So I went. But when I came downstairs from my place and got a taxi to start back to hers, I realized that I didn't know her name—and for the life of me I couldn't remember which of those fucking buildings she lived in. Kepesh, I was stymied," he says, and reaching across the table with a thumb and forefinger to get the strudel crumbs off my plate, manages to sweep my water glass into my lap with the cuff of his army coat. For some reason Baumgarten always eats in his coat. Maybe Jesse James did, too. "Oops," he cries, seeing the glass go down, but of course this isn't the first time; indeed, "oops" may be the four-letter word that most frequently falls from Baumgarten's lips, certainly while he is turning the table into his trough. "Sorry," he says; "you all right?" "It'll dry," I say, "it always does. Go on. What did you do?" "What could I do? Nothing. I started wandering from one building to the next, looking at the names on the directories. Jane was her first name, or so she said, so whenever I saw a 'J,' like a schmuck I rang the buzzer. Couldn't find her, of course, though I had several promising conversations. Anyway, a guard came up and asked me what I was looking for. I told him I must be in the wrong building, but when I went out he followed me into the portico area there, and so I hung around for about a minute or two, looking up and admiring the moon. And then I went home. And after that I bought the *Daily News* on the way to school every day. I looked in there for weeks to see if the cops had found a skeleton tied to a bed with dental floss over on the decadent

East Side. Finally I just gave up. Then this summer I was coming out of a movie down on Eighth Street, and there standing in line to get in for the next show is the same girl. Plain Jane. And you know what she says? She spots me, and a smile spreads across her face, and she says, 'Far out, man.'"

Skeptical, but laughing, I say, "That all happened, huh?"

"Dave, just walk the streets and say hello to the folks. *Everything* happens."

And then, after Baumgarten has asked the waitress—new to our restaurant, and whose aging, peasanty overflow he had decided he must get to know—whether she can recommend someone to give him Hungarian lessons; after he has taken her name and number—"Live alone there, do you, Eva?"—he excuses himself and goes to the back of the restaurant, where there is a pay phone. In order to write down Eva's telephone number, he has emptied his coat pocket of a handful of papers and envelopes, on which, I see, he already has recorded the names and whereabouts of those others of her sex who have crossed his path during the day. The number of whomever he is calling now he has carried off with him to the phone, leaving the little mess of personal papers for me to contemplate at my leisure, the papers and the life that goes with them.

With a fingernail, I am able to flick into view the last paragraph of a letter neatly typewritten on heavy cream-colored stationery.

. . . I've gotten you your fifteen-year-old (eighteen, actually, but fleshwise I'll swear you'd never know the difference, and anyway, fifteen is *jail*)—a succulent sophomore, and not just young but a real beauty besides, a sweet girl and worldly both, and altogether I can't see how you could improve on her. I found her for you all by myself, her name is Rona and we are having lunch next week, so if you meant it (assuming you do remember mentioning this fancy), I will open negotiations at this time. I feel reasonably confident of success. Kindly semaphore your intentions next time you're in the office, one blink for yes, two for no, if I should go ahead. So there's my half of the bargain—I'm procuring for you, as desired and with my heart somewhere up near my mouth—now *please* put me in touch with the orgiasts. The only good reasons for no that I can think of are (a) you are involved there yourself—and in that case I would simply abstain from those soirees, if you prefer—or (b) you're afraid of being compromised by somebody at the heart of the Kremlin—then just give me the name and I'll say I heard about it elsewhere than you. Otherwise, why not give your (slightly atrophied) faculty of human sympathy a little workout (I've read somewhere it was once believed to be an essential quality for a poet) as long as it won't cost you anything, and bring a little ray of sunshine into the dim life of a (rapidly) fading spinster.

Your chum,
T.

And who is "T," I wonder, in the "Kremlin"? The assistant to the provost or the director of student health? And who—on another piece of paper—is "L"? Her words crossed out and rewritten on every line; her felt-tipped pen on the brink of anemia—what does *she* want of the poet with the slightly atrophied heart? Is "L" 's the pleading voice Baumgarten is so patiently listening to in the telephone booth? Or is that "M," or "N" or "O" or "P"—?

Ralph, I refuse to be sorry about last night unless you can point out in a *believable* way there was something twisted or mean about my wanting to see you. I had thought that if I could only sit in the same room with a man who wasn't trying to push me or convince me or confuse me, someone whom I liked and respected, that I might get closer to something in myself that matters and is real. I was under the impression that you didn't live in a dream world, and have sometimes wondered since the baby whether I do. I didn't want to make love. Sometimes you act like someone who is adept at removing a lady's drawers and that's all. I certainly won't make any more spontaneous visits after 10 p.m. It is just that wanting and needing to talk to someone with whom I am *not* involved, I chose you, when, I admit, in some way I want to be involved, some part wanting to be in your arms, when the other part insists that what I really need is your friendship, your advice—*and* distance. I guess I don't quite want to admit that you move me. But that doesn't mean I don't think there is something crazy about you—

Inside the booth, Baumgarten hangs up the phone and so I stop reading his fan mail. We pay Eva, Baumgarten collects his property, and together—his "pal" on the phone is best left to herself this evening, he informs me—we head toward the nearest Bookmasters, where, as usual, one or the other of us will lay out five dollars for five remaindered books he most likely will never get around to reading. "Inebriate of cunt and print!" as my secret sharer exclaims somewhere in the song of himself behind, before, above, between, below.

It takes two full weeks, six whole sessions, before I am able to tell the psychoanalyst to whom I am supposed to tell everything that only a little later that evening we had met a high school girl shopping for a paperback for her English class. (BAUMGARTEN: Emily or Charlotte? GIRL: Charlotte. BAUMGARTEN: *Villette* or *Jane Eyre?* GIRL: I never heard of the first one. *Jane Eyre.*) Breezy, streetwise, and just a little terrified, she had accompanied us back to Baumgarten's one room, and there, on his Mexican rug, amid several piles of his own two erotic books of verse, she had auditioned for a modeling job for the new erotic picture magazine being started on the West Coast by our bosses, the Schonbrunns. Magazine to be called *Cunt.* "The Schonbrunns," he explains, "are sick and tired of pulling their punches."

A lanky strawberry blonde in fringed leather jacket and jeans, the girl had told us straight out, while being interviewed in the bookstore, that she would not be at all shy about taking off her clothes for a photographer—so, at Baumgarten's, she is given one of his Danish magazines to look at, for the inspiration in it.

"Could you do this, Wendy?" he asks her earnestly as she sits on the sofa leafing through the magazines with one hand and, with the other, holding the Baskin-Robbins ice cream cone that Baumgarten (the impeccable scenarist) couldn't resist buying for her on the way home. ("What's your favorite flavor, Wendy? Go ahead, please, have a double dip, have sprinkles, have everything. How about you, Dave? Want some Chocolate Ribbon, too?") Clearing her throat, she closes the magazine in her lap, bites into what remains of the cone, and casually as she can manage, says, "That's a little far for me." "What isn't?" he asks her; "just tell me what isn't." "Maybe something more along the lines of *Playboy*," she says.

Working together then, something like teammates moving the ball across the midcourt line against a tight defense, something like two methodical day laborers driving a post into the ground with alternating blows of their mallets—something like Birgitta and myself back on the continent of Europe during the Age of Exploration—we manage, by bringing her through a series of provocative postures in progressive stages of undress, to get her flat on her back in her bikini underpants and her boots. And that, says the seventeen-year-old senior from Washington Irving High—trembling ever so slightly as she gazes up at our four eyes looking down—that is as far as she will go.

What next? That her limit is to be *the* limit is understood by Baumgarten and myself without any consultation. I make that clear to Klinger—also point out that no tears were shed, no force used, not so much as a fingertip touched her flesh.

"And this happened when?" Klinger asks me.

"Two weeks ago," I say, and rise from the couch to get my coat. And leave. I have withheld my confession for two full weeks, and even now, until the end of the hour. Consequently, I am able just to walk out the door, and do not have to add—and never will—that it was not a recidivist's shame that deterred me from narrating the incident earlier, but rather the small color snapshot of Klinger's teenage daughter, in faded dungarees and school T-shirt, taken on a beach somewhere and displayed in a triptych frame on his desk between photographs of his two sons.

And then the summer after I return East I meet a young woman altogether unlike this small band of consolers, counselors, tempters, and provocateurs—the "influences," as my father would have it—off whom my benumbed and unsexed carcass has been careening since I've been a womanless, pleasureless, passionless man on his own.

I am invited for a weekend on Cape Cod by a faculty couple I have just gotten to know, and there I am introduced to Claire Ovington, their young neighbor, who is renting a tiny shingled bungalow in a wild-rose patch near the Orleans beach for herself and her golden Labrador. Some ten days after the morning we spend talking together on the beach—after I have sent her a painfully charming letter from New York, and consulted for several clammy hours with Klinger—I take the impulse by the horns and return to Orleans, where I move into the local inn. I am drawn at first by the same look of soft voluptuousness that had (against all seemingly reasonable reservations) done so much to draw me to Helen, and which has touched off, for the first time in over a year, a spontaneous surge of warm feeling. Back in New York after my brief weekend visit, I had thought only about her. Do I sense the renewal of desire, of confidence, of capacity? Not quite yet. During my week at the inn, I cannot stop behaving like an overzealous child at dancing class, unable to go through a door or to raise a fork without the starchiest display of good manners. And after the *self*-display of that letter, that bravura show of wit and self-assurance! Why did I listen to Klinger? "Of course, go—what can you lose?" But what does *he* have to lose if I fail? Where's his tragic view of life, damn it? Impotence is no joke—it's a plague! People kill themselves! And alone in my bed at the inn, after yet another evening of keeping my distance from Claire, I can understand why. In the morning, just before I am to leave for New York once again, I arrive at her bungalow for an early breakfast, and midway through the fresh blueberry pancakes try to redeem myself a little by admitting to my shame. I don't know how else to get out of this with at least some self-esteem intact, though why I will ever have to care about self-esteem again I cannot imagine. "I seem to have come all the way up here—after writing to you like that, and then arriving out of nowhere—well, after all that fanfare, I seem to have come upon the scene and . . . disappeared." And now moving over me—moving right up to the roots of my hair—I feel something very like the shame that I must have imagined I could avoid *by* disappearing. "I must seem odd to you. At this point I seem odd to myself. I've seemed odd to myself for some time now. I'm only trying to say that it's nothing you've done or said that's made me behave so coldly." "But," she says, before I can begin another round of apology about this "oddity" that I am, "it's been so pleasant. In a way it's been the sweetest thing." "It has?" I say, fearful that I am about to be humbled in some unforeseen way. "*What* has?" "Seeing somebody shy for a change. It's nice to know it still exists in the Age of Utter Abandon."

God, as tender within as without! The tact! The calm! The *wisdom!* As physically alluring to me as Helen—but there the resemblance ends. Poise and confidence and determination, but, in Claire, all of it marshaled in behalf of something more than high sybaritic adventure. At twenty-four, she has earned a degree from Cornell in experimental psychology, a master's from Columbia in education, and is on the faculty of a private school in Manhattan, where she teaches eleven- and twelve-year-olds, and, as of the coming semester, will be in charge of the curriculum-review committee. Yet, for someone who, as I come to learn, emanates in her professional role a strong aura of reserve, a placid, coolheaded, and seemingly unassailable presence, she is surprisingly innocent and guileless about the personal side of her life, and, as regards her friends, her plants, her herb garden, her dog, her cooking, her sister Olivia, who summers on Martha's Vineyard, and Olivia's three children, she has about as much reserve as a healthy ten-year-old girl.

In all, this translucent mix of sober social aplomb and domestic enthusiasms and youthful susceptibility is simply irresistible. What I mean is *no resistance is necessary*. A tempter of a kind to whom I can at last succumb.

Now it is as if a gong has been struck in my stomach when I recall—and I do, daily—that I had written Claire my clever, flirtatious letter, and then had very nearly been content to leave it at that. Had even told Klinger that writing out of the blue to a voluptuous young woman I had spoken with casually on a beach for two hours was a measure of just how hopeless my prospects had become. I had almost decided against showing up for breakfast that last morning on the Cape, so fearful was I of what my convalescent desire might have in store for me were I, with a suitcase in one hand and my plane ticket in the other, to try to put it to a crazy last-minute test. How ever *did* I manage to make it past my shameful secret? Do I owe it to sheer luck, to ebullient, optimistic Klinger, or do I owe everything I now have to those breasts of hers in that bathing suit? Oh, if so, then bless each breast a thousand times! For now, now I am positively exultant, thrilled, astonished— grateful for everything about her, for the executive dispatch with which she orders her life as for the patience that she brings to our lovemaking, that canniness of hers that seems to sense exactly how much raw carnality and how much tender solicitude it is going to require to subdue my tenacious anxiety and renew my faith in coupling and all that may come in its wake. All the pedagogic expertise bestowed upon those sixth-graders is now bestowed upon *me* after school—such a gentle, tactful tutor comes to my apartment each day, and yet always the hungry woman with her! And those breasts, those breasts—large and soft and vulnerable, each as heavy as an udder upon my face, as warm and heavy in my hand as some fat little animal fast asleep. Oh, the look of this large girl above me when she is still half stripped! And, mind you, an assiduous keeper of records as well! Yes, the history of each passing day in calendar books going back through college, her life's history in the photographs she has been taking since childhood, first with a Brownie, now with the best equipment from Japan. And those lists! Those wonderful, orderly lists! I too write out on a yellow pad what I plan to accomplish each day, but by bedtime I seem never to find a soothing little check mark beside each item, confirming that the letter has been dispatched, the money withdrawn, the article xeroxed, the call made. Despite my own strong penchant for orderliness, passed along through the maternal chromosomes, there are still mornings when I can't even locate the list I drew up the night before, and, usually, what I don't feel like doing one day, I am able to put off to the next without too many qualms. Not so with Mistress Ovington—to every task that presents itself, regardless of how difficult or dreary, she gives her complete attention, taking each up in its turn and steadfastly following it through to its conclusion. And, to my great good luck, reconstituting my life is apparently just such a task. It is as though at the top of one of her yellow pads she has spelled out my name and then, beneath, in her open spherical hand, written instructions to herself, as follows: "Provide DK with— 1. Loving kindness. 2. Impassioned embraces. 3. Sane surroundings." For within a year the job is somehow done, a big check mark beside each life-saving item. I give up the anti-depressants, and no abyss opens beneath me. I sublet the sublet apartment, and, without being wracked too much by memories of the handsome rugs, tables, dishes, and chairs once jointly owned by Helen and me and now hers alone, I furnish a new place of my own. I even accept an invitation to a dinner party at the Schonbrunns', and at the end of the evening politely kiss Debbie's cheek while Arthur paternally kisses Claire's. Easy as that. Meaningless as that. At the door, while Arthur and Claire conclude the conversation they'd been having at dinner—about the curriculum that Claire is now devising for the upper grades—Debbie and I have a moment to chat privately. For some reason—alcoholic intake on both sides, I think—we are holding hands! "Another of your tall blondes," says Debbie, "but this one seems a bit more sympathetic. We both find her very sweet. And very bright. Where did you meet?" "In a brothel in Marrakesh. Look, Debbie, isn't it about time you got off my ass? What does that mean, my 'tall blondes'?" "It's a fact." "No, it is not even a fact. Helen's hair was auburn. But suppose it was cut from the same bolt as Claire's—the fact is that 'blondes,' in that context, and that tone, is, as you may even know, a derogatory term used by intellectuals and other serious people to put down pretty women. I also believe it is dense with unsavory implication when addressed to men of my origin and complexion. I remember how fond you used to be at Stanford of pointing out to people the anomaly of a literate chap like myself coming from the 'Borscht Belt.' That too used to strike me as a bit reductive." "Oh, you take yourself too

seriously. Why don't you just admit you have a penchant for these
big blondes and leave it at that? It's nothing to be ashamed of.
They do look lovely up on water skis with all that hair streaming. I
bet they look lovely everywhere." "Debbie, I'll make a deal with
you. I'll admit I know nothing about you, if you'll admit you know
nothing about me. I'm sure you have a whole wondrous being and
inner life that I know nothing about." "Nope," she says, "this is it.
This is the whole thing. Take it or leave it." Both of us begin to
laugh. I say, "Tell me, what does Arthur see in you? It's really one
of the mysteries of life. What do you have that I'm blind to?" "Everything," she replies. Out in the car, I give Claire an abridged version of the conversation. "The woman is warped," I say. "Oh, no,"
says Claire, "just silly, that's all." "She tricked you, Clarissa. Silly is
the cover—assassination is the game." "Ah, sweetie," says Claire,
"it's *you* she's tricked."

So much for my rehabilitation back into society. As for my father
and his awesome loneliness, well, now he takes the train from Cedarhurst to have dinner in Manhattan once a month; he can't be
coaxed in any more often, but in truth, before there was the new
apartment, and Claire to help with the conversation and the cooking, I didn't work at coaxing him that hard, no, not so each of us
could sit and peer sadly at the other picking at his spareribs, two
orphans in Chinatown . . . not so I could wait to hear him ask over
the lichee nuts, "And that guy, he hasn't come back to bother you,
has he?"

And, to be sure, from the maw of that maelstrom called Baumgarten I withdraw my toes a little. We still have lunch together
from time to time, but the grander feasts I leave him to partake of
on his own. And I do not introduce him to Claire.

My, how easy life is when it's easy, and how hard when it's hard!

One night, after dinner at my apartment, while Claire is preparing her next day's lessons at the cleared dining table, I finally get
up the nerve, or no longer seem to need "nerve," to reread what
there is of my Chekhov book, shelved now for more than two years.
In the midst of the laborious and deadly competence of those fragmentary chapters intended to focus upon the subject of romantic
disillusionment, I find five pages that are somewhat readable—
reflections growing out of Chekhov's comic little story, "Man in a
Shell," about the tyrannical rise and celebrated fall—"I confess,"
says the goodhearted narrator after the tyrant's funeral, "it is a

great pleasure to bury people like Belikov"—the rise and fall of a
provincial high school official whose love of prohibitions and hatred
of all deviations from the rules manages to hold a whole town of
"thoughtful, decent people" under his thumb for fifteen years. I go
back to reread the story, then to reread "Gooseberries" and "About
Love," written in sequence with it and forming a series of anecdotal
ruminations upon the varieties of pain engendered by spiritual im-
prisonment—by petty despotism, by ordinary human complacency,
and finally, even by the inhibitions upon feeling necessary to support a scrupulous man's sense of decency. For the next month, with
a notebook on my lap, and some tentative observations in mind, I
return to Chekhov's fiction nightly, listening for the anguished cry
of the trapped and miserable socialized being, the well-bred wives
who during dinner with the guests wonder "Why do I smile and
lie?", and the husbands, seemingly settled and secure, who are "full
of conventional truth and conventional deception." Simultaneously I
am watching how Chekhov, simply and clearly, though not quite so
pitilessly as Flaubert, reveals the humiliations and failures—worst
of all, the destructive power—of those who seek a way *out* of the
shell of restrictions and convention, out of the pervasive boredom
and the stifling despair, out of the painful marital situations and the
endemic social falsity, into what they take to be a vibrant and desirable life. There is the agitated young wife in "Misfortune" who
looks for "a bit of excitement" against the grain of her own
offended respectability; there is the lovesick landowner in
"Ariadne," confessing with Herzogian helplessness to a romantic
misadventure with a vulgar trampy tigress who gradually transforms him into a hopeless misogynist, but whom he nonetheless
waits on hand and foot; there is the young actress in "A Boring
Story," whose bright, hopeful enthusiasm for a life on the stage,
and a life with men, turns bitter with her first experiences of the
stage and of men, and of her own lack of talent—"I have no talent,
you see, I have no talent and . . . and lots of vanity." And there is
"The Duel." Every night for a week (with Claire only footsteps
away) I reread Chekhov's masterpiece about the weaseling, slov-
enly, intelligent, literary-minded seducer Layevsky, immersed in his
lies and his self-pity, and Layevsky's antagonist, the ruthless punitive
conscience who all but murders him, the voluble scientist Von
Koren. Or so it is that I come to view the story: with Von Koren
as the ferociously rational and merciless prosecutor called forth to

challenge the sense of shame and sinfulness that is nearly all that Layevsky has become, and from which, alas, he no longer can flee. It is this immersion in "The Duel" that finally gets me writing, and within four months the five pages extracted from the old unfinished rehash of my thesis on romantic disillusionment are transformed into some forty thousand words entitled *Man in a Shell*, an essay on license and restraint in Chekhov's world—longings fulfilled, pleasures denied, and the pain occasioned by both; a study, at bottom, of what makes for Chekhov's pervasive pessimism about the methods —scrupulous, odious, noble, dubious—by which the men and women of his time try in vain to achieve "that sense of personal freedom" to which Chekhov himself is so devoted. My first book! With a dedication page that reads "To C.O."

"She is to steadiness," I tell Klinger (and Kepesh, who must never, never, never forget), "what Helen was to impetuosity. She is to common sense what Birgitta was to indiscretion. I have never seen such devotion to the ordinary business of daily life. It's awesome, really, the way she deals with each day as it comes, the attention she pays minute by minute. There's no dreaming going on there—just steady, dedicated *living*. I trust her, that's the point I'm making. That's what's done it," I announce triumphantly, "trust."

To all of which Klinger eventually replies goodbye then and good luck. At the door of his office on the spring afternoon of our parting, I have to wonder if it can really be that I no longer need bucking up and holding down and hearing out, warning, encouragement, consent, consolation, applause, and opposition—in short, professional doses of mothering and fathering and simple friendship three times a week for an hour. *Can* it be that I've come through? Just like that? Just because of Claire? What if I awaken tomorrow morning once again a man with a crater instead of a heart, once again without a man's capacity and appetite and strength and judgment, without the least bit of mastery over my flesh or my intelligence or my feelings . . .

"Stay in touch," says Klinger, shaking my hand. Just as I could not look squarely at him the day I neglected to mention the impact on my conscience of his daughter's snapshot—as though suppressing that fact I might be spared his unuttered judgment, or my own—so I cannot let his eyes engage mine when we say farewell. But now it is because I would prefer not to give vent to my feelings of elation and indebtedness in an outburst of tears. Sniffing all sentiment back up my nose—and firmly, for the moment, suppressing all doubt—I say, "Let's hope I don't have to," but once out on the street by myself, I repeat the incredible words aloud, only now to the accompaniment of the appropriate emotions: "I've come through!"

The following June, when the teaching year is over for the two of us, Claire and I fly to the north of Italy, my first time back in Europe since I'd gone prowling there with Birgitta a decade earlier. In Venice we spend five days at a quiet pensione near the Accademia. Each morning we eat breakfast in the pensione's aromatic garden and then, in our walking shoes, weave back and forth across the bridges and alleyways that lead to the landmarks Claire has marked on the map for us to visit that day. Whenever she takes her pictures of these palazzos and piazzas and churches and fountains I wander off a ways, but always looking back to get a picture of her and her unadorned beauty.

Each evening after dinner under the arbor in the garden, we treat ourselves to a little gondola ride. With Claire beside me in the armchair that Mann describes as "the softest, most luxurious, most relaxing seat in the world," I ask myself yet again if this serenity truly exists, if this contentment, this wonderful accord is real. *Is* the worst over? Have I no more terrible mistakes to make? And no more to pay on those behind me? Was all that only so much Getting Started, a longish and misguided youth out of which I have finally aged? "Are you sure we didn't die," I say, "and go to heaven?" "I wouldn't know," she replies; "you'll have to ask the gondolier."

Our last afternoon I blow us to lunch at the Gritti. On the terrace I tip the headwaiter and point to the very table where I had imagined myself sitting with the pretty student who used to lunch on Peanut Chews in my classroom; I order exactly what I ate that day back in Palo Alto when we were studying Chekhov's stories about love and I felt myself on the edge of a nervous collapse—only this time I am not imagining the delicious meal with the fresh, untainted mate, this time both are real and I am well. Settling back—I with a cold glass of wine; Claire, the teetotaling daughter of parents who overimbibed, with her *acqua minerale*—I look out across the gleaming waters of this indescribably beautiful toy town and I say to her, "Do you think Venice is really sinking? The place seems in vaguely the same position as last time I was here."

"Who were you with then? Your wife?"

"No. It was my Fulbright year. I was with a girl."

"Who was that?"

Now, how endangered or troubled would she feel, what, if anything, do I risk awakening if I go ahead and tell her all? Oh, how dramatically put! What did "all" consist of—any more, really, than a young sailor goes out to find in his first foreign port? A sailor's taste for a little of the lurid, but, as things turned out, neither a sailor's stomach nor strength . . . Still, to someone so measured and orderly, someone who has turned all her considerable energy to making normal and ordinary what had for her been heartbreakingly irregular in her childhood home, I think it best to answer, "Oh, nobody, really," and let the matter drop.

Whereupon the nobody who has been no part of my life for over ten years is all I can think of. In that Chekhov class the mismatched husband had recalled sunnier days on the terrace of the Gritti, an unbruised, audacious, young Kepesh still running around Europe scot-free; now on the terrace of the Gritti, where I have come to celebrate the triumphant foundation of a sweet and stable new life, to celebrate the astonishing renewal of health and happiness, I am recalling the earliest, headiest hours of my sheikdom, the night in our London basement when it is my turn to ask Birgitta what it is *she* most wants. What I most want the two girls have given me; what Elisabeth most wants we are leaving for last—she does not know . . . for in her heart, as we are to discover when the truck knocks her down, she wants none of it. But Birgitta has desires about which she is not afraid to speak, and which we proceed to satisfy. Yes, sitting across from Claire, who has said that my semen filling her mouth makes her feel that she is drowning, that this is something she just doesn't care to do, I am remembering the sight of Birgitta kneeling before me, her face upturned to receive the strands of flowing semen that fall upon her hair, her forehead, her nose. *"Här!"* she cries, *"här!"*, while Elisabeth, wearing her pink woolen robe, and reclining on the bed, looks on in frozen fascination at the naked masturbator and his half-clothed suppliant.

As if such a thing matters! As if Claire is withholding anything that *matters!* But admonish myself as I will for amnesia, stupidity, ingratitude, callowness, for a lunatic and suicidal loss of all perspective, the rush of greedy lust I feel is not for this lovely young woman with whom I have only recently emerged into a life promising the most profound sort of fulfillment, but for the smallish buck-toothed comrade I last saw leaving my room at midnight some thirty kilometers outside Rouen over ten years ago, desire for my own lewd, lost soul mate, who, back before my sense of the permissible began its inward collapse, welcomed as feverishly and gamely as did I the uncommon act and the alien thought. Oh, Birgitta, go away! But this time we are in our room right here in Venice, a hotel on a narrow alleyway off the Zattere, not very far from the little bridge where Claire had taken my picture earlier in the day. I tie a kerchief around her eyes, careful to knot it tightly at the back, and then I am standing over the blindfolded girl and—ever so lightly to begin with—whipping her between her parted legs. I watch as she strains upward with her hips to catch the bite of each stroke of my belt on her genital crease. I watch this as I have never watched anything before in my life. "Say all the things," Birgitta whispers, and I do, in a low, subdued growl such as I have never used before to address anyone or anything.

For Birgitta then—for what I would now prefer to dismiss as a "longish and misguided youth"—a surging sense of lascivious kinship . . . and for Claire, for this truly passionate and loving rescuer of mine? Anger; disappointment; disgust—contempt for all she does so marvelously, resentment over that little thing she will not deign to do. I see how very easily I could have no use for her. The snapshots. The lists. The mouth that will not drink my come. The curriculum-review committee. Everything.

The impulse to fly up from the table and telephone Dr. Klinger I suppress. I will not be one of those hysterical patients at the other end of the overseas line. No, not that. I eat the meal when it is served, and sure enough, by the time the dessert is to be ordered, yearnings for Birgitta begging me and Birgitta beneath me and Birgitta below me, all such yearnings have begun to subside, as left to themselves those yearnings will. And the anger disappears too, to be replaced by shame-filled sadness. If Claire senses the rising and ebbing of all this distress—and how can she not? how else understand my silent, icy gloom?—she decides to pretend ignorance, to talk on about her plans for the curriculum-review committee until whatever has cast us apart has simply passed away.

From Venice we drive a rented car to Padua to look at the Giottos. Claire takes more pictures. She will have them developed when we get home and then, sitting cross-legged on the floor—the posture of tranquillity, of concentration, the posture of a very good girl indeed—paste them, in their proper sequence, into the album for this year. Now northern Italy will be in the bookcase at the foot of the bed where her volumes of photographs are stored, now northern Italy will be forever *hers*, along with Schenectady, where she was born and raised, Ithaca, where she went to college, and New York City, where she lives and works and lately has fallen in love. And I will be there at the foot of the bed, along with her places, her family, and her friends.

Though so many of her twenty-five years have been blighted by the squabbling of contentious parents—arguments abetted, as often as not, by too many tumblers of Scotch—she regards the past as worth recording and remembering, if only because she has outlasted the pain and disorder to establish a decent life of her own. As she likes to say, it is the only past she has got to remember, hard as it may have been when the bombs were bursting around her and she was trying her best to grow up in one piece. And then, of course, that Mr. and Mrs. Ovington put more energy into being adversaries than into being the comforters of their children does not mean that their daughter must deny *herself* the ordinary pleasures that ordinary families (if such there be) take as a matter of course. To all the pleasant amenities of family life—the exchanging of photographs, the giving of gifts, the celebration of holidays, the regular phone calls—both Claire and her older sister are passionately devoted, as though in fact she and Olivia are the thoughtful parents and their parents the callow offspring.

From a hotel in a small mountain town where we find a room with a terrace and a bed and an Arcadian view, we make day trips to Verona and Vicenza. Pictures, pictures, pictures. What is the opposite of a nail being driven into a coffin? Well, that is what I hear as Claire's camera clicks away. Once again I feel I am being sealed up into something wonderful. One day we just walk with a picnic lunch up along the cowpaths and through the flowering fields, whole nations of minute bluets and lacquered little buttercups and unreal poppies. I can walk silently with Claire for hours on end. I am content just to lie on the ground propped up on one elbow and watch her pick wild flowers to take back to our room and arrange in a water glass to place beside my pillow. I feel no need for anything more. "More" has no meaning. Nor does Birgitta appear to have meaning any longer, as though "Birgitta" and "more" are just

different ways of saying the same thing. Following the performance
at the Gritti, she has failed to put in anything like such a sensational appearance again. For the next few nights she does come by
to pay me a visit each time Claire and I make love—kneeling, always kneeling, and begging for what thrills her most—but then she
is gone, and I am above the body I am above, and with that alone
partake of all the "more" I now could want, or want to want. Yes, I
just hold tight to Claire and the unbeckoned visitor eventually
drifts away, leaving me to enjoy once again the awesome fact of my
great good luck.

On our last afternoon, we carry our lunch to the crest of a field
that looks across high green hills to the splendid white tips of the
Dolomites. Claire lies stretched out beside where I am sitting, her
ample figure gently swelling and subsiding with each breath she
draws. Looking steadily down at this large, green-eyed girl in her
thin summer clothes, at her pale, smallish, oval, unmarred face, her
scrubbed, unworldly prettiness—the beauty, I realize, of a young
Amish or Shaker woman—I say to myself, "Claire is enough. Yes,
'Claire' and 'enough'—they, too, are one word."

From Venice we fly by way of Vienna—and the house of Sig-
mund Freud—to Prague. During this last year I have been teaching
the Kafka course at the university—the paper that I am to read a
few days from now in Bruges has Kafka's preoccupations with spiritual starvation as its subject—but I have not as yet seen his city,
other than in books of photographs. Just prior to our departure I
had graded the final examinations written by my fifteen students in
the seminar, who had read all of the fiction, Max Brod's biography,
and Kafka's diaries and his letters to Milena and to his father. One
of the questions I had asked on the examination was this—

In his "Letter to His Father" Kafka writes, "My writing is all about
you; all I did there, after all, was to bemoan what I could not
bemoan upon your breast. It was an intentionally long-drawn-out
leave-taking from you, yet, although it was enforced by you, it did
take its course in the direction determined by me . . ." What does
Kafka mean when he says to his father, "My writing is all about
you," and adds, "yet it did take its course in the direction determined by me"? If you like, imagine yourself to be Max Brod writing a letter of your own to Kafka's father, explaining what it is your
friend has in mind . . .

I had been pleased by the number of students who had taken my
suggestion and decided to pretend to be the writer's friend and
biographer—and, in describing the inner workings of a most unusual son to a most conventional father, had demonstrated a mature
sensitivity to Kafka's moral isolation, to his peculiarities of perspective and temperament, and to those imaginative processes by which
a fantasist as entangled as Kafka was in daily existence transforms
into fable his everyday struggles. Hardly a single benighted literature major straying into ingenious metaphysical exegesis! Oh, I am
pleased, all right, with the Kafka seminar and with myself for what
I've done there. But these first months with Claire, what hasn't
been a source of pleasure?

Before leaving home I had been given the name and telephone
number of an American spending the year teaching in Prague, and,
happily, as it turns out (and what doesn't these days?), he and a
Czech friend of his, another literature professor, have the afternoon
free and are able to give us a tour of old Prague. From a bench in
the Old Town Square we gaze across at the palatial building where
Franz Kafka attended Gymnasium. To the right of the columned
entry way is the ground-floor site of Hermann Kafka's business.
"He couldn't even get away from him at school," I say. "All the
worse for him," the Czech professor replies, "and all the better for
the fiction." In the imposing Gothic church nearby, high on one
wall of the nave, a small square window faces an apartment next
door where, I am informed, Kafka's family had once lived. So
Kafka, I say, could have sat there furtively looking down on the sinner confessing and the faithful at prayer . . . and the interior of
this church, might it not have furnished, if not every last detail, at
least the atmosphere for the Cathedral of *The Trial?* And those
steep angular streets across the river leading circuitously to the
sprawling Hapsburg castle, surely they must have served as inspiration for him too . . . Perhaps so, says the Czech professor, but a
small castle village in northern Bohemia that Kafka knew from his
visits to his grandfather is thought to have been the principal model
for the topography of *The Castle.* Then there is the little country
village where his sister had spent a year managing a farm and
where Kafka had gone to stay with her during a spell of illness.
Had we time, says the Czech professor, Claire and I might benefit
from an overnight visit to the countryside. "Visit one of those xeno-

phobic little towns, with its smoky taverna and its buxom barmaid, and you will see what a thoroughgoing realist this Kafka was."

For the first time I sense something other than geniality in this smallish, bespectacled, neatly attired academic—I sense all that the geniality is working to suppress.

Near the wall of the castle, on cobbled Alchemist Street—and looking like a dwelling out of a child's bedtime story, the fit habitation for a gnome or elf—is the tiny house that his youngest sister had rented one winter for Kafka to live in, another of her efforts to help separate the bachelor son from father and family. The little place is now a souvenir shop. Picture postcards and Prague mementos are being sold on the spot where Kafka had meticulously scribbled variants of the same paragraph ten times over in his diary, and where he had drawn his sardonic stick figures of himself, the "private ideograms" he hid, along with practically everything else, in a drawer. Claire takes a picture of the three literature professors in front of the perfectionist writer's torture chamber. Soon it will be in its place in one of the albums at the foot of her bed.

While Claire goes off with the American professor, and her camera, for a tour of the castle grounds, I sit over tea with Professor Soska, our Czech guide. When the Russians invaded Czechoslovakia and put an end to the Prague Spring reform movement, Soska was fired from his university post and at age thirty-nine placed in "retirement" on a minuscule pension. His wife, a research scientist, also was relieved of her position for political reasons and, in order to support the family of four, has been working for a year now as a typist in a meat-packing plant. How has the retired professor managed to keep up his morale, I wonder. His three-piece suit is impeccable, his gait quick, his speech snappy and precise—how does he do it? What gets him up in the morning and to sleep at night? What gets him through each day?

"Kafka, of course," he says, showing me that smile again. "Yes, this is true; many of us survive almost solely on Kafka. Including people in the street who have never read a word of his. They look at one another when something happens, and they say, 'It's Kafka.' Meaning, 'That's the way it goes here now.' Meaning, 'What else did you expect?' "

"And anger? Is it abated any when you shrug your shoulders and say, 'It's Kafka'?"

"For the first six months after the Russians came to stay with us I

was myself in a continuous state of agitation. I went every night to
secret meetings with my friends. Every other day at least I circu-
lated another illegal petition. And in the time remaining I wrote, in
my most precise and lucid prose, in my most elegant and thoughtful sentences, encyclopedic analyses of the situation which then cir-
culated in *samizdat* among my colleagues. Then one day I keeled
over and they sent me to the hospital with bleeding ulcers. I
thought at first, all right, I will lie here on my back for a month, I
will take my medicine and eat my slops, and then—well, then *what?*
What will I do when I stop bleeding? Return to playing K. to their
Castle and their Court? This can all go on interminably, as Kafka
and his readers so well know. Those pathetic, hopeful, striving K.'s
of his, running madly up and down all those stairwells looking for
their solution, feverishly traversing the city contemplating the new
development that will lead to, of all things, their success. Beginnings, middles, and, most fantastical of all, endings—that is how
they believe they can force events to unfold."

"But, Kakfa and his readers aside, will things change if there is
no opposition?"

The smile, disguising God only knows the kind of expression he
would *like* to show to the world. "Sir, I have made my position
known. The entire country has made its position known. This way
we live now is not what we had in mind. For myself, I cannot burn
away what remains of my digestive tract by continuing to make this
clear to our authorities seven days a week."

"And so what do you do instead?"

"I translate *Moby Dick* into Czech. Of course, a translation happens already to exist, a very fine one indeed. There is absolutely no
need for another. But it is something I have always thought about,
and now that I have nothing else pressing to be accomplished, well,
why not?"

"Why that book? Why Melville?" I ask him.

"In the fifties I spent a year on an exchange program, living in
New York City. Walking the streets, it looked to me as if the place
was aswarm with the crew of Ahab's ship. And at the helm of everything, big or small, I saw yet another roaring Ahab. The appetite
to set things right, to emerge at the top, to be declared a 'champ.'
And by dint, not just of energy and will, but of enormous rage. And
that, the rage, that is what I should like to translate into Czech . . .
if"—smiling—"that *can* be translated into Czech.

"Now, as you might imagine, this ambitious project, when completed, will be utterly useless for two reasons. First, there is no need for another translation, particularly one likely to be inferior to the distinguished translation we already have; and second, no translation of mine can be published in this country. In this way, you see, I am able to undertake what I would not otherwise have dared to do, without having to bother myself any longer worrying whether it is sensible or not. Indeed, some nights when I am working late, the futility of what I am doing would appear to be my deepest source of satisfaction. To you perhaps this may appear to be nothing but a pretentious form of capitulation, of self-mockery. It may even appear that way to me on occasion. Nonetheless, it remains the most serious thing I can think to do in my retirement. And you," he asks, so very genially, "what draws you so to Kafka?"

"It's a long story too."

"Dealing with?"

"Not with political hopelessness."

"I would think not."

"Rather," I say, "in large part, with sexual despair, with vows of chastity that seem somehow to have been taken by me behind my back, and which I lived with against my will. Either I turned against my flesh, or it turned against me—I still don't know quite how to put it."

"From the look of things, you don't seem to have suppressed its urgings entirely. That is a very attractive young woman you are traveling with."

"Well, the worst is over. *May* be over. At least is over for *now*. But while it lasted, while I couldn't be what I had always just assumed I was, well, it wasn't quite like anything I had ever known before. Of course you are the one on intimate terms with totalitarianism—but if you'll permit me, I can only compare the body's utter single-mindedness, its cold indifference and absolute contempt for the well-being of the spirit, to some unyielding, authoritarian regime. And you can petition it all you like, offer up the most heartfelt and dignified and logical sort of appeal—and get no response at all. If anything, a kind of laugh is what you get. I submitted my petitions through a psychoanalyst; went to his office every other day for an hour to make my case for the restoration of a robust libido. And, I tell you, with arguments and perorations no less involuted and tedious and cunning and abstruse than the kind of thing you find in *The Castle*. You think poor K. is clever—you should have heard me trying to outfox impotence."

"I can imagine. That's not a pleasant business."

"Of course, measured against what you—"

"Please, you needn't say things like that. It is *not* a pleasant business, and the right to vote provides, in this matter, little in the way of compensation."

"That is true. I did vote during this period, and found it made me no happier. What I started to say about Kafka, about reading Kafka, is that stories of obstructed, thwarted K.'s banging their heads against invisible walls, well, they suddenly had a disturbing new resonance for me. It was all a little less remote, suddenly, than the Kafka I'd read in college. In my own way, you see, I had come to know that sense of having been summoned—or of imagining yourself summoned—to a calling that turns out to be beyond you, yet in the face of every compromising or farcical consequence, being unable to wise up and relinquish the goal. You see, I once went about living as though sex were sacred ground."

"So to be 'chaste' . . ." he says, sympathetically. "Most unpleasant."

"I sometimes wonder if *The Castle* isn't in fact linked to Kafka's own erotic blockage—a book engaged at every level with not reaching a climax."

He laughs at my speculation, but as before, gently and with that unrelenting amiability. Yes, just so profoundly compromised is the retired professor, caught, as in a mangle, between conscience and the regime—between conscience and searing abdominal pain. "Well," he says, putting a hand on my arm in a kind and fatherly way, "to each obstructed citizen his own Kafka."

"And to each angry man his own Melville," I reply. "But then what are bookish people to do with all the great prose they read—"

"—but sink their teeth into it. Exactly. Into the books, instead of into the hand that throttles them."

Late that afternoon, we board the streetcar whose number Professor Soska had written in pencil on the back of a packet of postcards ceremoniously presented to Claire at the door of our hotel. The postcards are illustrated with photographs of Kafka, his family, and Prague landmarks associated with his life and his work. The handsome little set is no longer in circulation, Soska explained to us, now that the Russians occupy Czechoslovakia and Kafka is an outlawed writer, *the* outlawed writer. "But you do have another set, I hope," said Claire, "for yourself—?" "Miss Ovington," he said, with a courtly bow, "I have Prague. Please, permit me. I am sure that everyone who meets you wants to give you a gift." And here he suggested the visit to Kafka's grave, to which it would not, however, be advisable for him to accompany us . . . and motioning with his hand, he drew our attention to a man standing with his back to a parked taxicab some fifty feet up the boulevard from the door of the hotel: the plainclothesman, he informs us, who used to follow him and Mrs. Soska around in the months after the Russian invasion, back when the professor was helping to organize the clandestine opposition to the new puppet regime and his duodenum was still intact. "Are you sure that's him, here?" I had asked. "Sufficiently sure," said Soska, and stooping quickly to kiss Claire's hand, he moved with a rapid, comic stride, rather like a man in a walking race, into the crowd descending the wide stairs of the passageway to the underground. "My God," said Claire, "it's too awful. All that terrible smiling. And that getaway!"

We are both a little stunned, not least of all, in my case, for feeling myself so safe and inviolable, what with the passport in my jacket and the young woman at my side.

The streetcar carries us from the center of Prague to the outlying district where Kafka is buried. Enclosed within a high wall, the Jewish graveyard is bounded on one side by a more extensive Christian cemetery—through the fence we see visitors tending the graves there, kneeling and weeding like patient gardeners—and on the other by a wide bleak thoroughfare bearing truck traffic to and from the city. The gate to the Jewish cemetery is chained shut. I rattle the chain and call toward what seems a watchman's house. In time a woman with a little boy appears from somewhere inside. I say in German that we have flown all the way from New York to visit Franz Kafka's grave. She appears to understand, but says no, not today. Come back Tuesday, she says. But I am a professor of literature and a Jew, I explain, and pass a handful of crowns across to her between the bars. A key appears, the gate is opened, and inside the little boy is assigned to accompany us as we follow the sign that points the way. The sign is in five different tongues—so many peoples fascinated by the fearful inventions of this tormented ascetic, so many fearful millions: Khrobu/ К могиле /Zum Grabe/ To the Grave of/à la tombe de/FRANZE KAFKY.

Of all things, marking Kafka's remains—and unlike anything else in sight—a stout, elongated, whitish rock, tapering upward to its pointed glans, a tombstone phallus. That is the first surprise. The second is that the family-haunted son is buried forever—still!—between the mother and the father who outlived him. I take a pebble from the gravel walk and place it on one of the little mounds of pebbles piled there by the pilgrims who've preceded me. I have never done so much for my own grandparents, buried with ten thousand others alongside an expressway twenty minutes from my New York apartment, nor have I made such a visit to my mother's tree-shaded Catskill grave site since I accompanied my father to the unveiling of her stone. The dark rectangular slabs beyond Kafka's grave bear familiar Jewish names. I might be thumbing through my own address book, or at the front desk looking over my mother's shoulder at the roster of registered guests at the Hungarian Royale: Levy, Goldschmidt, Schneider, Hirsch . . . The graves go on and on, but only Kafka's appears to be properly looked after. The other dead are without survivors hereabouts to chop away the undergrowth and to cut back the ivy that twists through the limbs of the trees and forms a heavy canopy joining the plot of one extinct Jew to the next. Only the childless bachelor appears to have living progeny. Where better for irony to abound than à la tombe de Franze Kafky?

Set into the wall facing Kafka's grave is a stone inscribed with the name of his great friend Brod. Here too I place a small pebble. Then for the first time I notice the plaques affixed to the length of cemetery wall, inscribed to the memory of Jewish citizens of Prague exterminated in Terezin, Auschwitz, Belsen, and Dachau. There are not pebbles enough to go around.

With the silent child trailing behind, Claire and I head back to the gate. When we get there Claire snaps a picture of the shy little boy and, using sign language, instructs him to write down his name and address on a piece of paper. Pantomiming with broad gestures and stagy facial expressions that make me wonder suddenly just how childish a young woman she is—just how childlike and needy a man I have become—she is able to inform the little boy that when the photograph is ready she will send a copy to him. In two or three weeks Professor Soska is also to receive a photograph from Claire, this one taken earlier in the day outside the souvenir shop where Kafka had once spent a winter.

Now why do I want to call what joins me to her childish? Why do I want to call this happiness names? Let it happen! Let it be! Stop the challenging before it even starts! You need what you need! Make peace with it!

The woman has come from the house to open the gate. Again we exchange some remarks in German.

"There are many visitors to Kafka's grave?" I ask.

"Not so many. But always distinguished people, Professor, like yourself. Or serious young students. He was a very great man. We had many great Jewish writers in Prague. Franz Werfel. Max Brod. Oskar Baum. Franz Kafka. But now," she says, casting her first glance, and a sidelong, abbreviated one at that, toward my companion, "they are all gone."

"Maybe your little boy will grow up to be a great Jewish writer."

She repeats my words in Czech. Then she translates the reply the boy has given while looking down at his shoes. "He wants to be an aviator."

"Tell him people don't always come from all over the world to visit an aviator's grave."

Again words are exchanged with the boy, and, smiling pleasantly at me—yes, it is only to the Jewish professor that she will address herself with a gracious smile—she says, "He doesn't mind that so much. And, sir, what is the name of your university?"

I tell her.

"If you would like, I will take you to the grave of the man who was Dr. Kafka's barber. He is buried here too."

"Thank you, that is very kind."

"He was also the barber of Dr. Kafka's father."

I explain to Claire what the woman has offered. Claire says, "If you want, go ahead."

"Better not to," I say. "Start with Kafka's barber, and by midnight we may end up by the grave of his candlestick maker."

To the graveyard attendant I say, "I'm afraid that's not possible right now."

"Of course your wife may come too," she starchily informs me.

"Thank you. But we have to get back to our hotel."

Now she looks me over with undisguised suspiciousness, as though it well may be that I am not from a distinguished American university at all. She has gone out of her way to unlock the gate on a day other than the one prescribed for tourists, and I have turned out to be less than serious, probably nothing but a curiosity seeker, a Jew perhaps, but in the company of a woman quite clearly Aryan.

At the streetcar stop I say to Claire, "Do you know what Kafka said to the man he shared an office with at the insurance company? At lunchtime he saw the fellow eating his sausage and Kafka is supposed to have shuddered and said, 'The only fit food for a man is half a lemon.'"

She sighs, and says, sadly, "Poor dope," finding in the great writer's dietary injunction a disdain for harmless appetites that is just plain silly to a healthy girl from Schenectady, New York.

That is all—yet, when we board the streetcar and sit down beside each other, I take her hand and feel suddenly purged of yet another ghost, as de-Kafkafied by my pilgrimage to the cemetery as I would appear to have been de-Birgittized once and for all by that visitation on the terrace restaurant in Venice. My obstructed days are behind me—along with the *un*obstructed ones: no more "more," and no more nothing, either!

"Oh, Clarissa," I say, bringing her hand to my lips, "it's as though the past can't do me any more harm. I just don't have any more regrets. And my fears are gone, too. And it's all from finding you. I'd thought the god of women, who doles them out to you, had looked down on me and said, 'Impossible to please—the hell with him.' And then he sends me Claire."

That evening, after dinner in our hotel, we go up to the room to prepare for our early departure the next day. While I pack a suitcase with my clothes and with the books I have been reading on the airplanes and in bed at night, Claire falls asleep amid the clothing she has laid out on the comforter. Aside from the Kafka diaries and Brod's biography—my supplemental guidebooks to old Prague —I have with me paperbacks by Mishima, Gombrowicz, and Genet, novels for next year's comparative literature class. I have decided to organize the first semester's reading around the subject of erotic desire, beginning with these disquieting contemporary novels dealing with prurient and iniquitous sexuality (disquieting to students because they are the sort of books admired most by a reader like Baumgarten, novels in which the author is himself pointedly implicated in what is morally most alarming) and ending the term's work with three masterworks concerned with illicit and ungovernable passions, whose assault is made by other means: *Madame Bovary*, *Anna Karenina*, and "Death in Venice."

Without awakening her, I pick Claire's clothes off the bed and pack them in her suitcase. Handling her things, I feel overwhelmingly in love. Then I leave her a note saying that I have gone for a walk and will be back in an hour. Passing through the lobby I notice that there are now some fifteen or twenty pretty young prostitutes seated singly, and in pairs, beyond the glass doorway of the hotel's spacious café. Earlier in the day there had been just three of them, at a single table, gaily chatting together. When I asked Professor Soska how all this is organized under socialism, he had explained that most of Prague's whores are secretaries and shopgirls moonlighting with tacit government approval; a few are employed full-time by the Ministry of the Interior to get what information they can out of the various delegations from East and West that pass through the big hotels. The covey of miniskirted girls I see seated in the café are probably there to greet the members of the Bulgarian trade mission who occupy most of the floor beneath ours. One of them, who is stroking the belly of a brown dachshund puppy that lies cuddled in her arms, smiles my way. I smile back (costs nothing) and then am off to the Old Town Square, where Kafka and Brod used to take their evening stroll. When I get there it is after nine and the spacious melancholy plaza is empty of everything except the shadows of the aged façades enclosing it. Where the tourist buses had been parked earlier in the day there is now only the smooth, worn, cobblestone basin. The place is empty —of all, that is, except mystery and enigma. I sit alone on a bench beneath a street lamp and, through the thin film of mist, look past the looming figure of Jan Hus to the church whose most sequestered proceedings the Jewish author could observe by peering through his secret aperture.

It is here that I begin to compose in my head what at first strikes me as no more than a bit of whimsy, the first lines of an introductory lecture to my comparative literature class inspired by Kafka's "Report to an Academy," the story in which an ape addresses a scientific gathering. It is only a little story of a few thousand words, but one that I love, particularly its opening, which seems to me one of the most enchanting and startling in literature: "Honored Members of the Academy! You have done me the honor of inviting me to give your Academy an account of the life I formerly led as an ape."

"Honored Members of Literature 341," I begin . . . but by the

time I am back at the hotel and have seated myself, with pen in
hand, at an empty table in a corner of the café, I have penetrated
the veneer of donnish satire with which I began, and on hotel stationery am writing out in longhand a formal introductory lecture
(not uninfluenced by the ape's impeccable, professorial prose) that
I want with all my heart to deliver—and to deliver not in September but at this very moment!

Seated two tables away is the prostitute with the little dachshund; she has been joined by a friend, whose favorite pet seems to
be her own hair. She strokes away at it as though it is somebody
else's. Looking up from my work, I tell the waiter to bring a cognac
to each of these petite and pretty working girls, neither of them as
old as Claire, and order a cognac for myself.

"Cheers," says the prostitute pleasing her puppy, and after the
three of us smile at one another for a brief, enticing moment, I go
back to writing what seem to me then and there somehow to be
sentences of the most enormous consequence for my happy new
life.

Rather than spend the first day of class talking about the reading
list and the general idea behind this course, I would like to tell you
some things about myself that I have never before divulged to any
of my students. I have no business doing this, and until I came into
the room and took my seat I wasn't sure I would go through with it.
And I may change my mind yet. For how do I justify disclosing to
you the most intimate facts of my personal life? True, we will be
meeting to discuss books for three hours a week during the coming
two semesters, and from experience I know, as you do, that under
such conditions a strong bond of affection can develop. However,
we also know that this does not give me license to indulge what
may only be so much impertinence and bad taste.

As you may already have surmised—by my style of dress, as easily as from the style of my opening remarks—the conventions tradi-
tionally governing the relationship between student and teacher are
more or less those by which I have always operated, even during
the turbulence of recent years. I have been told that I am one of
the few remaining professors who address students in the classroom
as "Mr." and "Miss," rather than by their given names. And however you may choose to attire yourselves—in the getup of garage
mechanic, panhandler, tearoom gypsy, or cattle rustler—I still prefer to appear before you to teach wearing a jacket and a tie . . .

though, as the observant will record, generally it will be the same jacket and the same tie. And when women students come to my office to confer, they will see, if they should even bother to look, that throughout the meeting I will dutifully leave open to the outside corridor the door to the room where we sit side by side. Some of you may be further amused when I remove my watch from my wrist, as I did only a moment ago, and place it beside my notes at the beginning of each class session. By now I no longer remember which of my own professors used to keep careful track of the passing hour in this way, but it would seem to have made its impression on me, signaling a professionalism with which I like still to associate myself.

All of which is not to say that I shall try to keep hidden from you the fact that I am flesh and blood—or that I understand that you are. By the end of the year you may even have grown a little weary of my insistence upon the connections between the novels you read for this class, even the most eccentric and off-putting of novels, and what you know so far of life. You will discover (and not all will approve) that I do not hold with certain of my colleagues who tell us that literature, in its most valuable and intriguing moments, is "fundamentally non-referential." I may come before you in my jacket and my tie, I may address you as madam and sir, but I am going to request nonetheless that you restrain yourselves from talking about "structure," "form," and "symbols" in my presence. It seems to me that many of you have been intimidated sufficiently by your junior year of college and should be allowed to recover and restore to respectability those interests and enthusiasms that more than likely drew you to reading fiction to begin with and which you oughtn't to be ashamed of now. As an experiment you might even want during the course of this year to try living without any classroom terminology at all, to relinquish "plot" and "character" right along with those very exalted words with which not a few of you like to solemnize your observations, such as "epiphany," "persona," and, of course, "existential" as a modifier of everything existing under the sun. I suggest this in the hope that if you talk about *Madame Bovary* in more or less the same tongue you use with the grocer, or your lover, you may be placed in a more intimate, a more interesting, in what might even be called a more *referential* relationship with Flaubert and his heroine.

In fact, one reason the novels to be read during the first semester are all concerned, to a greater or lesser degree of obsessiveness, with erotic desire is that I thought that readings organized around a subject with which you all have some sort of familiarity might help you even better to locate these books in the world of experience, and further to discourage the temptation to consign them to that manageable netherworld of narrative devices, metaphorical motifs, and mythical archetypes. Above all, I hope that by reading these books you will come to learn something of value about life in one of its most puzzling and maddening aspects. I hope to learn something myself.

All right. This much said by way of stalling, the time has come to begin to disclose the undisclosable—the story of the *professor's* desire. Only I can't, not quite yet, not until I have explained to my own satisfaction, if not to your parents', why I would even think to cast you as my voyeurs and my jurors and my confidants, why I would expose my secrets to people half my age, almost all of whom I have never previously known even as students. Why for me an audience, when most men and women prefer either to keep such matters entirely to themselves or to reveal them only to their most trusted confessors, secular or devout? What makes it compellingly necessary, or at all appropriate, that I present myself to you young strangers in the guise not of your teacher but as the first of this semester's texts?

Permit me to reply with an appeal to the heart.

I love teaching literature. I am rarely ever so contented as when I am here with my pages of notes, and my marked-up texts, and with people like yourselves. To my mind there is nothing quite like the classroom in all of life. Sometimes when we are in the midst of talking—when one of you, say, has pierced with a single phrase right to the heart of the book at hand—I want to cry out, "Dear friends, cherish this!" Why? Because once you have left here people are rarely, if ever, going to talk to you or listen to you the way you talk and listen to one another and to me in this bright and barren little room. Nor is it likely that you will easily find opportunities elsewhere to speak without embarrassment about what has mattered most to men as attuned to life's struggles as were Tolstoy, Mann, and Flaubert. I doubt that you know how very affecting it is to hear you speak thoughtfully and in all earnestness about solitude, illness, longing, loss, suffering, delusion, hope, passion, love, terror, corruption, calamity, and death . . . moving because you are nineteen and twenty years old, from comfortable middle-class homes most of you, and without much debilitating experience in your dossiers yet—but also because, oddly and sadly, this may be the last occasion you will ever have to reflect in any sustained and serious way upon the unrelenting forces with which in time you will all contend, like it or not.

Have I made any clearer why I should find our classroom to be, in fact, the *most* suitable setting for me to make an accounting of my erotic history? Does what I have just said render any more legitimate the claim I should like to make upon your time and patience and tuition? To put it as straight as I can—what a church is to the true believer, a classroom is to me. Some kneel at Sunday prayer, others don phylacteries each dawn . . . and I appear three times each week, my tie around my neck and my watch on my desk, to teach the great stories to you.

Class, oh, students, I have been riding the swell of a very large emotion this year. I'll get to that too. In the meantime, if possible, bear with my mood of capaciousness. Really, I only wish to present you with my credentials for teaching Literature 341. Indiscreet, unprofessional, unsavory as portions of these disclosures will surely strike some of you, I nonetheless would like, with your permission, to go ahead now and give an open account to you of the life I formerly led as a human being. I am devoted to fiction, and I assure you that in time I will tell you whatever I may know about it, but in truth nothing lives in me like my life.

The two pretty young prostitutes are still unattended, still sitting across from me in their white angora sweaters, pastel miniskirts, dark net stockings, and elevating high-heel shoes—rather like children who have ransacked Mamma's closet to dress as usherettes for a pornographic movie house—when I rise with my sheaf of stationery to leave the café.

"A letter to your wife?" says the one who strokes the dog and speaks some English.

I cannot resist the slow curve she has thrown me. "To the children," I say.

She nods to the friend who is stroking her hair; yes, they know my type. At eighteen they know all the types.

Her friend says something in Czech and they have a good laugh.

"Goodbye, sir; nighty-night," says the knowing one, offering a harmless enough smirk for me to carry away from the encounter. I am thought to have gotten my kick by buying two whores a drink. Maybe I did. Fair enough.

In our room I find that Claire has changed into her nightdress and is sleeping now beneath the blankets. A note for me on the pillow: "Dear One—I loved you so much today. I *will* make you happy. C."

Oh, I *have* come through—on my pillow is the proof!

And the sentences in my hands? They hardly seem now to be so laden with implication for my future as they did when I was hurrying back to the hotel from the Old Town Square, dying to get my hands on a piece of paper so as to make *my* report to *my* academy. Folding the pages in two, I put them with the paperbacks at the bottom of my suitcase, there along with Claire's note that promises to make her dear one happy. I feel absolutely triumphant: capacious indeed.

When I am awakened in the early morning by a door slamming beneath our room—down where the Bulgarians are sleeping, one of them no doubt with a little Czech whore and a dachshund puppy— I find I cannot begin to reconstruct the meandering maze of dreams that had so challenged and agitated me throughout the night. I had expected I would sleep marvelously, yet I awaken perspiring and, for those first timeless seconds, with no sense at all of where I am in bed or with whom. Then, blessedly, I find Claire, a big warm animal of my own species, my very own mate of the other gender, and encircling her with my arms—drawing her sheer creatureliness up against the length of my body—I begin to recall the long, abusive episode that had unfolded more or less along these lines:

I am met at the train by a Czech guide. He is called X, "as in the alphabet," he explains. I am sure he is really Herbie Bratasky, our master of ceremonies, but I do nothing to tip my hand. "And what have you seen so far?" asks X as I disembark.

"Why, nothing. I am just arriving."

"Then I have just the thing to start you off. How would you like to meet the whore Kafka used to visit?"

"There is such a person? And she is still alive?"

"How would you like to be taken to talk with her?"

I speak only after I have looked to be sure that no one is eavesdropping. "It is everything I ever hoped for."

"And how was Venice without the Swede?" X asks as we step aboard the cemetery streetcar.

"Dead."

The apartment is four flights up, in a decrepit building by the river. The woman we have come to see is nearly eighty: arthritic hands, slack jowls, white hair, clear and sweet blue eyes. Lives in a rocking chair on the pension of her late husband, an anarchist. I ask myself, "An anarchist's widow receiving a government pension?"

"Was he an anarchist all his life?" I ask.

"From the time he was twelve," X replies. "That was when his father died. He once explained to me how it happened. He saw his father's dead body, and he thought, 'This man who smiles at me and loves me is no more. Never again will any man smile at me and love me as he did. Wherever I go I will be a stranger and an enemy all my life.' That's how anarchists are made, apparently. I take it you are not an anarchist."

"No. My father and I love each other to this day. I believe in the rule of law."

From the window of the apartment I can see the gliding force of the famous Moldau. "Why, there, boys and girls, at the edge of the river"—I am addressing my class—"is the *piscine* where Kafka and Brod would go swimming together. See, it is as I told you: Franz Kafka was real, Brod was not making him up. And so am I real, nobody is making me up, other than myself."

X and the old woman converse in Czech. X says to me, "I told her that you are a distinguished American authority on the works of the great Kafka. You can ask her whatever you want."

"What did she make of him?" I ask. "How old was he when she knew him? How old was she? When exactly was all this taking place?"

X (interpreting): "She says, 'He came to me and I took a look at him and I thought, "What is this Jewish boy so depressed about?"' She thinks it was in 1916. She says she was twenty-five. Kafka was in his thirties."

"Thirty-three," I say. "Born, class, in 1883. And as we know from all our years of schooling, three from six is three, eight from one doesn't go, so we must borrow one from the preceding digit; eight from eleven is three, eight from eight is zero, and one from one is zero—and that is why thirty-three is the correct answer to the question: How old was Kafka when he paid his visits to this whore? Next question: What, if any, is the relationship between Kafka's whore and today's story, 'The Hunger Artist'?"

X says, "And what else would you like to know?"

"Was he regularly able to have an erection? Could he usually reach orgasm? I find the diaries inconclusive."

Her eyes are expressive when she answers, though the crippled hands lie inert in her lap. In the midst of the indecipherable Czech I catch a word that makes my flesh run: Franz!

X nods gravely. "She says that was no problem. She knew what
to do with a boy like him."

Shall I ask? Why not? I have come not just from America, after
all, but out of oblivion, to which I shall shortly return. "What was
that?"

Matter-of-fact still, she tells X what she did to arouse the author
of—"Name Kafka's major works in the order of their composition.
Grades will be posted on the department bulletin board. All those
who wish recommendations for advanced literary studies will
please line up outside my office to be whipped to within an inch of
their lives."

X says, "She wants money. American money, not crowns. Give
her ten dollars."

I give over the money. What use will it be in oblivion? "No, that
will not be on the final."

X waits until she is finished, then translates: "She blew him."

Probably for less than it cost me to find out. There is such a thing
as oblivion, and there is such a thing as fraud, which I am also
against. Of course! This woman is nobody, and Bratasky gets half.

"And what did Kafka talk about?" I ask, and yawn to show just
how seriously I now take these proceedings.

X translates the old woman's reply word for word: "I don't remember any more. I didn't remember the next day probably. Look,
these Jewish boys would sometimes say nothing at all. Like little
birds, not even a squeak. I'll tell you one thing, though—they never
hit me. And they were clean boys. Clean underwear. Clean collars.
They would never dream to come here with so much as a soiled
handkerchief. Of course everybody I always would wash with a rag.
I was always hygienic. But they didn't even need it. They were
clean and they were gentlemen. As God is my witness, they never
beat on my backside. Even in bed they had manners."

"But is there anything about Kafka in particular that she re-
members? I didn't come here, to her, to Prague, to talk about nice
Jewish boys."

She gives some thought to the question; or, more likely, no
thought. Just sits there trying out being dead.

"You see, he wasn't so special," she finally says. "I don't mean he
wasn't a gentleman. They were all gentlemen."

I say to Herbie (refusing to pretend any longer that he is some
Czech named X), "Well, I don't really know what to ask next,

Herb. I have the feeling she may have Kafka confused with somebody else."

"The woman's mind is razor-sharp," Herbie replies.

"Still, she's not exactly Brod on the subject."

The aged whore, sensing perhaps that I have had it, speaks
again.

Herbie says, "She wants to know if you would like to inspect her
pussy."

"To what possible end?" I reply.

"Shall I inquire?"

"Oh, please do."

Eva (for this, Herbie claims, is the lady's name) replies at length.
"She submits that it might hold some literary interest for you.
Others like yourself, who have come to her because of her relationship with Kafka, have been most anxious to see it, and, providing of course that their credentials established them as serious, she
has been willing to show it to them. She says that because you are
here on my recommendation she would be delighted to allow you
to have a quick look."

"I thought she only blew him. Really, Herb, of what possible interest could her pussy be to me? You know I am not in Prague
alone."

Translation: "Again, she frankly admits she doesn't know of what
interest anything about her is to anyone. She says she is grateful for
the little money she is able to make from her friendship with young
Franz, and she is flattered that her callers are themselves distinguished and learned men. Of course, if the gentleman does not care
to examine it—"

But why not? Why come to the battered heart of Europe if not to
examine just this? Why come into the world at all? "Students of literature, you must conquer your squeamishness once and for all!
You must face the unseemly thing itself! You must come off your
high horse! There, *there* is your final exam."

It would cost me five more American dollars. "This is a flourishing business, this Kafka business," I say.

"First of all, given your field of interest, the money is tax-deduc-
tible. Second, for only a fiver, you are striking a decisive blow
against the Bolsheviks. She is one of the last in Prague still in business for herself. Third, you are helping preserve a national literary
monument—you are doing a service for our suffering writers. And

last but not least, think of the money you have given to Klinger.
What's five more to the cause?"

"I beg your pardon. What cause?"

"Your happiness. We only want to make you happy, to make you
finally you, David dear. You have denied yourself too much as it
is."

Despite her arthritic hands Eva is able on her own to tug her
dress up until it is bunched in her lap. Herbie, however, has to hold
her around with one arm, shift her on her buttocks, and draw down
her underpants for her. I reluctantly help by steadying the rocking
chair.

Accordioned kidskin belly, bare ruined shanks, and, as-
tonishingly, a triangular black patch, pasted on like a mustache. I
find myself rather doubting the authenticity of the pubic hair.

"She would like to know," says Herbie, "if the gentleman would
care to touch it."

"And how much does that go for?"

Herbie repeats my question in Czech. Then to me, with a courtly
bow, "Her treat."

"Thanks, no."

But again she assures the gentleman that it will cost him nothing.
Again the gentleman courteously declines.

Now Eva smiles—between her parted lips, her tongue, still red.
The pulp of the fruit, still red!

"Herb, what did she say just then?"

"Don't think I ought to repeat it, not to you."

"What was it, Herbie? I demand to know!"

"Something indecent," he says, chuckling, "about what Kafka
liked the most. His big thrill."

"*What was it?*"

"Oh, I don't think your dad would want you to hear that, Dave.
Or your dad's dad, and so on, all the way back to the Father of the
Faithful and the Friend of God. Besides, it may just have been a
malicious remark, gratuitously made, with no foundation in fact.
She may only have said it because you insulted her. You see, by refusing to touch a finger to her famous vizz you have cast doubt—
perhaps not entirely inadvertently either—on the very meaning of
her life. Moreover, she is afraid you will go back to America now
and tell your colleagues that she is a fraud. And then serious
scholars will no longer come to pay their respects—which, of course,

would mark the end for her, and if I may say so, the end too for private enterprise in our country. It would constitute nothing less than the final victory of the Bolsheviks over free men."

"Well, except for this new Czech routine of yours—which, I have to admit, could have fooled just about anybody but me—you haven't changed, Bratasky, not a bit."

"Too bad I can't say the same about you."

Here Herbie approaches the old woman, her face now sadly tear-streaked, and cupping his fingers as though to catch the trickle of a stream, he places his hands between her bare legs.

"Coo," she gurgles. "Coo. Coo." And closing her blue eyes, she rubs her cheek against Herbie's shoulder. The tip of her tongue I see protruding from her mouth. The pulp of the fruit, still red.

Upon returning from our travels through the beautiful cities—after I dreamed in Prague of visiting Kafka's whore, we flew the next morning to Paris, and three days later to Bruges, where at a conference on modern European literature I read the paper entitled "Hunger Art"—we decide to split the rent on a small house in the country for July and August. How better to spend the summer? But once the decision is made, all I can think about is the time I last lived in daily proximity to a woman, the tomb-like months just before the Hong Kong fiasco, when neither of us could so much as bear the sight of the other's shoes on the floor of the closet. Consequently, before I sign the lease for the perfect little house that we've found, I suggest that probably it would be best not to sublet either of our apartments in the city for the two months—a small financial sacrifice, true, but this way there will always be a place to retreat to if anything untoward should happen. I actually say "untoward." Claire—prudent, patient, tender Claire—understands well enough what I mean as I jabber on in this vein, the pen in my hand, and the agent who drew up the lease casting unamused glances from the other end of his office. Raised by heavyweight battlers from the day she was born until she was able to leave for school and a life of her own, an independent young woman now since the age of seventeen, she has no argument against having a nest to fly off to, as well as the nest that is to be shared, for so long as the sharing is good. No, we won't rent our apartments, she agrees. Whereupon, with the solemnity of the Japanese Commander-in-Chief sitting down aboard MacArthur's battleship to surrender an empire, I affix my signature to the lease.

A small, two-storied white clapboard farmhouse, then, set halfway up a hillside of dandelions and daisies from a silent, untraveled rural road, and twenty miles north of the Catskill village where I was raised. I have chosen Sullivan County over Cape Cod, and that too is fine with Claire—proximity to the Vineyard and to Olivia seems not to matter to her quite the way it did just the year before. And for me the gentle green hills and distant green mountains beyond the dormer windows take me back to the bedroom vista of my childhood—exactly my view from the room at the top of the "Annex"—and augment the sense I already have with her that I am living at last in accordance with my true spirit, that, indeed, I am "home."

And for the spirit what a summer it is! From the daily regimen of swimming in the morning and hiking in the afternoon we each grow more and more fit, while within, day by day, we grow fat as our farmer neighbor's hogs. How the spirit feasts on just getting up in the morning! on coming to in a whitewashed sunlit room with my arms encircling her large, substantial form. Oh, how I do love the size of her in bed! That *tangibility* of hers! And the weight of those breasts in my hands! Oh, very different, this, from all the months and months of waking up with nothing to hold on to but my pillow!

Later—is it not yet eleven? *really?* we have eaten our cinnamon toast, taken our dip, stopped in town to buy food for dinner, brooded over the newspaper's front page, and it is only ten-fifteen? —later, from the rocker on the porch where I do my morning writing, I watch her toil in the garden. Two spiral notebooks are arranged beside me. In one I work at planning the projected book on Kafka, to be called, after my Bruges lecture, *Hunger Art,* while in the other, whose pages I approach with far greater eagerness—and where I am having somewhat more success—I move on to the substance of the lecture whose prologue I had begun composing in the hotel café in Prague, the story of *my* life in its most puzzling and maddening aspects, *my* chronicle of the iniquitous, the ungovernable and the thrilling . . . or (by way of a working title), "How David Kepesh comes to be sitting in a wicker rocker on a screened-in porch in the Catskill Mountains, watching with contentment while a teetotaling twenty-five-year-old sixth-grade teacher from

Schenectady, New York, creeps about her flower garden in what appear to be overalls handed down from Tom Sawyer himself, her hair tied back with a snip of green twister seal cut from the coil with which she stakes the swooning begonias, her delicate, innocent Mennonite face, small and intelligent as a raccoon's, and soil-smudged as though in preparation for Indian night at the Girl Scout jamboree—and his happiness in her hands."

"Why don't you come out and help with the weeds?" she calls—"Tolstoy would have." "He was a big-time novelist," I say; "they have to do that sort of thing, to gain Experience. Not me. For me it's enough to see you crawling on your knees." "Well, whatever pleases," she says.

Ah, Clarissa, let me tell you, all that *is* pleases. The pond where we swim. Our apple orchard. The thunderstorms. The barbecue. The music playing. Talking in bed. Your grandmother's iced tea. Deliberating on which walk to take in the morning and which at dusk. Watching you lower your head to peel peaches and shuck corn . . . Oh, nothing, really, is what pleases. But what nothing! Nations go to war for this kind of nothing, and in the absence of such nothing, people shrivel up and die.

Of course by now the passion between us is no longer quite what it was on those Sundays when we would cling together in my bed until three in the afternoon—"the primrose path to madness," as Claire once described those rapacious exertions which end finally with the two of us rising on the legs of weary travelers to change the bed linens, to stand embracing beneath the shower, and then to go out of doors to get some air before the winter sun goes down. That, once begun, our lovemaking should have continued with un-diminished intensity for almost a year—that two industrious, re-sponsible, idealistic schoolteachers should have adhered to one another like dumb sea creatures, and, at the moment of overbrimming, have come to the very brink of tearing flesh with cannibalized jaws—well, that is somewhat more than I ever would have dared predict for myself, having already served beyond the call of duty—having already staked so much and lost so much—under the tattered scarlet standard of His Royal Highness, my lust.

Leveling off. Overheated frenzy subsiding into quiet physical affection. That is how I choose to describe what is happening to our passion during this blissful summer. Can I think otherwise—can I possibly believe that, rather than coming to rest on some warm plateau of sweet coziness and intimacy, I am being eased down a precipitous incline and as yet am nowhere near the cold and lonely cavern where I finally will touch down? To be sure, the faintly brutal element has taken it on the lam; gone is the admixture of the merciless with the tender, those intimations of utter subjugation that one sees in the purplish bruise, the wantonness one thrills to in the coarse word breathed at the peak of pleasure. We no longer *succumb* to desire, nor do we touch each other everywhere, paw and knead and handle with that unquenchable lunacy so alien to what and who we otherwise are. True, I am no longer a little bit of a beast, she is no longer a little bit of a tramp, neither any longer is quite the greedy lunatic, the depraved child, the steely violator, the helplessly impaled. Teeth, once blades and pincers, the pain-inflicting teeth of little cats and dogs, are simply teeth again, and tongues are tongues, and limbs are limbs. Which is, as we all know, how it must be.

And I for one will not quarrel, or sulk, or yearn, or despair. I will not make a religion of what is fading away—of my craving for that bowl into which I dip my face as though to extract the last dram of a syrup I cannot guzzle down fast enough . . . of the harsh excitement of that pumping grip so strong, so rapid, so unyielding, that if I do not moan that there is nothing left of me, that I am stupefied and numb, she will, in that stirring state of fervor bordering on heartlessness, continue until she has milked the very life from my body. I will not make a religion of the marvelous sight of her half-stripped. No, I intend to nurse no illusions about the chance for a great revival of the drama we would seem very nearly to have played out, this clandestine, uncensored, underground theater of four furtive selves—the two who pant in performance, the two who pantingly watch—wherein regard for the hygienic, the temperate, and the time of day or night is all so much ridiculous intrusion. I tell you, I am a new man—that is, I am a *new* man no longer—and I know when my number is up: now just stroking the soft, long hair will do, just resting side by side in our bed each morning will do, awakening folded together, mated, in love. Yes, I am willing to settle on these terms. This will suffice. No more *more*.

And before whom am I on my knees trying to strike such a bargain? Who is to decide how far from Claire I am going to slide?

Honored members of Literature 341, you would think, as I do, that it would, it should, it must, be me.

Late in the afternoon of one of the loveliest days of August, with nearly fifty such days already stored away in memory and the deep contentment of knowing that there are still a couple dozen more to come, on an afternoon when my feeling of well-being is boundless and I cannot imagine anyone happier or luckier than myself, I receive a visit from my former wife. I will think about it for days afterward, imagining each time the phone rings or I hear the sound of a car turning up the steep drive to the house that it is Helen returning. I will expect to find a letter from her every morning, or rather a letter about her, informing me that she has run off again to Hong Kong, or that she is dead. When I awaken in the middle of the night to remember how once I lived and how I live now—and this still happens to me, too regularly—I will cling to my sleeping partner as though it is she who is ten years my senior—twenty, thirty years my senior—rather than the other way around.

I am out by the orchard in a canvas lounge chair, my legs in the sun and my head in the shade, when I hear the phone ringing inside the house, where Claire is getting ready to go swimming. I have not yet decided—of such decisions are my days composed—whether I'll go along with her to the pond, or just stay on quietly doing my work until it is time to water the marigolds and open the wine. Since lunch I have been out here—just myself, the bumblebees, and the butterflies, and, from time to time, Claire's old Labrador, Dazzle—reading Colette and taking notes for the course known by now around the house as Desire 341. Leafing through a pile of her books, I have been wondering if there has ever been in America a novelist with a point of view toward the taking and giving of pleasure even vaguely resembling Colette's, an American writer, man or woman, stirred as deeply as she is by scent and warmth and color, someone as sympathetic to the range of the body's urgings, as attuned to the world's every sensuous offering, a connoisseur of the finest gradations of amorous feeling, who is nonetheless immune to fanaticism of any sort, except, as with Colette, a fanatical devotion to the self's honorable survival. Hers seems to have been a nature exquisitely susceptible to all that desire longs for and promises—"these pleasures which are lightly called physical"—yet wholly untainted by puritan conscience, or murderous impulse, or megalo-

mania, or sinister ambitions, or the score-settling rage of class or social grievance. One thinks of her as egotistic, in the sharpest,
crispest sense of the word, the most pragmatic of sensualists, her
capacity for protective self-scrutiny in perfect balance with the capacity to be carried away—

The top sheet of my yellow pad is spattered and crisscrossed
with the fragmentary beginnings of a lecture outline—running
down one margin is a long list of modern novelists, European as
well as American, among whom Colette's decent, robust, bourgeois
paganism still seems to me unique—when Claire comes out of the
kitchen's screen door, wearing her bathing suit and carrying her
white terry-cloth robe over her arm.

The book in her hand is Musil's *Young Törless*, the copy I'd just
finished marking up the night before. How delighted I am with her
curiosity about these books I will be teaching! And to look up at
the swell of her breasts above the bikini's halter, well, that is yet
another of this wonderful day's satisfactions.

"Tell me," I say, taking hold of the calf of her nearest leg, "why
is there no American Colette? Or could it be Updike who comes the
closest? It's surely not Henry Miller. It's surely not Hawthorne."

"A phone call for you," she says. "Helen Kepesh."

"My God." I look at my watch, for all the help that will give.
"What time would it be in California? What can she want? How
did she find me?"

"It's a local call."

"*Is* it?"

"I think so, yes."

I haven't yet moved from the chair. "And that's what she said,
Helen *Kepesh?*"

"Yes."

"But I thought she'd taken her own name back."

Claire shrugs.

"You told her I was here?"

"Do you want me to tell her you aren't?"

"What can she *want?*"

"You'll have to ask her," says Claire. "Or maybe you won't."

"Would it be so very wrong of me just to go in there and put the
phone back on the hook?"

"Not wrong," says Claire. "Only unduly anxious."

"But I *feel* unduly anxious. I feel unduly *happy*. This is all so perfect." I spread ten fingers across the soft swell of flesh above her halter. "Oh, my dear, dear pal."

"I'll wait out here," she says.

"And I *will* go swimming with you."

"Okay. Good."

"So wait!"

It would be neither cruel nor cowardly, I tell myself, looking down at the phone on the kitchen table—it would just be the most sensible thing I could do. Except, of the half-dozen people closest to my life, Helen happens still to be one. "Hello," I say.

"Hello. Oh, hello. Look, I feel odd about phoning you, David. I almost didn't. Except I seem to be in your town. We're at the Texaco station; across from a real-estate office."

"I see."

"I'm afraid it was just too hard driving off without even calling. How are you?"

"How did you know I was staying here?"

"I tried you in New York a few days ago. I called the college, and the department secretary said she wasn't authorized to give out your summer address. I said I was a former student and I was sure you wouldn't mind. But she was adamant about Professor Kepesh's privacy. Quite a moat, that lady."

"So how did you find me?"

"I called the Schonbrunns."

"My, my."

"But stopping off here for gas is really just accidental. Strange, I know, but true. And not as strange, after all, as the truly strange things that happen."

She is lying and I'm not charmed. Through the window I can see Claire holding the unopened book in her hand. We could already be in the car on the way down to the pond.

"What do you want, Helen?"

"You mean from you? Nothing; nothing at all. I'm married now."

"I didn't know."

"That's what I was doing in New York. We were visiting my husband's family. We're on our way to Vermont. They have a summer house there." She laughs; a very appealing laugh. It makes me remember her in bed. "Can you believe I've never been to New England?"

"Well," I say, "it's not exactly Rangoon."

"Neither is Rangoon any more."

"How is your health? I heard that you were pretty sick."

"I'm better now. I had a hard time for a while. But it's over. How are *you?*"

"My hard time is over too."

"I'd like to see you, if I could. Are we that far from your house? I'd like to talk to you, just for a little—"

"About what?"

"I owe you some explanations."

"You don't. No more than I owe you any. I think we'd both be better off at this late date without the explanations."

"I was mad, David, I was going crazy— David, these are difficult things to say surrounded by cans of motor oil."

"Then don't say them."

"I have to."

Out on my chair, Claire is now leafing through the *Times.*

"You better go swimming without me," I say. "Helen's coming here; with her husband."

"She's married?"

"So she says."

"Why *was* it Helen 'Kepesh' then?"

"Probably to identify herself to you. To me."

"Or to herself," says Claire. "Would you rather I weren't here?"

"Of course not. I meant I thought you'd *prefer* going swimming."

"Only if *you* prefer—"

"No, absolutely not."

"Where are they now?"

"Down in town."

"She came all this way ? I don't understand. What if we hadn't been at home?"

"She says they're on their way to his family's house in Vermont."

"They didn't take the Thruway?"

"Honey, what's happened to you? No, they didn't take the Thruway. Maybe they're taking the back roads for the scenery. What's the difference? They'll come and they'll go. You were the one who told *me* not to be unduly anxious."

"But I wouldn't want you to be hurt."

"Don't worry. If that's why you're staying—"

Here suddenly she stands, and at the edge of tears (where I have never before seen her!) she says, "Look, you so *obviously* want me

out of the way—" Quickly she starts toward where our car is parked
on the other side of the house, in the dust bowl by the old collaps-
ing barn. And I run after her, just behind the dog, who thinks it is
all a game.

Consequently we are beside the barn, waiting together, when the
Lowerys arrive. As their car makes its way up the long dirt drive to
the house, Claire slips her terry-cloth robe on over her bathing suit.
I am wearing a pair of corduroy shorts, a faded old T-shirt, battered sneakers, an outfit I've probably had since Syracuse. Helen
will have no trouble recognizing me. But will I recognize her? Can
I explain to Claire—should I have?—that really, all I want is to
see . . .

I had heard that, on top of all her debilitating ailments, she had
gained some twenty pounds. If so, she has by now lost all that
weight, and a bit more. She emerges from the car looking exactly
like herself. She is paler-complexioned than I remember—or rather,
she is not pale in the cleansed, Quakerish way to which I am now
accustomed. Helen's pallor is luminous, transparent. Only in the
thinness of her arms and neck is there any indication that she has
been through a bad time with her health, and, what is more, is now
a woman in her mid-thirties. Otherwise, she is the Stunning Creature once again.

Her husband shakes my hand. I had been expecting someone
taller and older—I suppose one usually does. Lowery has a close-
cropped black beard, round tortoise-shell glasses, and a compact,
powerful, athletic build. Both are dressed in jeans and sandals and
colored polo shirts and have their hair cut in the Prince Valiant
style. The only jewelry either wears is a wedding ring. All of which
tells me practically nothing. Maybe the emeralds are home in the
vault.

We walk around as though they are prospective buyers who have
been sent up by the real-estate agent to look at the house; as
though they are the new couple from down the road who have
stopped by to introduce themselves; as though they are what they
are—ex-wife with new husband, someone now meaning nothing, ar-
tifact of relatively little remaining historical interest uncovered during an ordinary day's archaeological excavation. Yes, giving her the
directions to our so perfect lair turns out to have been neither a
foolish nor, God knows, a *dangerous* mistake. Otherwise, how
would I have known that I have been wholly de-Helenized too,

that the woman can neither harm me nor charm me, that I am un-bewitchable by all but the most loving and benign of feminine spirits. How right Claire was to caution me against being unduly anxious; before, of course, she went ahead and—doubtless because of my own confusion upon hanging up the phone—became unduly anxious herself.

Claire is up ahead now with Les Lowery. They are headed toward the blackened, ruined oak tree at the edge of the woods. Early in the summer, during a dramatic daylong storm, the tree was struck by lightning and severed in two. While we all walked together around the house and through the garden, Claire had been talking, just a little feverishly, about the wild thunderstorms of early July; a little feverishly, and a little childishly. I had not imagined beforehand just how ominous Helen would seem to her, given the tales of her troublemaking that I have told; I suppose I had not realized how often I must have told them to her in the first months we were together. No wonder she has latched on to the quiet husband, who does in fact seem closer to her in age and spirit, and who, it turns out, is also a subscriber to *Natural History* and the *Audubon Magazine*. Some minutes earlier, on the porch, she had identified for the Lowerys the unusual Cape Cod seashells arranged in a wicker tray in the center of the dining table, between the antique pewter candlesticks that were her grandmother's gift upon her graduation from college.

While my mate and her mate are examining the burned-out trunk of the oak tree, Helen and I drift back to the porch. She is telling me all about him, still. He is a lawyer, a mountain climber, a skier, he is divorced, has two adolescent daughters; in partnership with an architect he has already made a small fortune as a housing developer; lately he has been in the news for the work he has been doing as investigating counsel for a California State Legislature committee unraveling connections between organized crime and the Marin County Police . . . Outside I see that Lowery has moved past the oak tree and onto the path that cuts up through the woods to the steep rock formations that Claire has been photographing all summer. Claire and Dazzle appear to be headed back down to the house.

I say to Helen, "He looks a bit young to be *such* a Karenin."

"I'm sure I'd be sardonic too," she replies, "if I were you and thought I was still me. I was surprised you even came to the phone.

But that's because you are a nice man. You always were, actually."

"Oh, Helen, what's going on here? Save the 'nice man' stuff for my tombstone. You may have a new life, but this lingo . . ."

"I had a lot of time to think when I was sick. I thought about—"

But I don't want to know. "Tell me," I say, interrupting her, "how was your conversation with the Schonbrunns?"

"I spoke to Arthur. She wasn't home."

"And how did he take hearing from you after all this time?"

"Oh, he took it quite well."

"Frankly I'm surprised he offered assistance. I'm surprised you asked him for it. As I remember, he was never a great fan of yours —nor you of theirs."

"Arthur and I have changed our minds about each other."

"Since when? You used to be very funny about him."

"I'm not any more. I don't ridicule people who admit what they want. Or at least admit to what they don't have."

"And what does Arthur want? Are you telling me that all along Arthur wanted *you*?"

"I don't know about all along."

"Oh, Helen, I find this hard to believe."

"I never heard anything easier to believe."

"And what exactly is it I'm supposed to be believing, again?"

"When we two got back from Hong Kong, when you moved out and I was alone, he telephoned one night and asked if he could come over to talk. He was very concerned about you. So he came from his office—it was about nine—and he talked about your unhappiness for nearly an hour. I said finally that I didn't know what any of it had to do with me any more, and then he asked if he and I might meet in San Francisco for lunch one day. I said I didn't know, I was feeling pretty miserable myself, and he kissed me. And then he made me sit down and he sat down and he explained to me in detail that he hadn't expected to do that, and that it didn't mean what I thought it meant. He was happily married still, and after all these years he still had a strong physical relationship with Debbie, and in fact he owed her his whole life. And then he told me a harrowing story about some crazy girl, some librarian he had almost married in Minnesota, and how she had once gone after him with a fork at breakfast and stabbed his hand. He'd never gotten over what might have happened to him if he had caved in and married her—he thinks it actually might have ended in a murder. He showed me the scar from the fork. He said his salvation was meeting Debbie, and that he owes everything he's accomplished to her devotion and love. Then he tried to kiss me again, and when I said I didn't think it was a good idea, he told me I was perfectly right and that he had misjudged me completely and he still wanted to have lunch with me. I really couldn't take any more confusion, so I said yes. He arranged for us to eat at a place in Chinatown where, I assure you, nobody he knew or I knew or *anybody* knew could possibly see us together. And that was it. But then that summer, when they moved East, he began writing letters. I still get them, every few months or so."

"Go on. What do they say?"

"Oh, they're awfully well-written," she says, smiling. "He must write some of those sentences ten times over before he's completely satisfied. I think they may be the kind of letters the poetry editor of the college magazine writes late at night to his girl friend at Smith. 'The weather, as clear and as sharp as a fish spine,' and so on. And sometimes he includes lines from great poems about Venus, Cleopatra, and Helen of Troy."

" 'Lo, this is she that was the world's desire.' "

"That's right—that's one of them. I thought it was a bit insulting, actually. Except I suppose it can't be because it's so 'great.' Anyway, he always somehow or other lets me know that I don't have to answer; so I don't. Why are you smiling? It's really rather sweet. Well, it's *something*. Who'da thunk it?"

"I smile," I say, "because I've had my own Schonbrunn letters—from her."

"Now, *that's* hard to believe."

"No, not if you saw them. No great lines of poetry for me."

Claire is still some fifty or so feet away, yet both of us stop speaking as she makes her way back to the house. Why? Who knows why!

And if only we hadn't! Why didn't I just talk nonsense, tell a joke, *recite* a poem, *anything* so that Claire hadn't to come through the screen door into this conspiratorial silence. Hadn't to come in to see me sitting across from Helen, charmed in spite of myself.

Immediately she becomes stony—and reaches a decision. "I'm going swimming."

"What's happened to Les?" asks Helen.

"Took a walk."

"You sure you don't want some iced tea?" I ask Claire. "Why don't we all have some iced tea?"

"No. Bye." That single adolescent syllable of farewell for the guest, then she's gone.

From where I am sitting I am able to watch our car pass down the hill to the road. What does Claire think we are plotting? What *are* we plotting?

Says Helen, when the car is out of sight, "She's terribly sweet."

"And I'm a 'nice man,'" I say.

"I'm sorry if I upset your friend by coming here. I didn't mean to."

"She'll be all right. She's a strong girl."

"And I mean you no harm. That isn't why I wanted to see you." I am silent.

"I did mean you harm once, that's true," she says.

"You weren't solely responsible for the misery."

"What you did to me you did without wanting to; you did because you were provoked. But I think now that I actually set out to torture you."

"You're rewriting history, Helen. It's not necessary. We tormented each other, all right, but it wasn't out of malice. It was confusion, and it was ignorance, and it was other things too, but had it been malice, we wouldn't have been together for very long."

"I used to burn that fucking toast on purpose."

"As I remember, it was the fucking eggs that were burned. The fucking toast never got put in."

"I used to not mail your letters on purpose."

"Why are you saying these things? To castigate yourself, to somehow absolve yourself, or just to try to get a rise out of me? Even if it's true, I don't want to know it. That's all dead."

"I just always hated so the ways that people killed their time. I had this grand life all planned out, you see."

"I remember."

"Well, that's all dead too. Now I take what I can get, and I'm grateful to have it."

"Oh, don't overdo the 'chastened' bit, if that's what this is. Mr. Lowery doesn't sound like the scrapings to me. He doesn't look it, either. He looks like a very forceful person who knows what he's about. He sounds like somebody to conjure with, taking on the Mafia *and* the police. He sounds like a rather courageous man of the world. Just right for you. It certainly looks like he agrees with you."

"Does it?"

"You look terrific," I say—and am sorry I said it. So why then do I add, "You look marvelous."

For the first time since Claire came onto the porch, we fall silent again. We look unflinchingly at one another, as though we are strangers who dare, finally, to stare openly and unambiguously—the prelude to leaping precipitously into the most shameless and exciting copulation. I suppose there is no way we can avoid a little—if not a little more than a little—flirtation. Maybe I ought to say that. And then again, maybe I ought not. Maybe I ought just to look away.

"What were you sick with?" I ask.

"Sick with? It seemed like everything. I must have seen fifty doctors. All I did was sit in waiting rooms and have X-rays taken and blood taken and have cortisone injections and wait around drugstores to have prescriptions filled, and then bolt down the pills, hoping they'd save me on the spot. You should have seen my medicine chest. Instead of Countess Olga's lovely creams and lotions, vials and vials of hideous little pills—and none of them did a thing, except to ruin my stomach. My nose wouldn't stop running for over a year. I sneezed for hours on end, I couldn't breathe, my face puffed up, my eyes itched all the time, and then I began breaking out in horrible rashes. I'd pray when I went to sleep that they'd just go away the way they came, that they'd be gone for good in the morning. One allergist told me to move to Arizona, another told me it wouldn't help because it was all in my head, and another explained in great detail to me how I was allergic to myself, or something very like that, and so I went home and got into bed and pulled the covers over my face and daydreamed about having all the blood drawn out of me and replaced by somebody else's blood, blood I could get through the rest of my life with. I nearly went crazy. Some mornings I wanted to throw myself out the window."

"But you did get better."

"I began seeing Les," Helen says. "That's how it seems to have happened. The ailments all began to subside, one by one. I didn't know how he could bear me. I was hideous."

"Probably not so hideous as you thought. It sounds as though he fell in love with you."

"After I got well I got frightened. I thought that without him I'd start getting sick again. And start drinking again—because somehow he even got me to stop that. I said to him the night he first came to pick me up, looking so strong and cocky and butch, I said, 'Look, Mr. Lowery, I'm thirty-four years old, and I'm sick as a dog, and I don't like to be buggered.' And he said, 'I know how old you are, and everybody gets sick some time, and buggering doesn't interest me.' And so we went out, and he was so marvelously sure of himself, and he fell in love with me—and of course in love with rescuing me. But I didn't love him. And I wanted time and again to be finished with him. Only when it was over, when it should have been over, I got so frightened . . . So we were married."

I don't reply. I look away.

"I'm going to have a baby," she says.

"Congratulations. When?"

"Soon as I can. You see, I don't care any more about being happy. I've given that up. All I care about is not being tortured. I'll do anything. I'll have ten babies, I'll have twenty if he wants them. And he might. There is a man, David, who has no doubts about himself at all. He had a wife and two children even while he was in law school—he was already in the housing business in law school—and now he wants a second family, with me. And I'll do it. What else *can* she do, who was once the world's desire? Own a smart little antique shop? Take a degree and go out and run something? Be one of those fading beauties?"

"If you can't be twenty years old and sailing past the junks at sunset . . . But we have had that discussion. It's no longer my business."

"What about your business? Will you marry Miss Ovington?"

"I might."

"What holds you back?"

I don't answer.

"She's young, she's pretty, she's intelligent, she's educated, and under that robe she seemed quite lovely. And as a bonus there's something childlike and innocent that I certainly never had. Something that knows how to be content, I would think. How do they get that way, do you know? How do they get so *good?* I wondered if she wouldn't be like that. Bright and pretty and good. Leslie is bright and pretty and good. Oh, David, how do you stand it?"

"Because I'm bright and pretty and good myself."

"No, my dear old comrade, not the way they are. They come by it naturally, naïvely. Resist as you will, it's not quite the same, not even for a master repressive like yourself. You're not one of them, and you're not poor Arthur Schonbrunn, either."

I don't reply.

"Doesn't she drive you even a little crazy being so bright and pretty and good?" asks Helen. "With her seashells and her flower bed and her doggie, and her recipes tacked up over the sink?"

"Is this what you came here to tell me, Helen?"

"No. It isn't. Of course it isn't. I didn't come here to say *any* of these things. You're a bright fellow—you know very well why I came. To show you my husband. To show you how I've changed, for the better, of course; and . . . and other assorted lies. I thought I might even fool myself. David, I came here because I wanted to talk to a friend, strange as that may sound right now. I sometimes think of you as the only friend I've got left. I did when I was sick. Isn't that odd? I almost called you one night—but I knew I was none of your business now. You see, I'm pregnant. I want you to tell me something. Tell me what you think I should do. Somebody has to. I'm two months pregnant, and if I wait any longer, well, then I'll have to go ahead and have it. And I can't stand him any more. But then I can't stand anyone. Everything everyone says is somehow wrong and drives me crazy. I don't mean I argue with people. I wouldn't dare. I listen and I nod and I smile. You should see how I please people these days. I listen to Les, and I nod and I smile, and I think I'll die of boredom. There's nothing he does now that doesn't irritate me nearly to death. But I can't be sick alone like that ever again. I couldn't take it. I can take loneliness, and I can take physical misery too, but I can't take them together like that ever again. It was too horrid and too relentless, and I haven't courage any more. I seem to have used it all up; inside me I feel there's no courage left. I have to have this baby. I have to tell him I'm pregnant—and have it. Because if I don't, I don't know what will happen to me. I can't leave him. I'm too terrified to be sick again like that, itching to death, unable to breathe—and it doesn't help to be told it's all in one's head, because that doesn't make it go away. Only he does. Yes, *he* made it all go away! Oh, this is all so crazy. None of this had to be! Because if that wife of Jimmy's had been run down when he had it all arranged, that would have been it. I would have had what I wanted. And I wouldn't have thought twice about her, either. Like it or not, that's the truth about me. I wouldn't have had a moment's stinking guilt. I would have been happy. And she would have gotten what she deserved. But instead I was good—and she's made them *both* miserable. I refused to be terrible, and the result is this terrible unhappiness. Each night I toss in my bed with the nightmare of how much I don't love *anybody*."

At last, at long last, I see Lowery coming out of the woods and descending the hill toward the house. He has removed his shirt and is carrying it in his hand. He is a strong and handsome young man, he is a great success in the world, and his presence in her life has somehow restored her to health . . . Only it is Helen's bad luck that she cannot stand him. Still Jimmy—still those dreams of what might and should have been, if only moral repugnance had not intervened.

"Maybe I'll love the baby," she says.

"Maybe you will," I say. "That happens sometimes."

"Then again, I may despise my baby," says Helen, sternly rising to greet her husband. "I would imagine that happens sometimes too."

After they leave—just like the new couple from down the road, with smiles and good wishes all around—I get into my bathing suit and walk the mile along our road to the pond. I have no thoughts and no feelings, I am numb, like someone at the perimeter of a terrible accident or explosion, who gets a brief, startling glimpse of a pool of blood, and then goes on his way, unharmed, to continue with the ordinary activities of the day.

Some small children are playing with shovels and pails at the edge of the pond, overseen by Claire's dog and by a mother's helper, who looks up and says "Hi." The girl is reading, of all things, *Jane Eyre*. Claire's terry-cloth robe is on the rock where we always put our things, and then I locate Claire, sunning herself out on the raft.

When I pull myself up beside her I see that she has been crying.

"I'm sorry I acted like that," she says.

"Don't be, don't be. We were both thrown way off. I don't believe those things can ever work out very well."

She begins to cry again, as noiselessly as it is possible to cry. The first of her tears that I've seen.

"What is it, lovely, what?"

"I feel so lucky. I feel so privileged. I love you. You've become my whole life."

"I have?"

This makes her laugh. "It frightens you a little to hear it. I guess it would. I didn't think it was true, till today. But I've never been happy like this before."

"Clarissa, why are you still so upset? There's no reason to be, is there?"

Turning her face into the raft, she mumbles something about her mother and father.

"I can't hear you, Claire."

"I wanted them to visit."

I'm surprised, but say, "Then invite them."

"I did."

"When was that?"

"It doesn't matter. It's just that I thought—well, I didn't think."

"You wrote them? Explain yourself, please. I'd like to know what's wrong."

"I don't want to go into it. It was foolish and dreamy. I lost my head a little."

"You telephoned them."

"Yes."

"When?"

"Before."

"You mean after you left the house? Before you came down here?"

"Down in town, yes."

"And?"

"I should never phone them without warning. I never do. It never works and it never will. But at night when we're having dinner, when we're so content and everything is so peaceful and lovely, I always start to think about them. I put on a record, and start cooking dinner, and there they are."

I hadn't known. She never speaks of what she does not have, never lingers for so much as a moment upon loss, misfortune, or disappointment. You'd have to torture her to get her to complain. She is the most extraordinary ordinary person I have ever known.

"Oh," she says, pushing up to a sitting position, "oh, this day will be fine when it's over. Do you have any idea when that will be?"

"Claire, do you want to stay out here with me, or do you want to be alone, or do you want to swim, or do you want to come home and have some iced tea and a little rest?"

"They're gone?"

"Oh, they're gone."

"And you're all right?"

"I'm intact. An hour or so older, but intact."

"How was it?"

"Not all that pleasant. You didn't take to her, I know, but the woman is in a bad way . . . Look, we don't have to talk about this now. We don't have to talk about it ever. Do you want to go home?"

"Not just yet," says Claire. She dives off the edge of the raft, remains out of sight for a long count of ten, and then surfaces by the ladder. When she sits back down beside me, she says, "There's one thing we'd better talk about now. One more thing I had better say. I was pregnant. I wasn't going to tell you, but I will."

"Pregnant by whom? When?"

A wan smile. "In Europe, love. By you. I found out for sure when we got home. I had an abortion. Those meetings I went to—well, I went to the hospital for the day."

"And the 'infection'?"

"I didn't have an infection."

Helen is two months pregnant, and I am the only person who knows. Claire has been pregnant, by me, and I've known nothing. I sense something very sad, all right, at the bottom of this day's confidences and secrets, but what it is I am too weak right now to fathom. Indeed, worn down more than I had thought from all that has surrounded Helen's visit, I am ready to think it is something about me that makes for the sadness; about how I have always failed to be what people want or expect; how I have never quite pleased anyone, including myself; how, hard as I have tried, I have seemed never quite able to be one thing or the other, and probably never will be . . . "Why did you do this alone?" I ask her. "Why didn't you tell me?"

"Well, it was just at the moment you were letting yourself go, and I thought that had to happen by itself. You were surrendering to something, and it always had to be clear to both of us exactly what it was. Is *that* clear?"

"But you did want to have it."

"The abortion?"

"No, the child."

"I want to have a child, of course. I want to have one with you—I can't imagine having anyone else's. But not until you're ready to with me."

"And when did you do all this, Claire? How could I *not* know it?"

"Oh, I managed," she says. "David, the point is that I wouldn't even *want* you to want it until you know for certain that it's me and my ways and this life that you can be content with. I don't want to make anybody unhappy. I don't want to cause anyone pain. I never want to be anyone's prison. That is the worst fate I can imagine. Please, let me just say what I have to—you don't have to say anything about what you would have said or wouldn't have said had I told you what I was doing. I didn't want any of the responsibility to be yours; and it isn't; it can't be. If a mistake was made, then I made it. Right now I just want to say certain things to you, and I want you to hear them, and then we'll go home and I'll start supper."

"I'm listening to you."

"Sweetheart, I wasn't jealous of her; far from it. I'm pretty enough, and I'm young, and thank God, I'm not 'tough' or 'worldly,' if that's what that's called. Truly, I wasn't afraid of anything she could do. If I were that uncertain I wouldn't be living here. I did get confused a little when you wanted to shoo me out of the way, but I came back to the house only to get my camera. I was going to take some pictures of the two of them together. All in all, I thought it was as good a way to get through that visit as any. But when I saw you sitting alone with her, I suddenly thought, 'I can't make him happy, I won't be able to.' And I wondered suddenly if anyone could. And that stunned me so, I just had to go. I don't know if what I thought was true or not. Maybe you don't either. But maybe you do. It would be agony leaving you right now, but I'm prepared to do it, if it makes sense. And better now than three or four years down the line, when you're absolutely in every breath I draw. It's not what I want, David; it's not anything I am even remotely proposing. Saying these kinds of things you take a terrible risk of being misunderstood, and, please, please, don't misunderstand me. I'm proposing nothing. But if you do think you know the answer to my question, I'd like to be told sometime soon, because if you can't be

truly content with me, then let me just go to the Vineyard. I know I
could get through up there with Olivia until school begins. And
after that I can manage on my own. But I don't want to give myself
any further to something that isn't going to evolve someday into a
family. I never had one that made the least bit of sense, and I want
one that does. I have to have that. I'm not saying tomorrow, or even
the day after tomorrow. But in time that's what I want. Otherwise,
I'd just as soon tear the roots up now, before the job requires a
hacksaw. I'd like us both to get away, if we can, without a bloody
amputation."

Here, though the bright sun has baked her body dry, she shud-
ders from head to foot. "I think that's everything I have the energy
left to say. And you don't have to say a word. I wish you wouldn't,
not just now. Otherwise, this will sound like an ultimatum, and it
isn't. It's a clarification, that's all. I didn't even want to make it, I
thought *time* would make it. But then it's time that just might do
me in. But, please, it doesn't require reassuring sounds to be made
in response. It's just that suddenly everything seemed as though it
might be a terrible delusion. It was so frightening. Please, don't
speak—unless there's something you know that I should know."

"No, there isn't."

"Then let's go home."

And last, my father's visit.

In the letter profusely thanking us for the Labor Day weekend
invitation extended to him on the phone, my father asks if he may
bring a friend along, another widower whom he has grown close to
in recent months and whom he says he wants me in particular to
meet. He must by now have discarded or used up the paper and
envelopes bearing the name of the hotel, for the request is written
on the back of stationery imprinted at the top with the words JEW-
ISH FEDERATION OF NASSAU COUNTY. Imprinted beneath is a brief,
pointed epistle to the Jews whose style is as easily recognizable to
me as Hemingway's or Faulkner's.

Dear

I am enclosing your pledge card from the Jewish Federation of
Nassau County. I, as a Jew, am making a personal appeal. There is

no need to recite our commitment to maintain a Jewish homeland. We need the financial aid of every Jew.

Never again must we allow a holocaust! No Jew can be apathetic!

I beg of you, please help. *Give before it hurts.*

> Sincerely,
> Abe Kepesh
> Garfield Garden Apartments
> Co-Chairman

On the reverse side is his letter to Claire and myself, written with a ball-point pen and in his oversized scrawl, though no less revealing than the printed message calling for Jewish solidarity (in those childlike hieroglyphics, all the more revealing) of the fanatically lavish loyalties that, now, in his old age, cause him to be afflicted throughout the waking day with the dull ache and shooting pain of wild sentiment ensnared.

The morning we get his letter I telephone him at my Uncle Larry's office to tell him that if he does not mind sharing our smallish guest room with his friend Mr. Barbatnik, he is of course welcome to bring him along.

"I hate like hell to leave him here alone on a holiday, Davey, that's the only thing. Otherwise I wouldn't bother you. See, I just didn't think it through," he explains, "when I rushed to say yes so quick like that. Only it's got to be no inconvenience for Claire, if he comes. I don't want to burden her, not with school starting up, not with all the work she must have to do to get ready."

"Oh, she's ready, don't worry about that," and I hand the phone over to Claire, who assures him that her school preparations were finished long ago and that it will be a pleasure to entertain the two of them for the weekend.

"He's a wonderful, wonderful man," my father quickly assures her, as though we actually have reason to suspect that a friend of his might turn out to be a rummy or a bum, "somebody who has been through things you wouldn't believe. He works with me when I go collecting for the UJA. And, I tell you, I need him. I need a hand grenade. Try to get money out of people. Try to get *feelings* out of people and see where you wind up. You tell them that what happened to the Jews must never happen again, and they look at

you like they never heard of it. Like Hitler and pogroms are something I am making up in order to fleece them out of their municipal
bonds. We got one guy in the building across the way, a brand-new
widower three years older than me, who already made himself his
bundle years ago in the bootleg business and God only knows what
else, and you should get a load of him since his wife passed away—
a new chippie on his arm every month. Dresses them up in expen-
sive clothes, takes them in to see Broadway shows, wouldn't be
caught dead driving them to the beauty parlor in anything but a
Fleetwood Caddie, but just try to ask him for a hundred dollars for
the UJA and he is practically in tears telling you how bad he has
been hit on the market. It's a good thing I can control my temper.
And between you and me, half the time I can't, and it is Mr. Barbatnik who has to call me off before I tell this s.o.b. just what I
think of him. Oh, this one guy, he really gets my goat. Every time I
leave him I have to go get a phenobarb from my sister-in-law. And
I'm somebody who don't even believe in an aspirin."

"Mr. Kepesh," Claire says, "please feel free to bring Mr. Barbatnik with you."

But he will not say yes until he has extracted a promise that if
they both come she will not think that she has to cook them three
meals a day. "I want a guarantee that you are going to pretend that
we're not even there."

"But what fun would that be? Suppose instead I take the easy
way out and just pretend that you are."

"Hey, listen," he says to her, "you sound like a happy girl."

"I am. My cup runneth over."

Even though Claire is holding the phone to her ear across the
kitchen table from me, I clearly hear what comes next. This results
from the fact that my father approaches long-distance com-
munication in much the way that he approaches so many of the rid-
dles that elude his understanding—with the belief that the electrical
waves transmitting his voice may not make it without his whole-
hearted and unstinting support. Without *hard work*.

"God bless you," he calls out to her, "for what you are doing for
my son!"

"Well—" beneath her tan, she has reddened—"well, he's doing
some nice things for me."

"I wouldn't doubt that," my father says. "I'm delighted to hear it.
But still and all he has practically gone out of his way to bring

trouble into his life. Tell me, does he realize how good he has got it with you? He is thirty-four years old, a grown man already, he can't afford any longer to go around wet behind his ears. Claire, does he know enough by now to appreciate what he's got?"

She tries laughing the question off, but he insists on an answer, even if finally he must give it himself. "Losing your bearings no one needs—life is confusing enough. You don't stick a knife in your own gut. But that is just what he did to himself with marrying that glamour girl, all dressed up like Suzie Wong. Oh, about her and those outfits of hers the less said the better. And those French perfumes. Pardon my language, but she smelled like a God damn barber shop. And what was he up to living in that sublet apartment with red walls made out of cloth, and with whatever else went on there, that I will never be able to fathom. I don't even want to think about it. Claire dear, listen to me, you at last are somebody worthwhile. If only you can get him to settle into a real life."

"Oh, my," she says, not a little flustered by all the emotion that is flowing her way, "if it were any more settled around here . . ."

Before she can quite figure out, at the age of twenty-five, how to conclude that sentence, my father is roaring, "Wonderful, wonderful, that is the most wonderful news about him since he finished that fellowship to be a gypsy in Europe and came back on that boat in one piece!"

In the lot behind the general store in town, he steps cautiously down from the high front step of the New York bus, but then, despite the scalding heat—despite his advanced age—*surges* forward, and not toward me, but on the wings of impulse, to the person who is no relation of his quite yet. There were those few evenings when she served him a meal in my new apartment, and then, when I gave my public lecture from *Man in a Shell* in the Scholar Series at the university, it was Claire who escorted him and my aunt and uncle into the library and sat beside him in the little auditorium there, identifying at his request which gentleman was the department chairman and which the dean. Nonetheless, now when he reaches out to embrace her, it is as though she is already pregnant with the first of his grandchildren, as though she is in fact *the* genetrix of all that is most estimable in that elite breed of creatures to which he is joined by blood and for which his admiration is overbrimming . . . if and when, that is, the membership does not go around shame-

lessly showing its fangs and its claws and leaving my father fit to
be tied.

Seeing Claire swallowed up by this stranger, Dazzle begins leaping crazily around in the dust at his mistress's sandals—and, though
my father has never had all that much trust, or found much to ad-
mire, in members of the animal kingdom who breed out of wedlock
and defecate on the ground, I am surprised to see that Dazzle's display of unabashed dogginess in no way seems to deflect his attention from the girl he is holding in his arms.

At first I do have to wonder if what we are witnessing is not designed in part at least to put Mr. Barbatnik at ease about visiting a
human couple who are not legally wed—if perhaps my father intends, by the very intensity with which he squeezes her body to his,
to put his own not entirely unexpected misgivings on that score to
rest. I cannot remember seeing him so forceful and so animated
since before my mother's illness. In fact, he strikes me as a little
nuts today. But that is still better than what I expected. Usually
when I call each week there is, in just about every upbeat thing he
says, a melancholy strain so transparent that I wonder how he finds
the wherewithal to keep going on, as he will, about how all is well,
wonderful, couldn't be better. The somber "Yeah, hello?" with
which he answers the phone is quite enough to inform me of what
underlies his "active" days—the mornings helping my uncle in his
office where my uncle needs no help; the afternoons at the Jewish
Center arguing politics with the "fascists" in the steam room, men
whom he refers to as Von Epstein, and Von Haberman, and Von
Lipschitz—the local Goering, Goebbels, and Streicher, apparently,
who give him palpitations of the heart; and then those interminable
evenings soliciting at his neighbors' doors for his various philan-
thropies and causes, reading again column by column through
Newsday, the *Post*, and the *Times*, watching the CBS News for the
second time in four hours, and finally, in bed and unable to sleep,
spreading the letters from his cardboard file box over the blanket
and reviewing his correspondence with his vanished, cherished
guests. In some cases more cherished, it seems to me, now that they
have vanished, than when they were around and there was too little barley in the soup, too much chlorine in the pool, and never
enough waiters in the dining room.

His letter writing. With each passing month it is getting harder
for him to keep track of who among the hundreds and hundreds of

old-timers is retired and in Florida, and thus capable still of writing him back, and who is dead. And it isn't a matter of losing his faculties, either—it's losing all those friends, "non-stop," as he graphically describes the decimation that occurred in the ranks of his former clientele during just this last year. "I wrote five full pages of news to that dear and lovely prince of a man, Julius Lowenthal. I even put in a clipping that I've been saving up from the *Times* about how they ruined the river over in Paterson where he had his law practice. I figured it would be interesting to him down there—this pollution business was made to order for the kind of man he was. I tell you"—pointing a finger—"Julius Lowenthal was one of the most civic-minded people you could ever want to meet. The synagogue, orphans, sports, the handicapped, colored people—he gave of his time to everything. That man was the genuine article, the *best*. Well, you know what's coming. I stamp and seal the envelope and put it by my hat to take to mail in the morning, and not until I brush my teeth and get into bed and turn out the light does it dawn on me that my dear old friend is gone now since last fall. I have been thinking about him playing cards alongside a swimming pool in Miami—playing pinochle the way only he could play with that legal mind of his—and in actuality he is underground. What is even left of him by now?" That last thought is too much, even for him, especially for him, and he moves his hand angrily past his face, as though to shoo away, like a mosquito that is driving him crazy, this terrible, startling image of Julius Lowenthal decomposing. "And, unbelievable as it may sound to a young person," he says, recovering most of his equilibrium, "this is actually becoming a weekly occurrence, right down to licking the envelope and pasting on the stamp."

It will be hours before Claire and I are finally alone together, and she is able at last to unburden herself of the enigmatic decree issued by him into her ear while we four stood grouped in the fumy wake of the departed bus. The sun is softening us like so much macadam; poor confused Dazzle (barely grown accustomed to this rival) continues carrying on in the air around my father's feet; and Mr. Barbatnik—a short leprechaunish gentleman, with a large, long-eared Asian face, and astonishing scoop-like hands suspended from powerful forearms mapped with a body builder's veins—Mr. Barbatnik hangs back, as shy as a schoolgirl, his jacket folded neatly over his arm, waiting for this living, throbbing valentine, my father, to make the introductions. But my father has urgent business to set-tle first—like the messenger in a classical tragedy, immediately as he comes upon the stage he blurts out what he has traveled all this way to say. "Young woman," he whispers to Claire, for so it would seem he has been envisioning her, allegorically, as all that and only that, "young woman," commands my father out of the power vested in him by his daydreams—"don't let—don't let—please!"

These, she tells me at bedtime, were the only words that she could hear, pinned as she was against his massive chest; most likely, I say, because these are the only words he uttered. For him, at this point, they say it all.

And having thus ordained the future, if only for the moment, he is ready now to move on to the next event in the arrival ceremonies he must have been planning now for weeks. He reaches into the pocket of the nubby linen jacket slung across *his* arm—and ap-parently finds nothing. Suddenly he is slapping at the lining of the jacket as though performing resuscitation upon it. "Oh Christ," he moans, "it's lost. My God, it's on the bus!" Whereupon Mr. Barbat-nik edges forward and, as discreetly as a best man to a half-dazed bridegroom, says in a soft voice, "Your pants, Abe." "Of course," my father snaps back, and reaching (still with a little desperation in the eyes) into the pocket of his houndstooth trousers—he is dressed, as they say, to the nines—extracts a small packet that he places in Claire's palm. And now he is beaming.

"I didn't tell you on the phone," he says to her, "so it would come as a total surprise. Every year you hold on to it I guarantee it will go up in value ten percent at least. Probably fifteen, and maybe more. It's better than money. And wait till you see the won-derful skill that goes into it. It's fantastic. Go ahead. Open it up."

So, while we all continue to cook away in the parking lot, my affable mate, who knows how to please, and loves pleasing, deftly unties the ribbon and removes the shiny yellow wrapping paper, not failing to remark upon its prettiness. "I picked that out too," my father tells her. "I thought that color would be up your alley—didn't I, Sol," he says, turning to his companion, "didn't I say I'll bet she's a girl who likes yellow?"

Claire takes from its velvet-lined case a small sterling-silver pa-perweight engraved with a bouquet of roses.

"David told me how hard you work in the garden you made, and

the way you love all the flowers. Take it, please. You can use it on
your desk at school. Wait till your pupils see it."

"It's beautiful," she says, and calming Dazzle with just a glance,
kisses my father on the cheek.

"Look at the handiwork," he says. "You can even see the little
thorns. Some person actually did that, by hand. An artist."

"It's lovely, it's a lovely gift," she says.

And only now does he turn and embrace me. "I got you something too," he says. "It's in my bag."

"You hope," I say.

"Wise guy," and *we* kiss.

At last he is ready to introduce his companion, dressed, I
now realize, in the same spanking-new, color-coordinated outfit, except where my father is in shades of tan and brown, Mr. Barbatnik
wears silver and blue.

"Thank God for this man," my father says as we drive slowly out
of town behind a farmer's pickup truck bearing a bumper sticker
informing the other motorists that ONLY LOVE BEATS MILK. The
bumper sticker on our car, affixed by Claire in sympathy with the
local ecologists, reads DIRT ROADS ARE DOWN TO EARTH.

Excited and garrulous as a small boy—much as *I* used to be when
he was doing the driving around these roads—my father cannot
stop talking now about Mr. Barbatnik: one in a million, the finest
person he has ever known . . . Mr. Barbatnik, meanwhile, sits
quietly beside him, looking into his lap, as humbled, I think, by
Claire's buoyant, summery fullness as by the fact that my father is
selling him to us much the way, in the good old days, he used to
sell the life-lengthening benefits of a summer in our hotel.

"Mr. Barbatnik is the guy who I tell you about from the Center.
If it wasn't for him, I would absolutely be a voice in the wilderness
there about that son of a bitch George Wallace. Claire, pardon me,
please, but I hate that lousy cockroach with a passion. You
shouldn't have to ever hear the kinds of things so-called decent
people think in their private thoughts. It's a disgrace. Only Mr. Barbatnik and me, we make a team, and we give it to them, but good."

"Not," says Mr. Barbatnik philosophically, in heavily accented
English, "that it makes much difference."

"And, tell me, what could make a difference with those ignorant
bigots? At least let them hear what someone else thinks of them!
Jewish people so full of hatred that they go out and vote for a

George Wallace—it's beyond me. *Why?* People who have lived and seen a whole lifetime as a minority, and the suggestion that they make in all seriousness is that they ought to line up the colored in front of machine guns and let them have it. Take actual people and mow them down."

"This of course isn't everybody that says that," Mr. Barbatnik puts in. "This is just one particular person, of course."

"I tell them, look at Mr. Barbatnik—ask him if that isn't the same thing that Hitler did with the Jews. And you know what their answer is, grown men who have raised families and run successful businesses and live in retirement now in condominiums like supposed civilized people? They say, 'How can you compare niggers with Jews?'"

"What's eating this particular person, and the group that he is the leader of—"

"And who appointed him leader, by the way? Of anything? Himself! Go ahead, Sol, I'm sorry. I just wanted to make clear to them what kind of a little dictator we're dealing with."

"What's eating them," Mr. Barbatnik says, "is that they owned homes, some of them, and businesses, and then came the colored, and when they tried to get out what they put in, they took a licking."

"Of course it's all economics when you get down to it. It always is. Wasn't it the same with the Germans? Wasn't it the same in Poland?" Here, abruptly, he breaks off his historical analysis to say to Claire and me, "Mr. Barbatnik only got here after the war." Dramatically, and yes, with pride, he adds, "He is a victim of the Nazis."

When we turn in the drive and I point out the house halfway up the hillside, Mr. Barbatnik says, "No wonder you look so happy, you two."

"They rent it," my father says. "I told him, he likes it so much, why don't he buy it? Make the guy an offer. Tell him you'll pay him cash. At least see if you get a nibble."

"Well," I say, "we're happy enough renting for now."

"Renting is throwing money down the drain. Find out from him, will you? What can it hurt? Cash on the barrelhead, see if he bites. I can help you out, Uncle Larry can help you out, as far as that goes, if it's a straight money deal that he's after. But definitely you ought to own a little piece of property at your stage of the game.

And up here, you can't miss, that's for sure. You never could. In my time, Claire, you could buy a little place like this for under five thousand. Today that little house and—and how far does the property go? To the tree line? All right, say four, say five acres—"

Up the dirt drive and in through the kitchen door—and right past the blooming garden he has heard so much about—he continues with his realtor's spiel, so delighted is the man to be back home in Sullivan County, and with his only living loved one, who by all outward appearances seems finally to have been plucked from his furnace and plunked down before the hearth.

Inside the house, before we can even offer a cold drink, or show them to their room or to the toilet, my father begins to unpack his bag on the kitchen table. "*Your* present," he announces to me.

We wait. His shoes come out. His freshly laundered shirts. His shiny new shaving kit.

My present is an album bound in black leather containing thirty-two medallions the size of silver dollars, each in its own circular cavity and protected on both sides by a transparent acetate window. He calls them "Shakespeare Medals"—a scene from one of the plays is depicted on the face side, and on the other, in tiny script, a quotation from the play is inscribed. The medals are accompanied by instructions for placing them in the album. The first instruction begins, "Put on a pair of lint-free gloves . . ." My father hands me the gloves last of all. "Always wear the gloves when you handle the medals," he tells me. "They come with the set. Otherwise, they say that there can be harmful chemical effects to the medals from being touched by human skin."

"Oh, this is nice of you," I say. "Though I don't quite know why now, such an elaborate gift—"

"Why? Because it's time," he answers, with a laugh, and, too, with a wide gesture that encompasses all the kitchen appliances. "Look, Davey, what they engrave for you. Claire, look at the outside."

Centered within the arabesque design that is embossed in silver and serves as a border to the album's funereal cover are three lines, which my father points out to us, word by word, with his index finger. We all read the words in silence—all except him.

FIRST EDITION STERLING SILVER PROOF SET
MINTED FOR THE PERSONAL COLLECTION OF
PROFESSOR DAVID KEPESH

I don't know what to say. I say, "This must have cost an awful lot. It's really something."

"Isn't it? But, no, the cost don't hurt, not the way they set it up. You just collect one medal a month, to begin with. You start off with *Romeo and Juliet*—wait'll I show Claire *Romeo and Juliet*— and you work your way up from there, till you've got them all. I've been saving for you all this time. The only one who knew was Mr. Barbatnik. Look, Claire, come here, you gotta look up close—"

It is a while before they can locate the medallion depicting *Romeo and Juliet*, for in its designated slot in the lower left-hand corner of the page labeled "Tragedies" it seems he has placed *Two Gentlemen from Verona*. "Where the hell is *Romeo and Juliet?*" he asks. The four of us are able to discover it finally under "Histories" in the slot marked *The Life and Death of King John*. "But then where did I put *The Life and Death of King John?*" he asks. "I thought I got 'em all in right, Sol," he says to Mr. Barbatnik, frowning. "I thought we checked." Mr. Barbatnik nods—they did. "Anyway," says my father, "the point is—what was the point? Oh, the *back*. Here, I want Claire to read what it says on the back, so everyone can hear. Read this, dear."

Claire reads aloud the inscription: "'. . . and a rose by any other name would smell as sweet.' *Romeo and Juliet*, Act Two, Scene Two."

"Isn't that something?" he says to her.

"Yes."

"And he can take it to school, too, you see. That's what's so useful. It's something not just for the home, but that he can have ten and twenty years from now to show his classes. And just like yours, it is sterling silver, and something that I guarantee will keep abreast of the inflation, and long after paper money is as good as worthless. Where will you put it?" This last asked of Claire, not me.

"For now," she says, "on the coffee table, so people can see. Come into the living room, everybody; we'll put it there."

"Wonderful," says my father. "Only remember, don't let your company take the medals out, unless they put on the gloves."

Lunch is served on the screened-in porch. The recipe for the cold beet soup Claire found in *Russian Cooking*, one of her dozen or so manuals in a Time-Life series on "Foods of the World" shelved neatly between the radio—whose dial seems set to play only Bach— and the wall hung with two of her sister's calm watercolors of the ocean and the dunes. The cucumber and yogurt salad, heavily flavored with crushed garlic and fresh mint from the herb garden just beyond the screen door, is out of the same set, the volume on the cuisine of the Middle East. The cold roast chicken seasoned with rosemary is a long-standing recipe of her own.

"My God," says my father, "what a spread!" "Excellent," says Mr. Barbatnik. "Gentlemen, thank you," says Claire, "but I'll bet you've had better." "Not even in Lvov, when my mother was cooking," says Mr. Barbatnik, "have I tasted such a wonderful borscht." Says Claire, smiling, "I suspect that's a little extravagant, but thank you, again." "Listen, my dear girl," says my father, "if I had you in the kitchen, I'd still be in my old line. And you'd get more than you get being a schoolteacher, believe me. A good chef, even in the old days, even in the middle of the Depression—"

But in the end Claire's biggest hit is not the exotic Eastern dishes which, in her Clairish way, she has tried today for the first time in the hope of making everybody—herself included—feel instantaneously at home together, but the hearty iced tea she brews with mint leaves and orange rinds according to her grandmother's recipe. My father cannot seem to get enough, cannot stop praising it to the skies, not after he has learned over the blueberries that Claire takes the bus to Schenectady every month to visit this ninety-year-old woman from whom she learned everything she knows about preparing a meal and growing a garden, and probably about raising a child too. Yes, it looks from the girl as though his renegade son has decided to go straight, and in a very big way.

After lunch I suggest to the two men that they might like to rest until the heat has abated somewhat and we can go for a little walk along the road. Absolutely not. What am I even talking about? As soon as we digest our food, my father says, we must drive over to the hotel. This surprises me, as it surprised me a little at lunch to hear him speak so easily about his "old line." Since moving to Long Island a year and a half ago, he has shown no interest whatsoever in seeing what two successive owners have made of his hotel, barely hanging on now as the Royal Ski and Summer Lodge. I had thought he would be just as happy staying away, but in fact he is boiling over again with enthusiasm, and after a visit to the toilet, is pacing the porch, waiting for Mr. Barbatnik to awaken from the little snooze he is enjoying in my wicker easy chair.

What if he should drop dead from all this fervor in his heart?

And before I have married the devoted girl, bought the cozy house, raised the handsome children . . .

Then what am I waiting for? If later, why not now, so he too can be happy and count his life a success?

What am I waiting for?

Down the main drag and through every last store still there and open for business my father leads the three of us, he alone seemingly oblivious to the terrific heat. "I can remember when there were four butchers, three barbershops, a bowling alley, three produce markets, two bakeries, an A&P, three doctors, and three dentists. And now, look," he says—and without chagrin; rather with the proud sagacity of one who imagines he actually knew to get out when the getting was good—"no butchers, no barbers, no bowling alley, just one bakery, no A&P, and unless things have changed since I left, no dentists and only one doctor. Yes," he announces, avuncular now, taking the overview, sounding a little like his friend Walter Cronkite, "the old, opulent hotel era is over—but it was something! You should have seen this place in summertime! You know who used to vacation here? You name it! The Herring King! The Apple King!—" And to Mr. Barbatnik and to Claire (who does not let on that she already made this same sentimental journey some weeks ago at the side of his son, who had explained at the time just what a herring king *was*) he begins a rapid-fire anecdotal history of his life's major boulevard, foot by foot, year by year, from Roosevelt's inauguration right on up through L.B.J. Putting an arm around his sopping half-sleeve shirt, I say, "I bet if you set your mind to it you could go back before the Flood." He likes that—yes, he likes just about everything today. "Oh, could I! This is some treat! This is *really* Memory Lane!" "It's awfully hot, Dad," I warn him. "It's nearly ninety degrees. Maybe if we slow down—" "Slow *down?*" he cries, and showing off, pulls Claire along on his arm as he breaks into a crazy little trot down the street. Mr. Barbatnik smiles, and mopping his brow with his handkerchief, says to me, "He's been hoping a long time."

"Labor Day weekend!" my father announces brightly as I swing into the lot next to the service entrance of the "main building." Aside from the parking lot, which has been resurfaced, and the tumescent pink the buildings have all been painted, little else seems to have been changed as yet, except of course for the hotel's name. In charge now are a worried fellow only a little older than myself and his youngish, charmless second wife. I met them briefly on the afternoon in June when I came down with Claire to conduct my own nostalgic tour. But there is no nostalgia for the good old days in these two, no more than those clutching at the debris in a swollen stream are able to feel for the golden age of the birch-bark canoe. When my father, having sized up the situation, asks how come no full house for the holiday—a phenomenon utterly unknown to him, as he quickly makes only too clear—the wife goes more bull-doggish even than before, and the husband, a hefty boyish type with pale eyes and pocked skin and a dazed, friendly expression—a nice, well-meaning fellow whose creditors, however, are probably not that impressed by plans extending into the twenty-first century —explains that they have not as yet been able to fix an "image" in the public mind. "You see," he says uncertainly, "right now we're still modernizing the kitchen—"

The wife interrupts to set the record straight: young people are put off because they think it is a hotel for the older generation (for which, it would seem from her tone, my father is to blame), and the family crowd is frightened away because the fellow to whom my father sold out—and who couldn't pay his bills by August of his first and only summer as proprietor—was nothing but a "two-bit Hugh Hefner" who tried to build a clientele out of "riffraff, and worse."

"Number one," says my father before I can grab an arm and steer him away, "the biggest mistake was to change the name, to take thirty years of good will and wipe it right off the map. Paint outside whatever color you want, though what was wrong with a nice clean white I don't understand—but if that's your taste, that's your taste. But the point is, does Niagara Falls change its name? Not if they want the tourist trade they don't." The wife has to laugh in his face, or so she says: "I have to laugh in your face." "You what? Why?" my outraged father replies. "Because you can't call a hotel the Hungarian Royale in this day and age and expect the line to form on the right, you know." "No, no," says the husband, trying to soften her words, and meanwhile working two Maalox tablets out of their silver wrapping, "the problem is, Janet, we are caught between life-styles, and that is what we have to iron out. I'm sure, as soon as we finish up with the kitchen—" "My friend, forget about the kitchen," says my father, turning noticeably away from the wife and toward someone with whom a human being can at least have a decent conversation; "do yourself a favor and change back the name. That is half of what you paid for. Why do you want to use in the name a word like 'ski' anyway? Stay open all winter if you think there's something in it—but why use a word that can only scare away the kind of people who make a place like this a going proposition?" The wife: "I have news for you. Nobody wants today to take a vacation in a place that sounds like a mausoleum." Period. "Oh," says my father, revving up his sarcasm, "oh, the past dies these days, does it?" And launches into a solemn, disjointed philosophical monologue about the integral relationship of past, present, and future, as though a man who has survived to sixty-six *must* know whereof he speaks, is *obliged* to be sagacious with those who follow after—especially when they seem to look upon him as the begetter of their woes.

I wait to intercede, or call an ambulance. From seeing his life's work mismanaged so by this deadbeat husband and his dour little wife, will my overwrought father burst into tears, or keel over, a corpse? The one—once again—seems no less possible to me than the other.

Why am I convinced that during the course of this weekend he is going to die, that by Monday I will be a parentless son?

He is still going strong—still going a little crazy—when we climb into the car to head home. "How did I know he was going to turn out to be a hippie?" "Who's that?" I ask. "That guy who bought us out after we lost Mother. You think I would have sold to a hippie, out of my own free will? The man was a fifty-year-old man. So what if he had long hair? What am I, a hard-hat, that I hold something like that against him? And what the hell did she mean by 'riffraff' anyway? She didn't mean what I think she meant, did she? Or did she?" I say, "She only meant that they are going under fast and it hurts. Look, she is obviously a sour little pain in the ass, but failing is still failing." "Yeah, but why blame *me?* I gave these people the last of the golden geese, I gave them a good solid tradition and a loyal clientele that all they had to do was stick to what was *there*. That was *all*, Davey! 'Ski!' That's all my customers have to hear, and they run like hell. Ah, some people, they can start a hotel in the Sahara and make a go of it, and others can start in the best of circumstances and they lose everything." "That's true," I say. "Now I look back in wonder that I myself could ever accomplish so much. A nobody like me, from nowhere! I started out, Claire, I was a short-order cook. My hair was black then, like his, and thick too, if you can believe it—"

Beside him Mr. Barbatnik's sleeping head is twisted to one side, as though he has been garrotted. Claire, however—amiable, tolerant, generous, and willing Claire—continues to smile and to nod yes-yes-yes as she follows the story of our inn and how it flourished under the loving care of this industrious, gracious, shrewd, slave-driving, and dynamic nobody. Is there a man alive, I wonder, who has led a more exemplary life? Is there an ounce of anything that he has withheld in the performance of his duties? Of what then does he believe himself to be so culpable? My derelictions, my sins? Oh, if only he would cut the summation short, the jury would announce "Innocent as a babe!" without even retiring from the courtroom.

Only he can't. Into the early evening his plea streams forth unabated. First he follows Claire around the kitchen while she prepares the salad and the dessert. When she retires to shower and to change for dinner—and to rally her forces—he comes out to where I am preparing to cook the steak on the grill behind the house. "Hey, did I tell you who I got an invitation to his daughter's wedding? You won't guess in a million years. I had to go over to Hempstead to get her blender fixed for your aunt—you know, the jar there, the top—and who do you think owns the appliance store that services now for Waring? You'll never guess, if you even remember him." But I do. It is my conjurer. "Herbie Bratasky," I say. "That's right! Did I tell you already?" "No." "But that's who it was—and can you believe it, that skinny *paskudnyak* grew up into a person and he is doing terrific. He's got Waring, he's got G.E., and now, he tells me, he is getting himself in with some Japanese company, bigger even than Sony, to be the sole Long Island distributor. And the daughter is a little doll. He showed me her picture—and then out of the blue two days ago I get this beautiful invitation in the mail. I meant to bring it, damn it, but I guess I forgot because I was already packed." Already packed two days ago. "I'll send it," he says; "you'll get a real kick out of it. Look, I was thinking, it's just a thought, but how would you and Claire like to come with me—to the wedding? That would be some surprise for Herbie." "Well, let's think about it. What does Herbie look like these days? What is he now, in his forties?" "Oh, he's gotta be forty-five, forty-six, easy. But still a dynamo—and as sharp and good-looking as he was when

he was a kid. He ain't got a pound on him, and still with all his hair
—in fact, so much, I thought maybe it was a rug. Maybe it was,
come to think of it. And still with that tan. What do you think of
that? Must use a lamp. And, Davey, he's got a little boy, just like
him, who plays *drums!* I told him about you, of course, and he says
he already knew. He read about when you gave your speech at the
school; he saw it in the *Newsday* calendar of what's happening
around the area. He said he told all his customers. So how do you
like that? Herbie Bratasky. How did you know?" "I took a guess."
"Well, you were right. You're psychic, kiddo. Whew, that's some
beautiful piece of meat. What are you paying up here by the
pound? Years ago, a sirloin cut like that—" And I want to enfold
him in my arms, bring his unstoppable mouth to my chest, and say,
"It's okay, you're here for good, you never have to leave." But in
fact we all must depart in something less than a hundred hours.
And—until death do us part—the tremendous closeness and the tremendous distance between my father and myself will have to continue in the same perplexing proportions as have existed all our
lives.

When Claire comes back down to the kitchen, he leaves me to
watch the coals heat up, and goes into the house "to see how beautiful she looks." "Calm down . . ." I call after him, but I might as
well be asking a kid to calm down the first time he walks into Yankee Stadium.

My Yankee puts him to work shucking the corn. But of course
you can shuck corn and still talk. On the cork bulletin board she
has hung over the sink, Claire has tacked up, along with recipes
out of the *Times,* some photographs just sent her from Martha's
Vineyard by Olivia. I hear them through the kitchen's screen door
discussing Olivia's children.

Alone again, and with time yet before the steak goes on, I at last
get around to opening the envelope forwarded to me from my box
at the university, and carried around in my back pocket since we
went into town hours ago to pick up the mail and our guests. I
hadn't bothered to open it, since it wasn't the letter I have been expecting daily now, from the university press to which I submitted
Man in a Shell, in its final revised version, upon our return from
Europe. No, it is a letter from the Department of English at Texas
Christian University, and it provides the first truly light moment of

the day. Oh, Baumgarten, you are a droll and devilish fellow, all right.

Dear Professor Kepesh:

Mr. Ralph Baumgarten, a candidate for the position of Writer in Residence at Texas Christian University, has submitted your name as an individual who is familiar with his work. I am reluctant to impose on your busy schedule, but would be most grateful if you would send me, at your earliest convenience, a letter in which you set forth your views on his writing, his teaching, and on his moral character. You may be assured that your comments will be held in the very strictest confidence.

I am most grateful for your help.

> Cordially yours,
> John Fairbairn
> Chairman

Dear Professor Fairbairn, Perhaps you would like my opinion of the wind as well, whose work I am also familiar with . . . I stick the letter back into my pocket and put on the steak. *Dear Professor Fairbairn, I cannot help but believe that your students' horizons will be enormously enlarged and their sense of life's possibilities vastly enriched* . . . And who next, I wonder. When I sit down at my place for dinner, will there be an extra plate at the table for Birgitta, or will she prefer to eat beside me, on her knees?

I hear from the kitchen that Claire and my father have got around finally to discussing her parents. "But *why?*" I hear him ask. From his tone I can tell that whatever the question, the answer is not unknown to him, but rather, wholly incompatible with his own passionate meliorism. Claire replies, "Because they probably never belonged together in the first place." "But two beautiful daughters; they themselves college-educated people; the two of them with excellent executive positions. I don't get it. And the drinking: *why?* Where does it get you? With all due respect, it seems to me stupid. I myself of course never had the advantages of an education. If I had—but I didn't, and that was that. But my mother, let me tell you, I just have to remember her to get a good feeling about the whole world. What a woman! Ma, I would say to her, what are you doing on the floor again? Larry and I will give you the money, you'll get somebody else in to wash the floors. But no—"

It is during dinner that, at last, in Chekhov's phrase, the angel of silence passes over him. But only to be followed quickly by the shade of melancholia. Is he teetering now at the brink of tears, having spoken and spoken and spoken and still not having *quite* said it? Is he at last about to break down and cry—or am I ascribing to him the mood claiming me? Why should I feel as though I have lost a bloody battle when clearly I have won?

We eat again on the screened-in porch, where, during the days previous, I have been making every effort, with pen and pad, to speak *my* it. Beeswax candles are burning invisibly down in the antique pewter holders; the bayberry candles, arrived by mail from the Vineyard, drip wax threads onto the table. Candles burn everywhere you look—Claire has a passion for them on the porch at night; they are probably her only extravagance. Earlier, when she went around from holder to holder with a book of matches, my father—already at the table with the napkin drawn through his belt—had begun to recite for her the names of the Catskill hotels that had tragically burned to the ground in the last twenty years. Whereupon she had assured him that she would be careful. Still, when a breeze moves lightly over the porch, and the flames all flicker, he looks around to check that nothing has caught fire.

Now we hear the first of the ripe apples dropping onto the grass in the orchard just beyond the house. We hear the hoot of "our" owl—so Claire identifies for our guests this creature we have never seen, and whose home is up in "our" woods. If we are all silent long enough, she tells the two old men—as though they are two children—the deer may come down from the woods to graze around the apple trees. Dazzle has been cautioned about barking and scaring them away. The dog pants a little at the sound of his name from her lips. He is eleven and has been hers since she was a fourteen-year-old high school girl, her dearest pal ever since the year Olivia went off to college, the closest thing to her, until me. Within a few seconds Dazzle is peacefully asleep, and once again there is only the spirited September finale by the tree toads and the crickets, most popular of all the soft summer songs ever heard.

I cannot take my eyes from her face tonight. Between the Old Master etchings of the two pouched and creased and candlelit old men, Claire's face seems, more than ever, so apple-smooth, apple-small, apple-shiny, apple-plain, apple-fresh . . . never more artless and untainted . . . never before *so* . . . Yes, and to what am I willfully blinding myself that in time must set us apart? Why continue to cast this spell over myself, wherein nothing is permitted to sift through except what pleases me? Is there not something a little dubious and dreamy about all this gentle, tender adoration? What will happen when the *rest* of Claire obtrudes? What happens if no "rest of her" is there! And what of the rest of me? How long will *that* be sold a bill of goods? How much longer before I've had a bellyful of wholesome innocence—how long before the lovely blandness of a life with Claire begins to cloy, to pall, and I am out there once again, mourning what I've lost and looking for my way!

And with doubts so long suppressed voiced at last—and in deafening unison—the emotions under whose somber portentousness I have been living out this day forge themselves into something as palpable and awful as a spike. *Only an interim,* I think, and as though I have in fact been stabbed and the strength is gushing out of me, I feel myself about to tumble from my chair. Only an interim. Never to know anything durable. Nothing except my unrelinquishable memories of the discontinuous and the provisional; nothing except this ever-lengthening saga of all that did not work . . .

To be sure, to be sure, Claire is still with me, directly across the table, saying something to my father and Mr. Barbatnik about the planets she will show them later, brilliant tonight among the distant constellations. With her hair pinned up, exposing the vulnerable vertebrae that support the stalk of her slender neck, and in her pale caftan, with its embroidered edging, sewn together early in the summer on the machine, and lending a tiny regal air to her overpowering simplicity, she looks to me more precious than ever, more than ever before like my true wife, my unborn offspring's mother . . . yet I am already bereft of my strength and my hope and my contentment. Though we will go ahead, as planned, and rent the house to use on weekends and school vacations, I am certain that in only a matter of time—that's all it seems to take, just time—what we have together will gradually disappear, and the man now holding in his hand a spoonful of her orange custard will give way to Herbie's pupil, Birgitta's accomplice, Helen's suitor, yes, to Baumgarten's sidekick and defender, to the would-be wayward son and all he hungers for. Or, if not that, the would-be *what?* When this too is gone in its turn, what then?

I can't, for the sake of us all, fall out of a chair at dinner. Yet
once again I am overcome by a terrible physical weakness. I am
afraid to reach for my wineglass for fear that I will not have
sufficient strength to carry it the distance to my mouth.

"How about a record?" I say to Claire.

"That new Bach?"

A record of trio sonatas. We have been listening to it all week.
The week before, it had been a Mozart quartet; the week before
that, the Elgar cello concerto. We just keep turning over one record
again and again and again until finally we have had enough. It is
all one hears coming and going through the house, music that almost seems by now to be the by-product of our comings and go-
ings, compositions exuded by our sense of well-being. All we ever
hear is the most exquisite music.

Seemingly with a good reason, I manage to leave the table before
something frightening happens.

The phonograph and speakers in the living room are Claire's,
carried up from the city in the back seat of the car. So are most of
the records hers. So are the curtains sewed together for the windows, and the corduroy spread she made to cover the battered
daybed, and the two china dogs by the fireplace, which once
belonged to her grandmother and became hers on her twenty-fifth
birthday. As a child on her way home from school she used to stop
and have tea and toast with her grandmother, and practice on the
piano there; then, armed at least with that, she could continue to
the battlefield of her house. On her own she decided to have that
abortion. So I would not be burdened by a duty? So I could choose
her just for herself? But is the notion of duty so utterly horrendous?
Why didn't she tell me she was pregnant? Is there not a point on
life's way when one yields to duty, *welcomes* duty as once one
yielded to pleasure, to passion, to adventure—a time when duty is
the pleasure, rather than pleasure the duty . . .

The exquisite music begins. I return to the porch, not quite so
pale as when I left. I sit back down at the table and sip my wine.
Yes, I can raise and lower a glass. I can focus my thoughts on another subject. I had better.

"Mr. Barbatnik," I say, "my father told us you survived the concentration camps. How did you do it? Do you mind my asking?"

"Professor, please let me say first how much I appreciate your
hospitality to a total stranger. This is the happiest day for me in a

very long time. I thought maybe I even forgot how to be happy with people. I thank you all. I thank my new and dear friend, your wonderful father. It was a beautiful day, and, Miss Ovington—"

"Please call me Claire," she says.

"Claire, you are beyond your years and young and adorable as well. And—and all day I have wanted to give you my deep gratitude. For all the lovey things you think to do for people."

The two elders have been seated to either side of her, the lover directly across: with all the love he can muster, he looks upon the fullness of her saucy body and the smallness of her face above the little vase of asters he plucked for her on his morning walk; with all the love at his command, he watches this munificent female creature, now in the moment of her fullest bloom, offer a hand to their shy guest, who takes it, grasps and squeezes it, and without relinquishing it begins to speak for the first time with ease and self-assurance, at last at home (just as she had planned it, just as she has made it come to pass). And amid all this, the lover does, in fact, feel more deeply implicated in his own life than at any moment in memory—the true self at its truest, moored by every feeling to its own true home! And yet he continues to imagine that he is being drawn away by a force as incontrovertible as gravity, which is no lie either. As though he is a falling body, helpless as any little apple in the orchard which has broken free and is descending toward the alluring earth.

But instead of crying, either in his mother tongue or with some rudimentary animalish howl, "Don't leave me! Don't go! I'll miss you bitterly! This moment, and we four together—this is what should be!" he spoons out the last of his custard and attends to the survival story that he has asked to hear.

"There was a beginning," Mr. Barbatnik is saying, "there has to be an ending. I am going to live to see this monstrosity come to an end. This is what I told myself every single morning and night."

"But how was it they didn't send you to the ovens?"

How do you come to be here, with us? Why is Claire here? Why not Helen and our child? Why not my mother? And in ten years' time . . . who then? To build an intimate life anew, out of nothing, when I am forty-five? To start over again with everything at fifty? To be forever a beweeper of my outcast state? I can't! I won't!

"They couldn't kill everybody," says Mr. Barbatnik. "This I knew. Somebody has to be left, if only one person. And so I would tell myself, this one person will be me. I worked for them in the coal mines where they sent me. With the Poles. I was a young man then, and strong. I worked like it was my own coal mine inherited from my father. I told myself that this was what I wanted to do. I told myself that this work I was doing was for my child. I told myself different things every single day to make it just that I could last till that night. And that's how I lasted. Only when the Russians started coming so quick all of a sudden, the Germans took us and at three in the morning started us off on a march. Days and days and days, until I stopped keeping track. It went on and on, and people dropping every place you looked, and sure, I told myself again that if one is left it is going to be me. But by then I knew somehow that even if I made it to the destination where we were going, when I got there they would shoot whoever of us was left. So this is how come I ran away after weeks and weeks of marching without a stop to wherever in God's name it was. I hid in the woods and at night I came out and the German farmers fed me. Yes, that's true," he says, as he stares down at his large hand, in the candlelight looking very nearly as wide as a spade and as heavy as a crowbar, and enfolding within it Claire's thin, fine fingers with their delicate bones and knuckles. "The individual German, he isn't so bad, you know. But put three Germans together in a room and you can kiss the good world goodbye."

"And then what happened?" I ask, but he continues looking down, as though to contemplate the riddle of this one hand in the other. "How were you saved, Mr. Barbatnik?"

"One night a German farm woman said to me that the Americans are here. I thought she must be lying. I figured, don't come back here to her, she's up to something no good. But the next day I saw a tank through the trees, rolling down the road, with a white star, and I ran out, screaming at the top of my lungs."

Claire says, "You must have looked so strange by then. How did they know who you were?"

"They knew. I wasn't the first one. We were all coming out of our holes. What was left of us. I lost a wife and two parents, my brother, two sisters, and a three-year-old daughter."

Claire groans, "Oh," as though she has just been pierced by a needle. "Mr. Barbatnik, we are asking you too many questions, we shouldn't . . ."

He shakes his head. "Darling, you live, you ask questions. Maybe it's why we live. It seems that way."

"I tell him," says my father, "that he should make a book out of all he went through. I can think of some people I'd like to give it to read. If they could read it, maybe they would shake their heads that they can be the way they are, and this man can be so kind and good."

"And before the war started?" I ask him. "You were a young man then. What did you want to be?"

Probably because of the strength of his arms and the size of his hands I expect to hear him say a carpenter or a mason. In America he drove a taxi for over twenty years.

"A human being," he answers, "someone that could see and understand how we lived, and what was real, and not to flatter myself with lies. This was always my ambition from when I was a small child. In the beginning I was like everybody, a good cheder boy. But I personally, with my own hands, liberated myself from all that at sixteen years. My father could have killed me, but I absolutely did not want to be a fanatic. To believe in what doesn't exist, no, that wasn't for me. These are just the people who hate the Jews, these fanatics. And there are Jews who are fanatics too," he tells Claire, "and also walk around in a dream. But not me. Not for a second since I was sixteen years old and told my father what I refuse to pretend."

"If he wrote a book," says my father, "it should be called 'The Man Who Never Said Die.'"

"And here you married again?" I ask.

"Yes. She had been in a concentration camp also. Three years ago next month she passed away—like your own mother, from cancer. She wasn't even sick. One night after dinner she is washing the dishes. I go in to turn on the TV, and suddenly I hear a crash from the kitchen. 'Help me, I'm in trouble.' When I run into the kitchen she is on the floor. 'I couldn't hold on to the ditch,' she says. She says 'ditch' instead of 'dish.' The word alone gave me the willies. And her eyes. It was awful. I knew then and there that she was done for. Two days later they tell us that cancer is already in her brain. And it happened out of nowhere." Without a trace of animus —just to keep the record straight—he adds, "How else?"

"Too terrible," Claire says.

After my father has gone around to each candle to snuff out the flame—blowing even at those already expired, just to be sure—we step into the garden for Claire to show them the other planets visible from the earth tonight. Talking toward their upturned eyeglasses she explains about the Milky Way, answers questions about shooting stars, points out, as she does to her sixth-graders—as she did with me on our first night here—that mere speck of a star adjacent to the handle of the Little Dipper which the Greek soldiers had to discern to qualify for battle. Then she accompanies them back into the house; if they should awaken in the morning before we do, she wants them to know where there is coffee and juice. I remain in the garden with Dazzle. I don't know what to think. I don't want to know. I want only to climb by myself to the top of the hill. I remember our gondola rides in Venice. "Are you sure we didn't die and go to heaven?" "You'll have to ask the gondolier."

Through the living-room window I see the three of them standing around the coffee table. Claire has turned the record over and put it back on the turntable to play. My father is holding the album of Shakespeare medals in his hands. It appears that he is reading aloud from the backs of the medallions.

Some minutes later she joins me on the weathered wooden bench at the top of the hill. Side by side, without speaking, we look up again at the familiar stars. We do this nearly every night. Everything we have done this summer we have done nearly every night, afternoon, and morning. Every day calling out from the kitchen to the porch, from the bedroom to the bath, "Clarissa, come see, the sun is setting," "Claire, there's a hummingbird," "Sweetheart, what's the name of that star?"

For the first time all day she gives in to exhaustion. "Oh, my," she says, and lays her head on my shoulder. I can feel the air she breathes slowly filling, then slowly leaving her body.

After inventing a constellation of my own of the sky's brightest lights, I say to her, "It's a simple Chekhov story, isn't it?"

"Isn't what?"

"This. Today. The summer. Some nine or ten pages, that's all. Called 'The Life I Formerly Led.' Two old men come to the country to visit a healthy, handsome young couple, brimming over with contentment. The young man is in his middle thirties, having recovered finally from the mistakes of his twenties. The young woman is in her twenties, the survivor of a painful youth and adolescence. They have every reason to believe they have come through. It looks and feels to both of them as though they have been saved, and in large part by one another. They are in love. But after dinner by candlelight, one of the old men tells of his life, about the utter ruination of a world, and about the blows that keep on coming. And that's it. The story ends just like this: her pretty head on his shoulder; his hand stroking her hair; their owl hooting; their constellations all in order—their medallions all in order; their guests in their freshly made beds; and their summer cottage, so cozy and inviting, just down the hill from where they sit together wondering about what they have to fear. Music is playing in the house. The most lovely music there is. 'And both of them knew that the most complicated and difficult part was only just beginning.' That's the last line of 'Lady with a Lapdog.'"

"Are you really frightened of something?"

"I seem to be saying I am, don't I?"

"But of what?"

Her soft, clever, trusting, green eyes are on me now. All that conscientious, schoolroom attention of hers is focused upon me—and what I will answer. After a moment I tell her, "I don't know really. Yesterday at the drugstore I saw that they had portable oxygen units up on the shelf. The kid there showed me how they work, and I bought one. I put it in the bathroom closet. It's back of the beach towels. In case anything should happen to anyone tonight."

"Oh, but nothing is going to happen. Why should it?"

"No reason. Only when he was going on like that about the past with that couple who own the hotel, I wished I had brought it along in the car."

"David, he isn't going to die just from getting heated up about the past. Oh, sweetheart," she says, kissing my hand and holding it to her cheek, "you're worn down, that's all. He gets so worked up, he *can* wear you to a frazzle—but he means so well. And he's obviously still in the best of health. He's fine. You're just exhausted. It's time for bed, that's all."

It's time for bed, that's all. Oh, innocent beloved, you fail to understand and I can't tell you. I can't say it, not tonight, but within a year my passion will be dead. Already it is dying and I am afraid that there is nothing I can do to save it. And nothing that you can do. Intimately bound—bound to you as to no one else!—and I will not be able to raise a hand to so much as touch you . . . unless first I remind myself that I must. Toward the flesh upon which I have been grafted and nurtured back toward something like mastery over my life, I will be without desire. Oh, it's stupid! Idiotic! Unfair! To be robbed like this of you! And of this life I love and have hardly gotten to know! And robbed by whom? It always comes down to myself!

And so it is I see myself back in Klinger's waiting room; and despite the presence there of all those *Newsweeks* and *New Yorkers*, I am no sympathetic, unspectacular sufferer out of a muted Chekhov tale of ordinary human affliction. No, more hideous by far, more like Gogol's berserk and mortified amputee, who rushes to the newspaper office to place a maniacal classified ad seeking the return of the nose that has decided to take leave of his face. Yes, the butt of a ridiculous, vicious, inexplicable joke! Here, you therapeutic con man, I'm back, and even worse than before! Did all you said, followed every instruction, unswervingly pursued the healthiest of regimens—even took it on myself to study the passions in my classroom, to submit to scrutiny those who have scrutinized the subject most pitilessly . . . and here is the result! I know and I know and I know, I imagine and I imagine and I imagine, and when the worst happens, I might as well know nothing! You might as well know nothing! And feed me not the consolations of the reality principle! Just find it for me before it's too late! The perfect young woman is waiting! That dream of a girl and the most livable of lives! And here I hand to the dapper, portly, clever physician the advertisement headed "LOST," describing what it looked like when last seen, its real and sentimental worth, and the reward that I will offer anyone giving information leading to its recovery: "My desire for Miss Claire Ovington—a Manhattan private-school teacher, five feet ten inches tall, one hundred and thirty-eight pounds, fair hair, silvery-green eyes, the kindest, most loving, and loyal nature—has mysteriously vanished . . ."

And the doctor's reply? That perhaps it was never in my possession to begin with? Or that, obviously, what has disappeared I must learn to live without . . .

All night long, bad dreams sweep through me like water through a fish's gills. Near dawn I awaken to discover that the house is not in ashes nor have I been abandoned in my bed as an incurable. My willing Clarissa is with me still! I raise her nightgown up along the length of her unconscious body, and with my lips begin to press and tug her nipples until the pale, velvety, childlike areolae erupt in tiny granules and her moan begins. But even while I suck in a desperate frenzy at the choicest morsel of her flesh, even as I pit all my accumulated happiness, and all my hope, against my fear of transformations yet to come, I wait to hear the most dreadful sound imaginable emerge from the room where Mr. Barbatnik and my father lie alone and insensate, each in his freshly made bed.